D1714844

N D

New Directions in Prose and Poetry 24

Edited by J. Laughlin

A New Directions Book

ACKNOWLEDGMENTS

Grateful acknowledgment is made to the editors and publishers of books
and magazines where some of the selections in this book first appeared:
for Jürgen Becker, *Dimension* (Copyright © 1968 by *Dimension*); for
Attila József, *Southern Poetry Review*.

The quotation from William Bronk in John Taggart's "The Room" is from
"The Dream of a World of Objects" in *The Empty Hands.* Copyright ©
1969 by William Bronk; published by the Elizabeth Press. The quotation
in the first three stanzas of John Taggart's "Liveforever: Of Actual Things
in Expansion" is from #27 of George Oppen's *Of Being Numerous.*
Copyright © 1968 by George Oppen. The quotation from Louis Zukofsky
in the same poem is from "A–2" in "A" *1–12.* Jonathan Cape, Ltd.,
London. All rights reserved.

Manufactured in the United States of America
First published clothbound and as New Directions Paperbook 332 in 1972
Published simultaneously in Canada by McClelland & Stewart, Ltd.

New Directions Books are published for James Laughlin
by New Directions Publishing Corporation,
333 Sixth Avenue, New York 10014

CONTENTS

THE VAMPIRES OF ISTANBUL:
A STUDY IN MODERN
COMMUNICATIONS METHODS

EDOUARD RODITI

Yeni Aksham, Istanbul, 7 February 1960, front page:

Our readers will be justifiably shocked to hear that cases of vampirism can still occur in the heart of a modern metropolis like Istanbul. Yesterday morning, the police of our city was suddenly called upon to investigate such a case and promptly arrested the chief culprit, Mahmut Osmanoglu, a carter, 48 years old, a native of Edirne, living in Fener at Küchük Gülhane Djaddesi 37.

While giving her ten-year-old son Hasan his weekly bath, Füreya Öztürk, a mother of five children living at Küchük Gülhane Djaddesi 11, noticed yesterday a suspicious scar on the child's upper arm. She recognized it at once as the mark left by the needle of a hypodermic syringe and began to question the boy. He then admitted that he and two of his companions had been accosted in the street the day before by an older man who promised to give them sweetmeats if they accompanied him to his room. The three boys agreed, in their innocence, and found themselves offered by the carter to two other vampires who had been waiting for him there while he went out to recruit their victims.

Hasan described to his mother in great detail the orgy of vampirism which then took place. The three men produced hypodermic

1

syringes with which each one extracted blood from the upper arm of his chosen victim, after which they drank this blood from ordinary tea glasses with great relish while the boys were given cordials and sweetmeats to help them recover from their fright.

Accompanied by her son, Füreya Öztürk went immediately to the nearest police station in the Fener district of our city, where she is well known as a respectable housewife, the pensioned widow of a Turkish war hero who was killed in Korea while fighting the Communists. To the sympathetic local police captain, she repeated her atrocious story. Quite understandably, the poor woman was in tears, as the police captain subsequently told our reporter. Two policemen, Muzafer Tavukdjuoglu and Ali Hamit, were sent out at once to investigate the case. Fortunately, the boy could still remember the house where he had been a victim of this disgusting orgy of vampirism. He was able to lead the police upstairs to the door of the very room which had been the scene of the crime. But the door was locked and the police found nobody there. Enquiries in the neighborhood revealed that the carter Mahmut Osmanoglu was probably still at work but could be found at home later in the evening.

The police waited till seven o'clock and then came again and found the carter alone in the lodging where he generally lives with his mother. He had just returned from work and, faced with an account of his crime, denied it. He admitted, however, that he and his two companions had practiced unnatural vices with the three boys and recompensed them as usual with sweetmeats. The three boys, he claimed, were regular visitors to his room, where they seemed to take pleasure in his company and in that of his friends. Mahmut Osmanoglu was then arrested on the charge of vampirism and the case is being investigated.

Yeni Aksham, 8 February 1960, p. 3, local news.

Mahmut Osmanoglu, the Vampire of Fener, has been unable or unwilling to identify for the police the two other vampires who perpetrated with him the disgusting crimes which we reported yesterday. After several hours of interrogation at the local police station and later at police headquarters, he finally alleged that he knew only one of the other two vampires, a member of our city's police force who visits him quite often in his room in the evening, often bringing an anonymous companion and threatening to arrest the carter for some past crime if he refuses to go out and recruit young victims for their orgies of blood-drinking. Police headquarters deny the validity of the carter's story, pointing out that it is an obvious attempt to discourage any further move on their part to uncover what now appears to be a secret network of vampires operating in this city.

Yeni Aksham, 10 February 1960, p. 3.

A second case of vampirism has been reported from Langna, where two young mothers saw an unknown old woman approach their little daughters in the street and offer sweetmeats to the children. The old woman was attacked and beaten by the indignant mothers and was already lying unconscious in the street when the police reached the scene of the incident and intervened. As it was impossible to question her on account of her condition, the woman was taken to hospital, pending further investigation of the matter. She has meanwhile been identified as Meriam Terzibashjian, 72 years of age, a native of Elazig and a widow, presently employed as a cleaning woman in the kitchens of the Armenian hospital in Psamatia.

Yeni Aksham, 12 February 1960, p. 1 of the Weekly Literary and Scientific Supplement.

*We have pleasure in offering to our readers today a scientific study on vampirism by Professor Reshat Allalemdji, the well-known authority whose recent proposals for solving Istanbul's traffic problems, by reducing the frequency of accident-proneness through psychoanalysis of all convicted violators of traffic regulations, caused so much comment when we published them here a few weeks ago. Professor Allalemdji studied medicine at Leipzig University, where a special course on vampirism is an integral part of the training of all medical students in the neuropsychiatric clinic of this world-famous university.—*THE EDITORS

Though fortunately rare as a vice or as what we scientists who are not moralists prefer to call a mental disease, vampirism is one of those evils that have continued to plague mankind since the very dawn of civilization. There exist among us a number of unfortunate men and women whose physical health requires that they absorb regularly certain quantities of fresh human blood. If deprived of this diet, they die within a few days of a rare kind of pernicious anemia for which no adequate cure has yet been discovered. Whether their dread disease is hereditary or not, we may never be able to ascertain, cases of vampirism being fortunately so rare that it has so far proven impossible to compare and investigate them scientifically. Besides, most vampires, when caught and questioned, remain extremely reticent about their ghoulish habits.

For many centuries, our knowledge of vampirism was thus founded almost exclusively on a few legendary cases that had so shocked popular imagination that they had been committed to memory in ballads, fairy tales and other forms of folklore. The well-known story of Little Red Ridinghood and the Wolf is thus but a disguised account of a legendary French case of vampirism. The famous German poet Goethe also refers to a case of vampirism, probably of German origin, in his poem entitled *Der Erlkönig*.

Modern anthropology has revealed, however, that "where there is smoke there must also be fire," and that folklore and legends are the repository of truths which have survived from prehistoric times when man was not yet able to record in writing the facts that he had observed. Subsequent generations gradually distorted or embellished these facts with the inevitable inaccuracies of oral tradition. Legendary tales of vampirism are therefore being investigated scientifically by modern anthropologists in order to find out whether we have to deal here with a mental or physical disease, or perhaps with the clandestine practices of some secret cannibalistic religious cult. The present case of the vampires of Fener may thus offer Turkish scientists a rare opportunity to study in real life and at first hand what they all too often know only from the very secondary sources of folklore and legend.

Fortunately, history has already recorded two famous cases of vampirism which led to sensational trials in periods which have left us reliable firsthand documents. The first of these cases is that of Gilles de Rais (1404–1440), a man who was a Marshal of France and the companion in arms of Joan of Arc. After her trial and execution on a false accusation of witchcraft, he appears to have become, in spite of his distinguished military past and the responsibilities of his position, involved in the most disgusting practices of sorcery. At the time of his arrest and trial in Nantes, it was proven beyond dispute that he had already tortured and murdered at least eight hundred male adolescents. Though it was alleged by the prosecution that he had sacrificed them to the Devil in the course of criminal Black Masses, it is now generally agreed that he was a vampire and that the elaborate ceremonies that he conducted served only as a setting for obscene sacraments in the course of which he drank the blood of his young victims.

The second case, that of Countess Elizabeth Batthyani (1580–1640), occurred in Hungary. At the time of her trial, it was proven that she had enticed over six hundred attractive peasant girls into her castle, from which not one of them had ever been seen to return alive. Witnesses at her trial testified that, whenever she saw a beautiful young girl, her mouth literally watered, so that the saliva could be seen dripping from her chin. Ever since the horrible revelations of her trial, human vampires have been believed to exist in quite large numbers in certain rural areas of Hungary, where cases of vampirism have again and again been denounced to the authorities, especially in those disputed frontier provinces, such as Transylvania and the Banat, where the feudal landowners were Hungarian nobles who ruthlessly exploited their Slavic or Rumanian serfs.

The Turkish vampires whose shocking practices have recently been revealed may thus prove, on further investigation, to be descendants of Hungarian vampires who came and settled in Istanbul when Hungary was still a province of our glorious Ottoman Empire, which might then add grist to the mills of those scientists who believe vampirism to be a hereditary disease. In any case, vampirism appears to be something utterly alien to our national character, since we find no mention of it in our native Turkish or Turanian folklore.

> Professor Fakir Allalemdji
> Psychiatrist,
> Bakirköy Mental Hospital

Yeni Aksham, 14 February 1960, p. 3.

The police continues to investigate the case of the vampires of Fener, diligently seeking to identify the two unknown accomplices who participated with the carter Mahmut Osmanoglu in the scenes of vampirism which he organized for them in his room. Yesterday, the three boys who had been victims of the orgy of drinking human blood that we had reported were brought face to face with the carter. Two of the boys failed to recognize him, declaring that they had never seen him before, which seems scarcely likely as they happen to be his neighbors, living in the same street where everyone knows everyone else, at least by sight. But these two boys also refuse to admit ever having been victims of any orgy of vampirism.

Only Hasan Öztürk continues to assert that he and his two companions had accompanied the carter to his room and met two other men there, after which the three older men took blood from the boys with hypodermic syringes and drank it fresh in tea glasses. Pressed by the police for a more detailed description of these two other men, Hasan Öztürk, who had already recognized and identified the carter Mahmut Osmanoglu as the man who first accosted him and his two companions in the street and organized in his room the whole orgy, now gave the following description of the two other unidentified culprits. One of them is tall and dark, about twenty-five years of age, wears a mustache and looks like a goalkeeper of the Fenerbahtche football team. The other is some ten years older and looks like the German film star Curd Jurgens. Police enquiries reveal, however, that Hamdi Kotcha, the well-known goalkeeper of the Fenerbahtche football team, was absent from Istanbul on the day of the crime, having accompanied his team to Izmir where they won a match against a team from Marash. Nor is the German film star Curd Jurgens recorded by our passport controls to have entered the country within the last two years, so that it is presumed that this may be a case of mistaken identities.

Yeni Aksham, Istanbul, 19 February 1960, Letter to the Editor, p. 3 of the Weekly Literary and Scientific Supplement.

Dear Sir,

I have been a faithful reader of *Yeni Aksham* for the past twenty years and have nearly always found myself warmly applauding its courageous and enlightened stand on all national issues. I was therefore all the more shocked when I read, in your issue of 12 February last, Dr. Allalemdji's deliberately obscurantist article on vampirism. Surely, such a sop thrown to the senile believers in the positivist historical science of fifty or more years ago was unworthy of a progressive newspaper.

I will take issue only on three points raised by Dr. Allalemdji in his article:

Firstly, all serious and objective students of medieval history now know, from the documents which have survived, what vested interests in religious prejudice and in reactionary feudalism were at work to conceal the real issues at stake in the trial of Gilles de Rais so as to avoid discrediting an outstanding member of the nobility in the eyes of its enemies. Gilles de Rais never practiced vampirism but was accused of it in order to cover up his other crimes. A homosexual debauchee, he had abducted countless young serfs from their modest peasant homes to serve him in his disgraceful orgies. But he soon tired of each one of them in turn and, instead of then allowing them to return to their villages and spread there the report of his debaucheries, preferred to castrate them and sell them as eunuchs to the Arab princes of the Maghreb. The Catholic Church, of course, could not tolerate the idea that Christians were thus being sold, beneath its very nose, by a Christian noble to more enlightened and less cruel Moslem masters, so that the truth was hushed up and a less politically dangerous accusation of vampirism formulated.

Secondly, reliable scholars have recently discovered in Hungary some of the documents of the trial of the infamous Countess Elizabeth Batthyani. From these it appears clearly that she was a paid agent of the Ottoman court, recruiting Hungarian peasant girls, famous for their milk, as wet nurses for unwanted Christian children who had been saved from dying of exposure when their parents had abandoned them. These children were being charitably brought up in Moslem orphanages to serve later as Janissaries in our Imperial regiments of converts to Islam. Here again, the Catholic Church and its feudal supporters refused to admit that such a clandestine trade existed in provinces that it claimed to control; again, it preferred to trump up a charge of vampirism, though the countess was known to suck milk from her victims and never blood, since she insisted on testing each one of them herself and had even acquired a somewhat infantile taste for human milk, which also explains why her mouth is reported to have watered at the mere sight of an opulent bosom.

On both these points, I am prepared to quote, should Dr. Allalemdji desire, all the relevant bibliographical sources in recent French or Hungarian scholarly publications. My third point is one of principle rather than of historical scholarship. Dr. Allalemdji quotes us cases of vampirism in which six hundred and even eight hundred victims were alleged to have been killed. In the recent Fener case, not a single victim has yet been reported to be missing or can be presumed to have been killed. Can the Fener case be compared in any way with these classical if somewhat unreliable cases of vampirism?

> Sincerely yours,
> Turgut Ekmekdjioglu
> Professor of European History
> Istanbul University

Yeni Aksham, 19 February 1960, Letter to the Editor, same page as the preceding one.

Dear Sir,

For many years I have deplored, like other devout patriots, the Godless policies of the successive governments of our unfortunate Republic. The present Fener case of vampirism proves how right I have been.

Had our nation remained faithful to its Moslem traditions, Turks of today would not have acquired as they have a taste for the red meat of animals which have not been slaughtered according to the strict rules of our religion. One sin leads to another and guzzling underdone steaks like the Infidels at the Istanbul Hilton Hotel or elsewhere in our increasingly degenerate cities has now led some of our more decadent compatriots to acquire a taste for human blood too. No restaurant in Turkey should be allowed to serve European-style steaks, especially that typically Infidel dish that is so blasphemously called Steak Tartare, as if our Moslem Tartar brethren could be suspected of ever having made a practice of eating anything as monstrously unclean.

> Sincerely yours,
> Hodja Ibrahim Hadjikaraosmanoglu

Yeni Aksham, Istanbul, 26 February 1960, Letter to the Editor, same page as the preceding letter.

Dear Sir,

I have read with great interest Dr. Allalemdji's article and the curious correspondence that it has provoked in your columns. All this reveals how ignorant most Turks have become of Turcology in general and, in particular, of the ancient customs and beliefs of our Turanian ancestors.

Let me assure you and your readers, as a professor of Turanian and Turkish folklore, that vampirism is an ancient and honorable

Turkish and Turanian custom, originally a form of medicine once practiced in Central Asia by Shamanistic priests before our ancestors were converted to Islam. By sucking the sick blood out of their patients, these Shamanistic priests cured them of their diseases, all illnesses being, according to their doctrine, diseases of the blood.

Sincerely yours,
Turhan Tashkent
Professor of Turcology
University of Ankara

Yeni Aksham, 4 March 1960, Letter to the Editor, p. 3 of the Weekly Literary and Scientific Supplement.

Dear Sir,

Professor Tashkent is perfectly right. I come of a family that has for countless generations earned 'an honest livelihood, even after its conversion to Islam, by practicing Shamanistic medicinal vampirism in the Vilayet of Afyon Karahissar. When I was still a boy, long before my parents moved to Istanbul where my father subsequently became a well-known pedicure, I used to see hundreds of sick people brought to our house by their family and friends for treatment at the hands of my grandfather. He was generally content to accept modest fees and had specialized in the treatment of obesity. Our home had thus become a kind of clinic where my grandfather's cures of vampirism saved many a high Ottoman dignitary from becoming an ungainly old man and the laughingstock of his inferiors. When Turks of the more privileged classes began to go abroad for more expensive and often less effective cures in well-publicized European watering places, my father solved the problem of our dwindling family practice by moving to Istanbul and setting himself up as a pedicure in the Passage in Beyoglu, where he still cured many a badly infected toe, however, by merely sucking it. I am sure that a number of your older readers will still remember having been treated by him.

Sincerely yours,
Boghatsch Hakimoglu

Yeni Aksham, Istanbul, 4 March 1960, same page as preceding letter.

Dear Sir,

As President of the Pan-Turanian Association of Shamanistic Vampires, I have been authorized by a quorum of our National Board to applaud and corroborate on its behalf every word of Professor Tashkent's remarkably objective letter. All our members have graduated from the last existing schools of ancient Shamanistic medicine. In Turkey, the last of these schools is now situated in Urfa, in Anatolia; in recent years, we have no longer received any correspondence from the schools which still existed in the Russian Turkestan before the Soviet Revolution, so that we are not able to report on the present state of our science in Soviet Russia, where it may have been suppressed as a manifestation of Pan-Turanian nationalism in the course of the Stalinist persecutions which decimated the Moslem intelligentsia of the Central-Asian Soviet Republics.

Our school in Urfa had first been founded and endowed in the thirteenth century by Korkhut Seljuk, one of the last of the ruling princes of the Oghuz Beylik. Though our faculty still graduates a few selected Shamanistic physicians every year, these are now trained only in the theory of their science, without any practical experience of the treatment of human patients, if only to avoid all possible conflicts with existing Turkish laws regulating the practice of medicine. As an association, we therefore limit our activities to the organization of campaigns to promote a more enlightened appreciation of the value of our science and thus hope soon to obtain public support for changes in our legislation in order to prevent our venerable and valuable science from becoming extinct.

Yours sincerely,
Tchinghiz Hulaghuoglu

Yeni Aksham, Istanbul, 4 March 1960, same page as preceding letter.

Dear Sir,

I hope other readers of *Yeni Aksham* have realized as I did at once that all these countless cases of shameless vampirism which now disgrace our once beautiful and peaceful city in the eyes of the civilized world are the work of a small but well organized band of fanatical Armenians. It has long been known that Armenians require the blood of Moslem children to prepare the meat pies that they eat at their annual Easter celebrations. All too often, they have relied in the past on corrupt Turkish or Kurdish accomplices to procure them their victims. My point is proven by the fact that an Armenian hag who works in the kitchens of the Armenian hospital has also been arrested in the present campaign to eradicate this wave of terrorism which, as always, is seasonal. Though Turks, the other vampires were surely employed as her agents.

Sincerely yours,
Atilla Bayraktutan

Yeni Aksham, Istanbul, 4 March 1960, same page as preceding letter.

Dear Sir,

I'm a hospital nurse and midwife. In all these stories about vampires, one thing worries me. How could the mother of one of the three victims recognize immediately the mark on her son's arm as having been left there by a hypodermic syringe? Unless she had special training as a nurse, how could she distinguish it from a mere scratch or a fleabite?

Respectfully yours,
Fazilet Bashkurt

Yeni Aksham, Istanbul, 4 March 1960, same page as preceding letter.

Dear Sir,

My kind Turkish neighbor is writing this letter for me because I never attended a Turkish school and learned to write only Italian in the old days. Because I am a Christian, some Turkish vampires think they can steal my cats with impunity but we all worship one and the same God and there is justice now in our glorious Republic for all its citizens, regardless of race or religion. My cats are very beautiful and well fed and in the past ten years three of them have disappeared. I know that they have been victims of vampires and now my good Turkish neighbor shares my suspicion but we don't know what we should do about it. Isn't it illegal to steal cats and drink their blood like the blood of human beings? Are they the same vampires who drink the blood of both or are there two kinds of vampires, those who drink human blood and those who drink the blood of cats? Perhaps Professor Allalemdji can answer my questions.

Sincerely yours,
Daria Genovesi

Yeni Aksham, Istanbul, 6 March 1960, p. 3, local news.

The case of the vampires of Fener is still being diligently investigated by the police. Prompted by the interest which so many of our readers have displayed, our reporter went yesterday to police headquarters to find out what progress has been made in solving this remarkable mystery. As we had previously reported, Hamdi Kotcha, the well-known goalkeeper of the Fenerbahtche football team, was able to supply a satisfactory alibi when Hasan Öztürk, one of the victims of the vampires, described him as one of the three men who had participated in this orgy of drinking human blood. Hamdi Kotcha happened on that day to be with his team in Izmir, playing a match against a team from Marash. Through Interpol, our police has now been able to ascertain that the German film star Curd Jurgens happened that day to be working in a Hollywood studio, so that he too has now submitted a satisfactory alibi.

The boy Hasan Öztürk remains the only witness of the actual orgies of vampirism which his mother, on the basis of his reports, denounced to the police. The other two boys whom he named as witnesses and co-victims continue to deny that the alleged vampires drank their blood. For lack of sufficiently conclusive evidence, the public prosecutor may therefore be obliged to drop the case against the carter Mahmut Osmanoglu, the only vampire who has so far been identified and who is now under arrest. Though Mahmut Osmanoglu has meanwhile admitted having practiced unnatural vices with the three boys, the latter and their parents hotly deny any such degenerate tendencies in their families. For lack of a complaint, the public prosecutor cannot prosecute Mahmut Osmanoglu for the only crime that he has so far confessed.

As for the other vampire, the Armenian cleaning woman Meriam Terzibashjian who had been suspected of attempted vampirism in Langna, we regret to report that she died yesterday in the Armenian Hospital without having sufficiently recovered from her injuries, since February 10th, to be questioned by the police. Though all these investigations have so far proven to be somewhat confusing, it is believed at police headquarters that we may soon expect sensational revelations concerning the wave of vampirism that has swept our city.

Yeni Aksham, Istanbul, 11 March 1960, Letter to the Editor, p. 3 of the Weekly Literary and Scientific Supplement.

Dear Sir,

I am an unmarried mother and support myself, my little girl and my invalid mother on my earnings as a *tchivtiteli* dancer. I used to earn high fees in the most expensive night clubs in Beyoglu and many of your readers will remember the film in which I starred, *The Girl with the Golden Belly*. It told the story of my life and was elected as the most popular Turkish film of the year for the Berlin Film Festival. Unfortunately, a jury of foreigners in Berlin was unable to understand the significance of *The Girl with the Golden Belly* as an artistic milestone in the history of the emancipation of Turkish womanhood, so it failed to get a prize.

But this was not my only misfortune in that year when my stars gave me every indication that I should stay at home and never expose myself unnecessarily to alien forces and influences. One winter night, as I was walking home from work, I slipped on the ice of the frozen Beyoglu sidewalk and fell and injured my hip. My left buttock soon began to swell and is now much larger than my right buttock. I have tried every medical treatment available, but modern science has been of no assistance. My professional life is now ruined. When I dance the *tchivtiteli*, men only laugh at me and I'm lucky if I find work in a low water-front café in Tophane instead of the better Beyoglu night clubs. Can you recommend me a reliable Shamanistic vampire whose treatments might solve my problem?

Sincerely yours,
Djevrieh Holivutlu

Yeni Aksham, Istanbul, 11 March 1960, p. 3 of the Weekly Literary and Scientific Supplement.

Dear Sir,

I'm a devout Moslem and was shocked to read your Christian correspondent's suggestion that Turks could kill and eat cats. After all the years that she has lived in Turkey, Daria Genovesi, who appears to be a Turkish citizen, should really know that our Prophet taught us to respect cats above all other animals. No devout Turk, for instance, will ever drown a kitten, as the Infidels so frequently do. If there exist Turkish vampires that live on the blood of cats, they must surely be Kurdish Yazids who worship fire and the Devil. But with the constant influx of ignorant Anatolian villagers who seek work in our city, I would not be surprised to hear that Istanbul now harbors a secret community of Kurdish Yazids.

Another explanation for the disappearance of your correspondent's three cats might be that they were not really cats but cannibalistic weremice, in fact mice that adopt the appearance of cats only during the daytime and resume their natural form as mice at night. It is a scientific fact that when mice become too numerous for their own convenience they regulate their population by means of cannibalistic massacres. Some of the survivors then become weremice and continue to prey on other mice. But it sometimes happens that weremice also get attacked and killed by real cats. I witnessed such a case once with my own eyes. I was living in Cairo in a house that was infested by mice, in an old building in Mousky. I acquired a cat, but she could not cope with the situation. All she ever did was eat, sleep and purr. One day, I bought some poison and placed pieces of poisoned cheese at strategic points on the floor in the kitchen. When I came home late that night from the movies, I found a dead mouse on the floor near the kitchen sink. Instead of picking it up and throwing it at once into the garbage can, I left it there and went to bed. The next morning, in the middle of the kitchen floor where I had seen the dead mouse, I found the corpse of my cat. It was perhaps a weremouse which, while it had been a mouse again at night, had eaten the poison and died; but at dawn its body had then assumed the form of a cat. Or had it died from eating a poisoned mouse? Weremice are very rare, however, and your correspondent's story of her vanished cats would constitute the first recorded case of a cat-lover being afflicted with three weremice. May I ask your correspondent if her three lost cats happened to be of the same family? It would be interesting to know whether this phenomenon is hereditary.

> Sincerely yours,
> Yilmaz Arslan, author of
> *Cats and their Ghosts,*
> (Istanbul, Kirmizi Gül Kitapevi, 1954.)

Yeni Aksham, Istanbul, 18 March 1960, Letter to the Editor, p. 3, of the Weekly Literary and Scientific Supplement.

Dear Sir,

One of the oldest and most honorable members of our association of Shamanistic medical vampires has been authorized by us to treat your correspondent Miss Djevrieh Holivutlu as a charity patient and solely in order to demonstrate the usefulness and efficacity of our art. But she must first sign a notarized statement to the effect that she is willingly allowing herself to be used as a test case for scientific purposes and will make no claims on us should the experiment fail to give the desired results.

Sincerely yours,
Tchinghiz Hulaghuoglu

Yeni Aksham, Istanbul, 25 March 1960, Letter to the Editor, p. 3, of the Weekly Literary and Scientific Supplement.

Dear Sir,

You sent me a disgusting old fraud who claimed to be a member in good standing of the National Shamanistic Order of Pan-Turanian Vampires. I am now writing to warn your readers against him. Not only was his treatment painful, humiliating and quite useless, but I now have a scar that is recognizably that of a vicious human bite further disfiguring my already swollen left buttock. Instead of curing me, his treatment leaves me worse off than I was before.

Sincerely yours,
Djevrieh Holivutlu

Yeni Aksham, Istanbul, 1 April 1960, Letter to the Editor, p. 3 of the Weekly Literary and Scientific Supplement.

Dear Sir,

As President of the Pan-Turanian Association of Shamanistic Vampires I must protest against your irresponsible publication of Miss Djevrieh Holivutlu's absurd and vicious allegations.

She had previously signed a notarized statement, as requested, to the effect that she willingly allowed herself to be used as a test case in a scientific experiment and would make no claims if it failed to produce the desired results. As an eyewitness, I must now state that she did not behave, during the experiment, with the proper scientific objectivity. Instead of keeping her composure, she giggled, wriggled and squealed, so that it was almost impossible for our distinguished member to draw blood from the affected buttock. After the experiment, she even had the effrontery to demand a fee, thus revealing that she believed she was engaging in some curious form of prostitution. Finally, if anyone now has a right to complain, it would surely be our distinguished member who, in his devotion to our venerable science, lost a tooth while trying to treat, free of charge, a silly and immoral woman who refused, as requested, to keep still while he was treating her. Throughout the experiment, she indeed behaved as if she were merely displaying

her charms to her customary water-front audience in a low Tophane
café.

Sincerely yours,
Tchinghiz Hulaghuoglu

Yeni Aksham, Istanbul, 1 April 1960, Letter to the Editor, same
page as the preceding one.

Dear Sir,

My wife and I are much disturbed by the articles and letters you
have published about the Fener vampires and about the plague of
vampirism that threatens our children. As parents of five growing
boys, we feel that everything should be done to protect the health
and morals of those on whose shoulders rests the future of our
nation. As for me, if I should ever chance to meet one of these vile
and subversive vampires, I would tear him or her apart, regardless
of age or sex, limb from limb with my own unarmed hands, then
gladly lap up the blood and chew the liver of such a satanic crea-
ture. Any other fate would be too good for one of these monsters
and I'm sure all other patriotic Turkish parents will agree with me.
Long live our glorious Republic,

Alp Karagöz

Yeni Aksham, Istanbul, 1 April 1960, Letter to the Editor, same
page as the preceding one.

Dear Sir,

I appeal to your kindness and to the mercy of your readers. Be-
cause I have never learned to read or write, I paid the writer in our
neighborhood market in Fener to write this letter to all of you, from
the widowed mother of the carter Mahmut Osmanoglu who was
arrested over a month ago and accused of being a vampire. All my
neighbors in Fener know what a good son he has always been, a
devout Moslem and kind to all boys and cats in our neighborhood.
People have read to me articles and letters you print and I can
swear to you on all the Holy Writings of Our Prophet that my son
has never stolen and eaten any cats nor does he drink the blood of
any boys.

My husband was killed fighting rebel Kurds in the army. A few
months later my son was born and never knew his father. We were
starving in Edirne and I came to Istanbul with my baby to find

work. Many years, I worked all day and half the night in a laundry till I thought I would break my back. Then my boy grew up and went to work and he is a good boy and let me stay at home and said to me: Mother, you have worked long enough. After that he worked and we both lived on his pay.

Like many other sons who have never known their father my boy is devoted to his mother and has little use for the silly girls of today who think only of movies and gossip. But he has a good heart and would be a wonderful father. All the boys in our neighborhood know him. In summer he takes them to the beach on Sundays and teaches them to swim. In winter he teaches them useful things like how to mend a leaking roof or how to mend their own shoes.

This whole vampire business started when I was away visiting my sister in Edirne. A silly mother in our neighborhood then accused my son of drinking her son's blood. The truth of it is that this evil boy and his two companions are vampires. They came to our lodgings while I was away and threatened to denounce my son to the police if he didn't give them all his week's pay. They said he had taught them to smoke hashish with him in the vacant lot behind the ruins of the old Koranic school in the next street but that isn't true because my son never smokes hashish or even tobacco. After my son was arrested these three boys could no longer agree among themselves what they had accused my son of doing with them. One of them still says he is a vampire and drank their blood but the other boys say nothing. But these three boys are real vampires and you need only see my son now to know that they have been sucking his blood.

Yesterday I was allowed to visit my son for the first time in prison. Every day the police beat him and he now looks like a ghost. Believe me the real vampires are these lying boys and of course the police too. I'm only an old woman but I know a vampire when I see one and they don't suck blood, they drive good men like my son to despair and to their death. What we need now in Turkey is a caliph like King Solomon to render justice to the poor from his emerald and ruby throne. May God bless you if you print my letter,

Fatima Osmanoglu

Yeni Aksham, Istanbul, 1 April 1960, Letter to the Editor, same page as the preceding one.

Dear Sir,

Vampires, schmampires. Each time I read your newspaper I'm more ashamed of being a Turk. For well over a month, you have now been feeding us hair-raising stories about vampires attacking our children of both sexes. Then you published yesterday a front-page editorial describing how the deputies of the Government party, in our National Parliament in Ankara, had attacked the deputies of the Opposition in a violent free-for-all in the course of which they tore the furniture of the House of Representatives apart and beat each other with the remains of their seats. Such behavior disgraces our national politicians in the eyes of the civilized world. The only vampires that we have in Turkey are our politicians of both parties.

As long as you could recognize the Jews, the Armenians, the Greeks or the Shiah Moslems in our midst by their headdresses, we used to have massacres whenever our tempers rose to boiling point. Now we all wear more or less the same hats and massacre each other at random. The only solution to this problem of Turkish national unity would be to allow only two kinds of hat in Turkey: one hat for the sadists and another hat for the masochists, and no hat at all for the majority of neutrals. Tit for tat and hit for hat, everybody would then be happy, the sadists beating up the maso-chists and the masochists being merrily beaten up by the sadists with no complaints later, while the rest of us would go about our daily business in peace or sit back and applaud the massacre like a football match in the Beziktash Stadium.

Perhaps we need to be psychoanalyzed as a nation. We're all too bloodthirsty, all of us vampires at heart. It may be useful to be bloodthirsty in times of war, but we're a failure in peacetime as a democratic nation. As for me, I've made my choice and become a vegetarian. If all Turks could only shift their attention from blood to chlorophyll, we might become a civilized nation within a couple of generations. Boys and girls would then be safe in our midst, but God protect a cabbage when I'm around! Vegetables already trem-ble when they see me approach them.

Sincerely yours,
Harun Pezevenkoglu

Yeni Aksham, Istanbul, 4 September 1960, p. 3 local news.

Our readers will remember that, six months ago, *Yeni Aksham* was the only daily newspaper in Istanbul to denounce as nonsense, from the very start, the absurd panic caused in our city by entirely unfounded rumors of vampirism. Thanks to our enlightened campaign, the innocent victim of this malicious gossip was finally proven to be no vampire and was released from prison.

But the press of other nations appears to be more credulous than ours. Foreign news agencies thus distributed to American newspapers distorted versions of our published reports of the investigation of the case of the alleged vampires of Fener. Thanks to our courageous press campaign, the carter Mahmut Osmanoglu, the only alleged vampire who had been arrested, has now been a free man again for many months. He was working peacefully at his old job as a carter, willing to forgive and forget, when he suddenly received two weeks ago a letter from America. After reading in the American press its somewhat sensational reports of alleged Turkish vampirism, an American research institute was offering Mahmut Osmanoglu a generous grant to come to America and cooperate there with a group of scientists on an important project to determine the physical and psychological causes of both hereditary and environmental vampirism. Yesterday morning, Mahmut Osmanoglu, accompanied by his aged mother, left Yesilköy airport for Chicago, where he will henceforth work as a kind of piece of human litmus paper to detect, by his reactions, who is a potential vampire and who is not.

Our reporter interviewed Mahmut Osmanoglu at the airport, a few minutes before he boarded the plane. A man of few words, he declared only that he plans to spend much of his spare time in Chicago as a voluntary missionary to convert Americans to Islam. "I've been told," he declared, "that most of them live on a diet of pork and whisky, though they would actually prefer to suck the blood of Communists. Every once in a while, however, they are obliged to send some of their more bloodthirsty vampires on raids to Cuba, San Domingo or Vietnam to suck the blood of Communists as they no longer have enough of them at home. It was high time I went to America to wean them away from their unclean diet and their propensity for political cannibalism."

Mahmut Osmanoglu's mission to America can thus be interpreted as Turkey's first attempt at technical assistance to an overdeveloped nation. We may soon expect other such idealistic Turkish pioneers to leave our country on similar UNESCO-sponsored projects to solve the problems of France, Western Germany, Sweden, Switzerland and the United Kingdom, nations which are equally infested, it seems, with the kind of vampirism that develops all too easily in an economy of leisure and plenty.

CHARTRES

ALEKSIS RANNIT

Translated by Henry Lyman

For ages you sought the coveted isle.
Then Chartres neared you and stood still.

Now you set ashore, and the Western Gate at once
hails the wanderer from the distant coast.

Keen emotion lashes stone to stone.
The whole temple is a single sculptured form,

the overlasting fervour of a thousand hands
and a single, restlessly tender mind.

Here dwells the olden god. His warm breath burns
with the silvery candescence of the moon,

and as from the beginning, his fingers are strewn
with the first, fragrant dust of creation.

The tread of his retinue is thicker than bone,
and theirs is the gaze of ancestral storms.

Their robes are unendingly carven through time,
born on the light of creative reason.

Aye where does faith begin and art expire?
And who is here to broach the inmost door?

You touch the source that moved your soul,
you bathe in its insistent splendour —

But wait, await the face within,
await the still more vivid fire!

Enter the pure, melodious room,
whose colours mellow in the dusk.

The windows above sing wondrous music
through their myriad lights, and the trembling mosaic,

descending the space, casts ethereal flame
where the columns of archways grow dim.

And the air is revealed in a blaze of song,
and its blaze has the fragrance of spring —

of another, sublime and distant spring,
which turns you to glittering ash.

Deadly, this craving desire for perfection.
More deadly still the achieved aim.

You have sought and struggled and won.
Now yours is the victory where all is forgone.

MARGINS

JÜRGEN BECKER

Translated by A. Leslie Willson

There hangs the map, all the walls are white, this is the land, these are the coasts, this is history, that is the high window with the trees in the park, above it is the sky, that is the daily D-C 8, that is Nina the cat, today is Friday, no summer, no change, that is the heartbeat just past, there comes what is called hope again, that is the duration of a cigarette, a deadline approaches now, that is Münchhausen, who drags a wild boar along behind him, that is the nearness of what they're talking about, then the name Mila Schön is heard, that was doubtless the city of Milan, the full glass, the empty glass, there a figure sits and sits looking up from the table surface at the table, there is something else, that is the interior of the earth, it is as clean as an Opel by Opel, there Kaiser Wilhelm is hanging, red plaster, it is 10 P.M. there, and there it is 8 A.M., the fly there does not fly, that's the important thing, that's what you forget, this is the Mississippi, that's the word that names a river, here an empty, cold oven stands, there a good portable radio, there and there, on each spot, a piece of a column, there is something to sit on and there something to sit and lie on.

And outside the storm wind howls through the region, and a flock of birds struggles until it gets dark.

All the things that can happen tomorrow: That the mail won't come and a letter from yesterday is still lying in the mailbox. Schnellinger will visit a fellow countryman. A change of wind. An excuse to go back to bed. That Nina will go out again and never come back. A strike in Italy. Nothing but ideas that earn no money. Raquel Welch will be here again. Always new interruptions. A pilot will get drunk and fall asleep. The president's wife will take a walk. That we'll make a mess and will start from the beginning. A trip together to the supermarket. Buy a new shirt. Die. Six cups of tea. A splendid horoscope for day after tomorrow. The Chinese will be at the gate. Ingeborg will call up in the rain. That you'll have forgotten everything again and you'll think, why, you've seen all that once already.

A trip away: that will cheer us up soon enough. The flat countryside is really almost completely desolate. A road with picturesque views at many places links the many typical points where fine views can be had and permits us to drive around the lake. In the center of the white desert we find a white hotel in which we spend the night awake, for whoever goes to sleep is seen no more. Beyond the mountains must be the ocean with havens of rescue. In a description of the route we read of people who have only one leg and whose one foot is so big that, lying on their backs, they find protection from the burning sun in its shade. Our tongues are swollen; our feet, garnished with thorns, are swelling; the sight of the beauties of Acapulco makes us forget both. This lake was once a crater. A few kilometers from Anguillara two great pines stand right and left of a road which leads through a great plain. Toward noon we turn into an inn whose hostess is just washing off the blood. In the next village many children are dancing to the playing of a flute. The plain is larger than we thought. There, a village, and there, another, and there, one is on fire. The cattle, the forest, the earth become smaller and smaller. We promise to keep quiet about everything. Since the gate fell shut behind us we are in night. Next morning on our way early, and the first ones out into the middle of the lake. The clouds over the mountains bode no good; with effort we keep watch. There is the car, right, there is no water or air. Air doesn't boil over and doesn't freeze. We find the bed of a river and are happy about the deliverance. Then we see the capital of the province. A few railway stations, practice fields, once-flourishing trade, the great palace of the prince, the shot-up sentry huts, bathhouses, the plague cemetery, Herbert Street, a museum that was formerly a camp for enemies, some catacombs, a dozen warning signs, many thistles and other greenery, some footprints, lizards in abundance, several well-kept houses. Tired and happy we return home in the evening. Many guests are already there, and we tell how it was in the province.

Some Names in the Series of Memories of Events:
Divorce. M. grins through tears.
September, Hannes, near Campi.
Ludovica Nagel introduces Monica Vitti.
My name is Hans Stahl.
S. Way, as in subway.
Flirting, always flirting, said Mr. Düvelius.
When it was said the Americans were here, Charlie Tümmler put on his white chef's hat.
Paffrath, the iceman there?
Huth, said Hofer, said Huth, said Sotrop.
Mr. Zimmermann, yes, Mr. Zimmermann.
Finally Hilde showed her passport, and then there was really no more doubt.
Watch out, said Liesbeth.
Fritz Herkenrath is catching a ball.
On 1 May 1950 the night in Dellbrück was as delightful as the May night of Lenau.
Boris asks his father why he isn't coming back.
Hoary Stan Kenton.
Lilo also suddenly looked different.
When one after another fell over, Panna Grady displayed only an ironic smile.
But Pyla had then already taken a taxi.
The wind is changing. Haussmann puts his sport cap on backward.
Adrion makes a coin disappear.
Andy Warhol sat quite still when the noise got louder and louder.
Natasha Ungeheuer.
At first he said his name was unpronounceable. Then he gave a false name.
At dinner he said he was living under a pseudonym. Helen Stauffacher wasn't about to believe all that.
Häppel.

Shortly before our move away from Annen Street, Walter tore up the apartment again.
We're still arguing about whether Sandra got into the little Fiat or the big one.

And why not?
Because anywhere else everything starts at the beginning. Because my back is hurting so much. Because it's raining. Because the conductor said it was all the same in the end. Because you don't even want it yourself. Because nobody's going to come anyway. Because I just can't stand it anymore. Because everything's too late, and nobody ever said anything. Because he didn't keep quiet. Because then finally there'll be some peace. Because nobody knows at the moment. Because it turned out that it won't work that way either. Because you always make such a fool of yourself doing that. Because it's always about the same thing, and because they always say, yeah, well, that'll change. Because nothing's ever changed. Because today, no, because even yesterday not another word was said about it. Because today you just can't interfere anymore. Because nothing's the matter that's worth the effort. Because it's always them again. Because nobody's going to join in and because it stinks. Because there's no reason given to be for it or against it. Because I don't care. Because it's still raining. Because you'll go away otherwise. Because it'll quit anyway all by itself pretty soon.

The room is getting bigger and bigger, it isn't even a room, it's a hall, now it's even snowing too and summer's near enough to pluck, and outside the gravel path crunches because somebody keeps going back and forth, now he's even whistling, that's the end of quiet, when is it going to get dark anyway, it *is* dark, it isn't snowing either and nobody's whistling, the gravel is quiet on the path, one mistake after another today.

Where is Nassau? There, past the table, past the folding screen, under the window in front of the door, that's where Nassau is.

Right after breakfast it begins. After one hour there are already three. During the next, two more join in. Little peace until noon, finally noon.

After lunch it really lets loose. Once doesn't count. Come on, we're going walking in the park. In the park the air is fresh and healthy. It's never too late for a new start. A new start.

New fights at the table, defeat, despair, start over again. Away from the table, to the couch, into the stuffed chair, round the table, at the table again. You can't stand on one leg for long. Life is hard enough. There's not much fun either. What for, anyway? All good things come in—well, how many are there anyway?

Contrite at supper, how many were there anyway, now the company's coming too, but that's a diversion; greetings, delight, hello. Everybody's standing around, relaxed, at ease, and why not, everybody's tried it once and knows how that is, don't give it another thought, you'll die one way or another. Well, and you, too, and everybody as they've lived. The windows open, clear night, take a deep breath, in the bathroom the coughing begins, starting tomorrow, a new try, no more smoking.

When it began, there was no way of telling what it was all about. When it had gotten that far, everybody said it was good that it had gotten that far. Then when it kept on, the first problems naturally began. When it suddenly stopped, they tried here and there until it suddenly started up again. Then when it had been working pretty long, nobody had anything against it any longer.

Tell some more.

Yeah, well, and when nothing occurred to prevent it, nobody thought any more about it. Then when a couple of small incidents happened again, well, who pays any attention to small incidents. When it got worse, people were a little worried about it. But when they saw what was the matter, who could do anything about it then anyway. You see, when it suddenly got involved, then everybody had other worries on his mind. Then, when it was all over, it looked entirely different than had been thought in the beginning. Anyway, when it started, there was no way of understanding what it really was all about. Only when it got so far, only then did everybody say, it's just fine that it has come to that. Sure, when it went on then, the first troubles started, too. But when it suddenly stopped, they tried here and there until it started up again. And when it had been working pretty long, then, no, nobody had anything against it any longer.

Tell some more.

And when it was long gone and forgotten, the first ones began all over again.

There the runaway runs through the park.

And what'll we do now? Norway is still a little early. We ought to call up the Rosenbergs. How would it be if, no, not that either. Nobody goes to Piper at the club anymore. Something simple maybe, if there were still anything like that. How about the East Sector? It would have to be the same kind of rain like that time when we lay in the huts in Hennestrand. Nothing's going on in Rome at any rate. Something's going on at Marlborough. We just came from there. Raddatz would definitely know something. Preferably sleep until September. What was the name of it anyway, that town up there with the people and the transistor radios at their ears? Not that. Isn't there a hotdog stand here? But we could . . . you know. And whom would you suggest? Hours on end, just like that, hours on end. And then? Then the other way round. Well, who's gonna go along? It's the day of departure at the Harrimann's. Then Gütz. He's dead. You'd have to have a forest, a really green, great forest. Or simply roar, loud, louder and louder. Well, we had all of that yesterday already. Then let's roast an apple now. You can do that only on the Lüneburg Heath. All right then, what are we gonna do, anyway?

Why not sing. I'm a little foreign devil . . .

Everything's so gloomy today, so melancholy, senseless and bleak. Everything's so indolent and dull, so oppressive and so slow, everything's just dragging along. Nothing's beginning, nothing's continuing, there's no more purpose, there's no help for it, no sun is rising, neither in the sky nor in my heart. Everything's so loud, it's so cold, it's so silent, it's blinding, nothing helps. It's no fun, it gets on my nerves, it's deadly, it's an indescribable situation. Nothing's new, it's unexplainable, it doesn't stop, it's everywhere. It makes my head ache, it constricts my breathing, it hurts my eyes so, it's so inane, it's nothing. Everything's so uneasy, it's so hot, it's so horribly bright, it's so exhausting, it rushes and rushes. Time isn't passing by, there's no fresh air, nothing's stirring, there's such a noise, it's flickering so much, nobody comes and says that everything is so bleak today, so cold and so still and that it's not bearable anymore.

A new visitor has been announced, from Munich, he says, in Bavaria, no longer young, no longer dangerous, doesn't eat much, drinks moderately, doesn't intend to stay long either, knows only stories about the old days, forgets immediately whatever is thrown at him, supposed to smile when he's tossed out, is grateful for everything, asks nothing, mostly invisible, seldom gets dirty, attempted assassination once, knew the king, recites ballads when he's asked to, doesn't like to come, somewhere or other said that he was a little afraid of us, already declined a couple of times, again today he declined.

Is it bright enough now, then? No, it's not. But, of course, we can sit and wait, we have patience. Early tomorrow, it will be bright enough again then.

After the first step now comes the second. A start is made. Just keep on. Can't turn back now. And it's not that bad either. Now there's one more taken. Like that, and then like that. Just don't let anyone interrupt. Everything comes to an end eventually. Just keep on like that. And don't think too much about it. Stop, who's saying stop, anyway? It's getting better and better. Soon nobody will even ask about it any longer.

And how was it? Well, when we arrived nothing much more was going on. Everything gotten rid of, orderly again, only a couple of marks on the walls, there was still a bit of a smell, of course, the floor almost dry, the weather was really ideal, everything clean, everything as though nothing had happened.

Today is a day in February. The quiet gravel paths in the park crunch under the steps of the first gardeners. In the icy water of the fountains the light male frogs, singly or fighting in twos or threes, are climbing onto the heavy bodies of the female frogs. They'll remain sitting there for weeks, even when the threads of eggs, in pairs, leave the bodies of the female frogs which slowly become flatter. Whoever hasn't gotten a female looks for a male that also has not gotten a female. The males soon leave one another alone. Soon the branches which fell from the trees into the fountains during the last storms will be so entangled and entwined by the egg clusters that they will no longer be recognizable as branches.

Before it gets to the point where countless thousands of tadpoles develop from the eggs, there will be an order for the gardeners to pull the branches out of the now warmer water of the fountains, throw them on an out-of-the-way heap, let them dry, set them afire, and burn them. The gardeners push their pushcarts ahead of them. The park suffered severely from the storms of winter. The cleanup proceeds a bit further every day; nobody hesitates.

There goes somebody running again, but that's not our park at all, that's, it's that enigmatical Monica running, and whom is she chasing now anyway, the trees just whiz by, or is she being chased again herself?

Well, we will just have to get used to it gradually. Well, you see, not much can be done about it anyway. Well, you're not going to manage it any other way either. Well, best thing to do is just keep your hands off. Well, you see, you can get mixed up with who knows what. Well, best thing is just not talk about it. Well, it won't get you anything anyway. Well, we won't get a feather in our hats anyway. And why always forever after? Well, you see, in the meantime we've changed our minds completely. Well, you see, there are altogether different matters. Well, you could have seen it with your own eyes, after all. Well, they didn't even say, so what does that mean. Well, you'll think about it altogether differently all over again. Well, they'll be saying again—yes, they'll be saying that again. Well, they'll just have to get used to it gradually, you see.

You can look out now for hours, that is at the trees that tower into the sky and that the wind always shakes, back and forth, the trees that you can look out at for hours, because there's nothing else outside, only the trees that tower into the sky and that the wind is always shaking, back and forth, the trees and nothing else.

New Realizations:
The company who just arrived there is, of course, altogether different from the one who was announced.
So Nina the cat is going to have kittens.
In a Roman alley five Londoners have now opened up shops.
Too much, last night, too much.

Last year at this time it was already much warmer.
So Arndt inherited the unfortunate talent of his great-grandfather.
Everything was not so bad, after all.
The Roman cat population is estimated at 120,000.
When somebody comes and says, come along, we have no inclina-
tion to, and when we are of a mind to go along if somebody comes
and says, come along, nobody comes and says, come along.
Somewhere somebody's always suffering.
The pope remains the pope.
The new Dino is real hot stuff.
The day you do everything right, you'll grow a second head.
Youth was never so young.
Aha. So that's the way it was with Farouk.
It's not closed season anymore.
The novel lives on and on.
None of that matters much to us.

That was once altogether different. The cities were all much larger
and the towns were still towns. There used to be justice, and who-
ever wouldn't listen had to take the consequences. Our teachers
then were still the teachers of our parents. Sundays we still put on
our Sunday clothes. The church was still standing in the town. The
watch was still kept on the Rhine. We once knew that God was
with us. Hans Muff used to come, too. Whomever we caught
wound up on the martyr's stake. The summers were real summers.
Vacation always seemed endless. Milk was still healthy. We once
knew what we had to hold on to. People went on hikes then. Who-
ever sat in a tavern soon was also sitting in the jug. People used to
walk a lot still. They protected their parks then. There was no such
thing then. There were still enemies then who had eyes to see the
whites of. Wherever you went, you always met people who thought
the way you did. Whoever didn't know better kept his mouth shut
too, and whoever absolutely could not adapt himself, well, he could
just stay far away. Once there were Moors, Indians, and Chinese.
All that used to be much simpler. A thing like that would never
have happened then. There was none of that then, after all. Once
people listened when you told about once.

There they are, sitting around, everywhere, on the steps, on the
walls, on the tops of cars, on the beach and in the woods, and
whenever you haul off at them, they don't stir even then.

Quick, forget everything, right now.

A look at a city, right on to the next, not here either, all right, the third, again nothing, on, maybe yet, just keep going.

All barriers out of the way, we can begin, begin, all day long we say begin.

Now we are standing in a room, you can even say in a hall, the north wall a gigantic window, right, the view of sky and trees. We know our way around here. The rough, golden table, tree stumps, the folding screen, more tables, an animal jumps out of the wardrobe. Under the window a puddle of water, we cross the room and find ourselves on the bank of the lake. In any case the lake is new. We go on and find out for sure that a forest has grown up. We expect fish and birds, but nothing emerges. What else has changed? We've been away a long time, I guess. Nothing has changed, all as usual, except that somebody's sitting at the table there and is thinking about returning after many years.

A few abandoned residences lie beyond, train platforms never set foot on again in a yellow railway station, stacks of unanswered letters, absolute mountains of shards, these vain attempts at reconciliation, these vain trial flights, a couple of good cities, yes, splendid bars, moor willows, dunes, coasts seen from above, a whole heap of hope, scratches on the fenders, odors, sounds, reminiscent of all that.

Some questions:
Are you happier now?
Is your father flying in that airplane?
How did all that come about?
What are we going to do in September, if the money's all gone?
What's gotten into John and the others?
Why are your marriages all breaking up?
Barthelme, why doesn't anyone know Barthelme?
Whom would you rather have, then: the fascists or the Chinese?
What are a biochemist, a city planner, a forester doing at IBM?
Is our route really right?
Why, if we doubt so, do we keep on?

Who will be the first to stop?
Have we at least grown wiser?
Would you like to be, let's say, ten years younger?
Who all is running back and forth again today on the gravel path
anyway?
Who is going to tell you what might help things along a bit?

This place, no, is not our place; we are not at home here, and we're
not guests exactly either. We are here, and we won't remain forever.
Often nice days; the winter harsher than expected. Once we had
the intention of describing the place but the orientation is failing,
the eye dims, too much confusion, too, stage scenery, no memory
here, we insulate more and more, no love, not a word about it
anymore. At times you want to run off screaming. Why we *are*
here, we just don't reflect about that anymore at all; you live half-
way comfortably anyway. What is going on in the old homeland?
Whoever hears something covers his ears up at once. Once outside,
they say, you're better off right away staying outside. Nobody's
going to go crazy here, because memory can sleep damned well
here. Yes, we sleep half the day away. At night, that's when we
have fun. There's only half as much scolding, although there's al-
ways a reason. The guests who come here often don't bark and
don't bite; we have nothing to tell. Sometimes we are very con-
fused; what we think we see disappears again instantly; a delirium
in the head; blurred world. Time of proverbs. Life with maps.
There is California. Where is our spot? Not here, not here either,
but there, we'd like to go there, there, too. Now time has passed
again, and we have forgotten a lot again. Mornings it is often the
worst; it takes a while until we know again where we are now,
what we're about to do, where to now. Indefinite, whatever we say;
wasn't different before: at the end of undetermined days it started
all over again, of course. But the trips made us very happy, and
we're going to describe a few still. Yesterday we made a trip to the
coast. There, on the sand, we stayed sleeping till the wind nudged
clouds in front of the sun. The cold doesn't kill here. The location
doesn't kill. Yes, where there's so much history, nothing much hap-
pens anymore, everything has already happened. Let's say today.
Today is not the Friday on which we began, and the spot on which
we are sitting is a great distance away.

NINE POEMS

ATTILA JÓZSEF

Translated by John Batki

TRANSLATOR'S NOTE: Attila József was born in Budapest in 1905 and died, a suicide, thirty-two years later under the wheels of a freight train at the small Hungarian village of Balatonszárszó. His father, a factory worker, abandoned the family in 1908, and for the following ten years József's mother, a frail woman suffering from cancer, tried to support her three children by doing washing and house cleaning. After her death in 1919, József was put through high school by his older sister's husband, a lawyer. He published his first volume of poems at the age of seventeen; from 1925 to 1929 he studied at the universities of Szeged, Vienna, Paris, and Budapest, without obtaining a degree. József survived on odd jobs and aid from relatives and friends; he had to rely on patronage all his life. Attempts at establishing a stable life met with failure, and after a breakdown in 1929 he was hospitalized several times. He became affiliated with the underground Communist party around 1930, but after a few years he was forced out because of ideological and personal conflicts. During the early 1930s he was deeply involved with Freudian psychoanalysis; in an essay and in some poems he strove for a synthesis of Marx and Freud. The six volumes of his poems published in his lifetime brought him only a peculiar notoriety and harassment from the literary and political establishments—confiscation of a volume on publication; police in-

terference at readings. The prestigious Baumgarten Prize was awarded him one month after his death, and his work by now has been translated into more than twenty languages.

THAT'S NOT ME SHOUTING

That's not me shouting, it's the earth that roars.
Beware, beware, for Satan is raving.
Lie low on the bottom of clear streams,
flatten yourself into a pane of glass,
hide behind the light of diamonds,
under stones with the small insects,
hide away in the fresh baked bread,
you poor man, you poor man.
Seep into the ground with cool showers.
Only in others can you wash your face,
it's no use trying it alone.
Become the edge on a little blade of grass
and you'll be greater than the world's axis.

O machines, birds, leaves, stars!
Our barren mother is praying for a child.
My friend, my dear, beloved friend,
whether it's horrible, whether it's splendid,
that's not me shouting. It's the earth that roars.

(1924)

SUMMONING THE LION

I've had cigars between my teeth,
and a knife stuck in my wrist.
I've been washed by foaming storms,
and could sleep with flies in my mouth.
Once, an old aunt used my bed:
some dreams she must have had.
I coughed blood and became respected,
but I never spat on snow.
I have howled and I have gloated:
let us hear the dead men laugh!
Or could the dead be, really, alive?
So I drank some good, cheap wine,
chewed on boiled shoulder of pig,
shook hands with my left hand only.
Twanged my eyetooth, sold my gods.
My clothes belonged to someone else—
let the pip-squeak search for me!
With my spindly, overgrown heart,
with love hiding behind my mirror,
I am waiting for the lion.
The first time, his rich mane
should buff the polish on my shoes.
The second time, he must caress me;
his claws must tear out my throat.
The third time, he must lick me
on my bed, with his eyes closed.
Then, when I lie in state,
he will be the peerless, roaring
guard over my catafalque.

(1926)

TISZAZUG

Pine needles stitch
lambskin shadows to the trees.
The puli moment runs by,
its claws clicking on ice.

The mesmerized folk hem and haw.
The little houses brood
and pull down greasy hats
of thatch over their windows.

A hen clucks desperately
under the eaves, as if
already an old woman's ghost,
returned to complain.

Indoors, other speckled beasts:
bluish, beaten old men squat there
grunting aloud from time to time
so they won't sink into thought.

For there is much to think about
when a man is too old for the hoe.
Pipesmoke is a fine, soft care,
cotton thread between cracked fingers.

What good is an old man? He drops
the spoon, he drools, has to be fed.
And when he tries to feed the pigs,
they knock him down and spill the foamy slops.

The farm is soft, the pigsty warm.
Twilight hangs there from a star.
Heaven is hard. A wagtail hobbles
on a twig, and whimpers out a cry.

(1929)

SUMMER

Golden plain, marigold, streaming
and weightless meadow. The small
breeze shakes silver laughter
from a birch. The sky sways.

Here comes a wasp. It sniffs me,
growls, lands on a wild rose.
The angry rose bows.
This summer is red, but still too slender.

More and more soft stirrings.
Blood-red berries on the sand.
The ripe wheat nods and rustles.
A storm is perched upon the treetops.

My summer's end is here so fast!
The wind arrives on tumbleweeds—
and as the heavens crash, my friends,
the blade of a scythe flashes out.

(1930)

MOTHER

She held her mug with both hands
one Sunday, and with a quiet smile
she sat a little while
in the growing dusk.

She brought home in a tiny skillet
the food they gave her where she worked.
We went to bed marveling how
the rich always fill their bellies.

My mother was a small woman.
She died early, for washerwomen die early:
their legs tremble from carrying,
their heads ache from ironing.

For scenery, they have mountains of laundry,
cloudscapes of steam to soothe their nerves.
For a change of climate they
only have to climb the attic stairs.

I see her pausing with the iron.
Her frail body, grown thinner and thinner,
was broken by capital.
Think about this, proletarians.

She was slightly stooped from all that laundry.
I didn't realize she was a young woman.
In her dreams she wore a clean apron
and even the mailman said hello.

(1931)

THE WASTELAND

Water smokes and withered rushes
droop in the flatlands.
The heights are tucked into feathery puffs.
A thick silence crackles
in the snowy fields.

Dusk is fat, greasy, quiet.
The lowlands are flat, orderly, and round.
Only a rowboat
clucks to itself
in the pond's freezing mush.

The forest gives birth to shivering times
among its icy branches.
This is where frost snaps
and finds moss for its bony horse
and ties him up.

Vineyards, with a plum tree here and there.
On the vinestalks, soggy straw.
Skinny stakes stand in a row,
waiting for old peasants
to take a walk.

This landscape revolves
around a farmhouse.
Winter's playful claws
crack some more plaster
from its walls.

The pigsty's gate hangs wide open.
It creaks as the wind toys with it.
Perhaps a pig will wander inside
or a cornfield will come running
with its corn!

Small peasants in a small room.
One of them smokes, but only dry leaves.
No prayer is going to help these.
They sit, full of thought,
in the dark.

The vineyard freezes—it's the landlord's.
The shots in the forest are also his.
The pond is his, too, and under the ice,
the fat fish wait
for him.

  (1932)

YELLOW GRASS

Yellow grass grows on the sand,
this wind is a bony old woman,
this puddle is a nervous beast,
the sea is calm and tells a tale.

I softly hum my inventory.
My home is an overcoat for sale,
a sunset fallen on the dunes.
I cannot go on like this.

Everything shines: time's teeming
coral reef, the lifeless world,
birch tree, woman, tenement—
through the blue currents of the sky.

                              (1933)

CONSCIOUSNESS

I
Dawn has untied the sky from the earth
and at its clear soft word
insects and children, like ripe grain,
roll out into the daylight.
There is no haze in the air,
this sparkling clarity floats everywhere.
Overnight, like small moths,
leaves have covered the trees.

II
In my dreams I saw paintings
splashed with blue, red, yellow
and I thought this was the order of the world,
not a speck of dust out of place.
Now my dreams seem to be pale shadows
in my limbs, and the iron world is the rule.
During day a moon rises within me
at at night a sun shines inside.

III

I am thin. At times I eat only bread.
Among the idle chatter of some minds
I search, free and free of charge, for
something more certain than the fall of dice.
True, I have no roast beef kissing my lips,
or a small child cuddled near my heart—
but even the trickiest cat is unable to catch
mice in and outdoors at the same time.

IV

Just like a pile of split wood,
the world lies in a heap.
Each thing is pushed and squeezed
and held in place by others
so that everything is determined.
Only what isn't can turn into bush,
only what will be can become flower.
The things that exist fall into pieces.

V

At the freight station I had
flattened myself against a tree
like a piece of silence. Gray weeds
touched my mouth, raw and strangely sweet.
Dead still, I watched the watchman, trying
to outguess him, afraid of his shadow
on the silent boxcars, his stubborn shadow
on the shiny, dewy lumps of coal.

VI

You see, the suffering is deep inside,
but the reasons for it lie out there.
The world is your wound. It burns and throbs,
and you feel the fever, your soul.
You are a slave as long as you have to
rebel. You will be free when you stop
building yourself the kind of house
into which landlords like to settle.

VII

I looked up in the night
and saw the cogwheel of the stars.
The loom of the past was weaving laws
from glittering threads of chance.
Then, from my steaming dreams,
I looked up at the sky again,
and saw that the fabric of the law
would somehow always have its flaw.

VIII

Silence listened as the clock struck one.
You could look up your childhood—
even among these damp cinder blocks
it's possible to imagine some freedom—
so I thought. But just as I stood up,
the constellations and the stars
lit up like prison bars
above a silent cell.

IX

I have heard iron crying,
I have heard the rain laugh.
I have seen the past shattered, and know
that only ideas can be forgotten.
Now I see all I can do is love
and submit to the weight of my burden.
But why must I forge a weapon
out of you, golden consciousness!

X

An adult is someone who has
no father and no mother in his heart,
who knows that he receives life
as something extra on death's part,
and, like a found object, can return it
any time—that's why he keeps it.
He is nobody's god or priest,
not even his own.

XI

I have seen happiness face to face:
it was flabby, blond, and weighed a ton.
Its curly smile wavered
above the harsh grass of the farmyard.
It plopped down into a lukewarm puddle,
blinked and grunted in my direction.
I can still see the hesitant light
fumbling with its fluffy hair.

XII

I live by the railroad tracks.
I watch the trains go by.
The shining windows fly
in the swaying flax darkness.
This is how in eternal darkness
the lit-up days speed by,
and I stand in the light of each compartment,
leaning on my elbows, silent.

(1934)

KÖLTÖNK ÉS KORA (The Poet and His Age)

Well, here is my poem.
And the second line.
Its title sounds hard with
those K's: "Költönk és Kora."
And inside it, nothingness
hovers as if it were something,
dust . . .

Nothingness hovers in it,
like something. The world,
floating in expanding space,
sets out for the future
amidst the murmuring of leaves and seas,
the howling of dogs
at night . . .

I on my chair, the chair on the earth,
the earth under the sun,
the sun's satellites, imprisoned
galaxies, everything progresses—
into nothingness.
In me, a movement in reverse,
this thought . . .

My mind is empty. It would fly
up to the great mother emptiness above.
But I tied it to my body
like a balloon to its gondola.
This is not real, not a dream;
it's called sublimating the
instincts . . .

Come, my friend, and look around.
You work in the world,
and inside you works pity.
It's no use to lie.
Leave it behind, leave it behind.
Look at the evening light, how it dies
with evening . . .

The stubble fields stand in red blood,
and the slopes stretch away
in bluish clots. The tiny weak grass
cries and bends.
Soft death spots appear
on happy hills.
Night is here.

(1937)

TAKE YOUR OWN SWEET SORROW

JAY PETER OLWYLER

It wasn't so tough taking them. But you wondered does it start at the toes and spread up and flame out fingers . . .

The bedclothes caught fire from the tiny blazes and became a bigger one. The flames wrapped his body. His hair disappeared in a puff and from his mouth the screams formed. Flame laved his mouth with passion and cooked his lungs. Hot dogs, so help me god, cooked guts.

Who cares for the blackened face?

Would the skin slough off?

Like scraping the slime coating from the surface of the river?

Oh god, oh agony!

Oh god!

Take it off.

He sat up. There was a sad smile on his face.

Grave, not sad, perhaps. Perhaps deep eyes, perhaps wondering. No . . . not wondering—waiting.

Not waiting, but *knowing*.

The hell with the pills. Puke them. After all, you can undo it if you're not dead.

He went into the bathroom and knelt at the side of the white toilet bowl. He placed his hands on the edges and leaned over the porcelain funnel of water. There was the familiar heave of the stomach, the constriction of the throat, the force tearing up from his stomach. It left him weak and gasping. There was the stink in his nostrils, the awful retching noise.

He looked out the window of the bus and there was a woman, shapeless, old, gray-head, with a funnel in her hand. A tin funnel. The base was wrapped in long brown paper or was it a stick? A broom? But there was the funnel.

She stood by the sink and somehow, vaguely, the water flowed from the faucet into the funnel. It was fixed. The funnel remaining under the sink till Christ comes!—but it's fixed and there it will stay until the house disappears in a puff of dust.

Can she even feel success over so small a thing? I could have fixed it. She's satisfied in her fat, crotchy way. She bought it for that, didn't she? and she knew beforehand it would work. The old woman didn't smile, but on her face there was the same look as of the boy playing secretly, cautiously with his dog, the dog uneasy, the dog resisting, but nothing bad because what does one do wrong when one is so little?

Let the old woman pass. Maybe she wants it for something else. He pulled the cord and got off. It yanked to a stop. On purpose he brushed his hand behind him as she swung suspended from her hand, the other holding her package.

Go ahead, look around you bitch! It was an accident. And if it wasn't? And why?

Take it home or——hell, once again doesn't matter. There are so many times. . . .

She looked at him with deep eyes. He smiled dark secret deep smile and together they climbed from the iron step into the sharp, pointed street, the blind street, into the dark coolness of the doorway.

Why? Darling?

Can't you see it? she said. No, he said. You can't go yet, she said. The hell I can't you bitch, he said. I couldn't help it, she said. The hell you couldn't.

No, he didn't say that. He stared at her, and her eyes were closer, and then only eyes, and yet, below, the swaying body, the bulging body, and the close body, and this body under his hands, the fat—not fat—her neck in his fingers. She loved him anyway. He could see it in her eyes. Her bulging eyes.

There were noises, these noises. His fingers tightened and there was no sound. Only her eyes asking him.

Please.

Please. Not now. Not here.

The hell with you, he thought. He squeezed.

She fell between his legs. A pressure. I've got to get out of here. He was sick.

You couldn't turn your eyes this way and have the street bat them in the face. In fact where could you turn them? Brightness and this damn dull fist smacking him in the back of the neck.

A dull fist pounding him over the head like jelly. Maybe the pills after all.

Never mind what for. I want them— No I want them for my dog. He's old, and the naked skin along his side is from eczema. He's an old dog. Let him die.

Ahhhh, you poor fool, he thought. He took the brown package. In his pocket.

Why me? I go on. I'm *worth* saving. I have to say so much.

Somehow it can't be what you want. He pulled the door open and watched her. She was reading her goddam magazine again. She looked up.

—You look so funny darling.

Yes.

—It makes me feel funny when you look that way.

I'm silent.

She put the magazine down. There's so much to do, she said. She wriggled in her mind. Change him. Stop him. Make him think of something else. Please god make him think of something else.

He walks closer. The pills in his hand. He holds them out. She takes them from his palm. Her eyes ask.

No.

And he replies, no. Take them. She takes them.

We'll have a wonderful life. Think of it. I'm so glad I married you.

He smiled.

He was silent. He held out the pills. They were in her hand. Her own hand carrying them toward her mouth.

Please.

No.

The hand moving upward. Her eyes in a frozen smile, her mouth talking but never mind, it doesn't fool us baby.

Of course not.

—I have such a good dinner for you. What you like.

Oh pray you damn goddamned eyes. Talk, mouth.

They talked of other things. They knew. The pills disappeared inside the mouth. It started with the toes. Spread upward in small flames before she sank. Her dress to her waist. Rot, you stinking bastard. A puddle on the floor. Even *ants*.

He felt the pity start in a low flood in his bladder and spread behind his forehead.

Or loneliness? The hell with it. You go on.

She opened the door and he raised his head.

What we said this morning—it was kind of dumb.

He knew she knew, but he wouldn't ask her.

There was the pounding, the old retching. His bowels ran loose and she saw.

—Nothing, he said.

—Nothing at all? she said.

—Nothing at all. He sat on the bed.

The doctor came in with her as she entered.

Of course I love you. How much? How goddam much?

He couldn't ask her. Never mind the doctor. Two were enough. I do love you goddamit! How much?

He looked at the knife dully. He felt it sinking into his finger below the second joint. It bit and scraped on the bone.

She looked at him. There was contempt in her voice. It doesn't prove a goddam thing.

What had he done it for? Too late now. Too late for good, this time.

Waiting for her to get back he sat on the edge of the bed and stared at his finger. The blood puddled on the carpet and his guts seemed to be draining out of him, seeping into the mattress beneath him, spreading in a wide, white ring.

He sat on the bed and said Hopeless.

She sneered as he waited for her to come back. He heard her.

And as he waited, dumbly, numbly, he felt the beginnings of the terror. . .

FOUR POEMS

JOHN RATTI

FALLING

for R.T.

> *"Amid all the beauty and splendour of*
> *Peterborough Cathedral, the thing which in-*
> *trigued me most was the 12th century carv-*
> *ing at the base of a pillar . . . of a man*
> *tormented by devils— . . . the headlong*
> *plunge of Simon Magus, the magician, who*
> *attempted to fly from the top of a building.*
> *High above him . . . stands the serene figure*
> *of St. Peter. . . ."*
>
> *—from a letter to* Country Life

Let there be no mistake,
I am Simon Magus,
curly-haired and wild-eyed,
brought to earth:
tormented living
by Christ's harsh wood
and rusty nails;

tormented
as I fall,
dying,
by live demons
who make my headlong
plunge
continue
after I have ceased
to fall,
who tear at me
endlessly,
giving me an immortality
of pain.
For the more they take,
the more I am;
Heaven reconstitutes me
for Hell's pleasure,
shuttlecock
in the loveplay
of God and Devil.
Divinely titillated,
Prince Lucifer
spends himself
in my open wounds,
flashing his arrogant
teeth in steely
satisfaction.
From a parapet,
from a tower,
I tried to fly
beyond them all,
telling my words and spells
from my lips,
making a web
of threadlike
incantations—
only
to have it cut
at the instant of escape

by the knife of
divine reason,
and I fall
trying to hold up
my sinking stomach
with my hands.
Triumphant and serene,
St. Peter
weathers on a gable,
his eyes eaten out
by the wind.
And I,
eternally
reaching
bottom
retain the full
definition
of my pain,
each stroke
of the master carver
still cut deep
and true.

RECURRENT DREAM

after Francis Bacon

I dreamed of you
in that recurrent dream
where
a lily-scented
three day corpse
is laid out
in a jewel box coffin
in the other room,
a horror just beyond the door,
half, quarter seen.
In all this time
I had forgotten
the white parts
of your body
and their dark words,
risen bubbling
on your lips.
Now it returns
at the moment
when
we were flayed
alive and screaming
on your rumpled bed,
skinned down
to our teeth and skulls.
And your pleasure of me
and my tearing hunger
spawned the horror
in the room
beyond the door.

FAMILY FUNERAL

for my cousin

At twelve I went to sleep
with your face,
a dream mask,
pressed to my face;
the weight,
I could have, would have sworn,
of your mouth
resting on my mouth;
your heavy hair
thick
between my sleep-padded
fingers.

Now I find you again
risen
from beside your mother's grave,
come away with her hair,
her face,
buried deep inside
her insulated woman's body.

We touch carefully,
standing in the iced,
raw clay;
your voice has changed
to her voice
and yet remains
enough your own
to bring the sleeping
lovesick child in me
to tears and hopeless
fear of waking.

THERE   AND THERE

There—
at the soft place
behind the ear,
close to the hair
where it is warm,
stung by the metal
tongue,
the neck
is lashed off
tight
by the black calf
leather.
They asked how
he managed to bring
his belt with him
into the cell;
there will be
an investigation
about bringing belts
into the cells.
And there—
the young blue arteries
feeding the groin
choked
at the impact;
the shriek
of his manhood
startled, falsetto,
then clotted
to silence.

THE UGLY DEVILS

YUMIKO KURAHASHI

Translated by Samuel Grolmes and Yumiko Tsumura

I spent the summer of that year in the villa on the cape. The breeze from the sea was soft, like a woman's tongue, and the sea and sky were sewn securely together by the horizon, parting only at morning like a frayed eyelid to vomit out its scarlet eyeball of sun. I was an ugly devil shut up in a shell. Ugly, I suppose, because of my love of despair. That love, of course, had been created by hatred. Hatred for the stable world with its daily-life pace that existed outside my shell. But a girl pulled me out with the hook "love," and managed to pin me firmly to the real world. My actual despair started with that. Today, the only bright past I can call to mind is in that decisive summer, in that word "love." A radiant past! An armload of maw-worms. I was seventeen that summer.

The cape was shaped like a stegosaurus trying to pull its tail up onto the shore. Those nights I spent at the villa, I used to caress that tail over and over in my dreams, especially where the notched part was about to slip back into the sea. And my fingers repeatedly groped for the tip of the stegosaurus's tail, trying with all my strength to drag the emerging monster back into the sea. Then, my will in those dreams turned into a demon standing blackly in the way. The monster was torn from the earth with a terrifying ob-scene roar, and after that the entire world slithered into the sea as its thick skin was stripped off— At that point I always woke up in sweet wet convulsions. But outside the window, like a lie, there was always the peaceful morning light. The smooth wax-yellow cape lay stretched out at full length in the shape of a woman's leg. My dream had not changed the world at all.

M often came by on mornings like that. The first time, for example, she brought the collie that had been raised in my own home. M and the collie with their heads sticking side by side out of the car window looked somehow alike. I greeted M (she was my cousin) with a mixture of morning drowsiness, the intimate arrogance of an older brother, and the sullenness a young man would show his mistress. I asked why she came. M brought her lashes neatly together and raised her eyes, forcing a laugh as though looking into the sun. *On an errand!* she answered. It was always an errand. In fact, she was a messenger. A messenger from whom? *A messenger from the Emperor,* M said, *to the Prince.* M liked to pretend that I was a Prince. It let her pretend to be the enamored Princess. *Orders from Him,* I said meekly, my tongue numb with shame, *or Her?* Shaking her head, M just pointed in the direction she had come from. An outstretched arm reaching back toward town, business, school. Actually she came with a report of what went on there to conceal her own spying. But it was perfectly clear that nothing could happen there. He and She—what other way is there to refer to them—had been in the process of divorce ever since I can remember. The case was still pending that summer, and it appeared that it would go on forever, because She absolutely would not give in to His demand for a divorce. They had been building an indestructible tower out of the hatred they shared. I grew up crawling around in that tower. I was not the son of either of them. I fed from my own breast. I ate nothing but my own flesh. And after spending a childhood as one of that breed of monsters known as prodigies, I was becoming as harmless a young man as any in the world. Just like all prodigies do. Wisdom's devil, with the soul of a globular cactus. I had begun to read voluminously, but it did nothing to expand the hollowness inside the cactus, to fertilize that darkness. It produced nothing. I was the kind of person who cringed at the idea of expressing himself to another in any form whatsoever. The instinct for self-expression was by nature lacking in me. In spite of that, I read and read, fattening myself to the point that my own bulk became more than I could move. My eyes ate up everything, like a mouth takes in food. My cerebrum must have been inflated by that morbid, chronic hunger. Even after I went to the villa, my daily routine (more than studying for the entrance examination) had been to continue devouring books like some insane sheep.

Seeing me so, this spy was undoubtedly reporting to them. I had continuous phone calls from Him and from Her, He telling me to concentrate only on study for the examination, and She asking me to study less and exercise more. What the hell should I exercise for! I am not ever going to do anything. M delivered her message, *She says, fatten up! your mother's getting marvelously fat! in the hospital!* That was the funny part of it. I knew that She had gone into the hospital with insomnia. But according to M's story, She was getting unbelievably fat. Her life under the insomnia treatment amounted to sleeping a few days, waking to eat her fill, and then going back to sleep again. At the same time, it seemed that He had taken up with another woman. *And lately he worries about cancer, is going into the hospital for check-ups all the time.*

How much I had wanted to hear a report of destruction from the mouth of this messenger! Of Her going insane, of Her flesh rotting, of His strangling to death, of His testes exploding, spurting out radioactive sperm, of the end of the world. . . But nothing at all happened. Nothing at all.

M came by frequently, bringing the collie, like a formal envoy. At some time or other, that giant collie had become completely M's. He would not eat from the palm of any other human being. And as for me, he merely pointed a sharp face out of his rich fur in my direction. He didn't even wag his tail at me anymore. My guess is that M had converted him by some trick of manipulation of the arrow concealed beneath his stomach.

Sensing that I was giving her a quiet brush-off, M attended to the salt-wind- and sand-stained car and to the dog, and left. The dry echo of the engine and the three histrionic barks of the dog lingered after her. But I should write about M as fairly as I can. She was between sixteen and seventeen that summer. I can say truthfully that she was a girl who had been raised exclusively on the milk of virtue peculiar to our social class, a girl both graceful and coquettish. I fell in love first with her eyes. They were obviously feline in shape, but judging by the color, they were finally canine eyes. No, that's not it. It was more than that. . .

I used to talk with M a lot before that summer. I talked on and on about a universe that existed inside my head—where else would a universe exist—of its countless nebulae, its exploding nebulae, its radio stars, its quasars, about a receding universe, I mean about the terrifying expansion of my universe. And M disagreed. She objected to the theory of an expanding universe, a universe going insane. She fell back on the hypothesis that the universe is eternally stable. In my universe, Nothingness was exactly the purpose of Existence. But according to M, Nothingness had given birth to Existence. The universe remained stationary.

So, we always clashed on this point, and stared into each other's faces. I looked inside M's eyes at those times, but there was no hint of a star there. Her eyes were an elemental substance, a theory of existence, a self-illuminated lake. Yet, if I stared into her eyes too long, they seemed to secrete a thin, salty liquid. When I tasted it, I felt a hunger for her that resembled sadness. At the beginning M was a mermaid when I held her in my arms, because I had arbitrarily decided that the lower half of this long-haired girl's body was enclosed in scales of virtue, was sealed in a perfect cone, had nowhere in it a symptom of sex. But my hand parted her legs effortlessly. M did open completely. I acted more from fear than hatred— And I became M's possession. I mean just that. I did not possess M. I became M's possession.

M walked softly to the window with a sheet wrapped around her. Even to the way a lock of her hair fluttered, her movements, gestures, her mannerisms indicated she was fully conscious that she was being watched. Stretching out her arms to push the windows open left and right, she filled the room with moonlight, letting the sheet slide "casually" off her body (the sort of casualness one sees on the stage), exposing her apricot-colored nakedness.

M was simply showing me her body. I don't know where she got the idea of showing herself to me. M was following M's script. But I realized then that my idea of her as a sexless creature was mistaken. M stood there with her crossed arms supporting the weight of her breasts. She looked thoroughly "petrified." Ordinarily, such a staring match would end in my defeat—I mean, I was looking at her with eyes while she was glaring back at me with her entire naked body—she could take advantage of the instant my eyes were diverted, melted, and fall on her prey like a wild beast. But she pretended to succumb, to leap of her own will into the arms of the hunter. And then, an explosive sigh of distress, a rough embrace, a delirious vow of "love"— But I refused to go by the script like that. I felt I ought to step back into the dark, become an observer, and watch M. Then she would not be able to leap with flapping arms into the heart of her audience. I was watching M from a safe distance. But the tide of my consciousness (or I might say, attention) was sucked out by M's magnetism, and before long the bleakness of my sea floor lay exposed. I looked at everything. Then, an audience of one, I applauded in a way that could not be misunderstood as simple flirting. In fact, the words "I love you" came out. I jabbed these words as my spear of pure irony into her chest. The curtain fell immediately. M covered her delighted face and left. . . .

But when I saw her again, she showed no inclination to make any fuss about this "love." She had the most innocent face in the world. Still, it was my mistake not to have taken precautions against her innocence, her pure artlessness. When I did come to my senses, I recognized that at some time or another she had started wearing the spearhead I had stabbed into her as a pendant. The medal "love." Because I said "I love you," M's behavior became "I am loved." I think that to her it amounted to the same thing as "I love." And when M and I faced each other across the table at the villa (the collie all the while seated politely beside M with his white face sticking up above the table, as if to certify that he was faithful to M only), I tried somehow to slice that sticky word with my knife and fork, but it was the world's worst *taffy*. Its very nature made it adhere to the tools I was using to try to cut it. The more I struggled against the spell of this "love" the more entangled I became. For example, to prevent M's "I am loved" behavior, I switched the signal to "I do not love you." This, M took as a sort of code. She deciphered it to mean in fact "I love you." So, as a result of her misreading, she had the right to act with confidence. I glared at the collie instead of her. M was feeding him cheese from her lips. She stopped, reading the look in my eyes. A very subtle movement of her own eyes. She clearly pretended to read the color of jealousy in my look.

One morning when M dropped by again, her face was red in the ominous fiery glow of the morning sky. The black birds that nested on the cliff of the cape were dancing boisterously in flocks in the sky. The klaxon that announced her arrival was different. It blared on and on like an alarm. M got out of the car wearing a dress the color of fire. *The dog?* I asked. M answered, *He's gone.* As if it had some deep meaning. She put her arm through mine and invited me for a walk. While we walked barefoot along the narrow beach below the cliff, I had the feeling some stone the size of an infant's head had reproduced itself in mounds. M was in unusually high spirits, bouncing up and down like a buoy.

M was a rather reticent girl, she seldom laughed. When she did, her smiling face was like the sudden appearance of the sun in the middle of the night, but she laughed loudly during our walk that morning, reaching out her arm to me for support every time she stumbled on a rock. Her wrist was burning cold. *They say there's a typhoon close,* M said, sticking out her lips at me. When I looked up, the morning glow had disappeared. The wind had stopped completely, and the world looked absolutely suffocated.

We had planned to go for a swim in the inlet before noon. As we walked along the level sand that was filled with sea shells, the fishermen's wives and the old men were dragging seine. They turned toward this "pair of lovers" and in unison let out some harsh roar. It may have been nothing but a friendly warning though, since the typhoon was close. But the inlet was as calm as if anesthetized. We undressed on the sand at the base of the inlet where a few shabby patches of weeds were growing. There was a tombstone standing at an angle with a barely legible inscription, and a hut of nothing but pillars and roof was half buried in the invading sand.

The fishermen's children who were usually screaming and romping around were not there that day. So, that gloomy morning, the two of us alone eased our bodies into the tepid water. There was a leaden membrane stretched across the ceiling of sky, making it difficult to locate where the sun was. When I raised my neck up out of the water, the sea as a whole was rocking slowly up and down, like a cradle in a dream, endlessly raising little obtuse-angled pyramid waves. It was clear that the smooth skin of the sea was animal matter. The sea is not an inorganic substance. I scanned the surface of the water for M so I could tell her of this discovery, but there was only her yellow hat bobbing up and down beyond the countless wrinkles of waves. When I tried to shout, I only gulped in fishy water. I felt I was bathing in amniotic fluid.

I stretched out on the bow of a rotting boat half sunk in the sand, and closed my eyes. I began to grow heavy, wings of sleep spread over me. My head began to sink in mucilage. Then, the cape came into my half-paralyzed mind as it always did at such times. I wonder what is on the other side of that cape. It goes on forever. The closer I come to the tip, the rougher the waves become. Fear always broke off these dream swims. But the one thing I did know was that what should have been on the other side of that cape could not be there. M was dropping sand onto my chest while she listened to me. The refrain she mouthed was like a lullaby to soothe my desperate questioning, *There is nothing.* Of course, it did not mean that the world literally stopped there, that nothing existed beyond. How wonderful it would be if there were no world beyond that cape, if the birds that flew away did not return. But I knew without the help of a map that the world went on as usual beyond the cape. Beyond the cape the same waves and sand interlock even more firmly than in my world, and an infinite number of fishing boats, nets, rocks and bits of driftwood, and even capes just like this one exist. Like saw teeth. That was the most intolerable thing of all. M's refrain, *There is nothing,* amounted to no more than the sound of the wind.

I was rowing on a dream ocean with weighted oars. I continued to round cape after cape in spite of the toil that accumulated like mud. The voyage toward "future" in which I could not round one single cape in spite of having passed countless others, the vertical fall of "time" at the end of the ocean that only the dead can go beyond— Suddenly I became a bird of ecstasy, soared up and saw the other side of the cape. Why was it I hadn't been able to do such a simple thing before? There I could see dead stars. A burnt-out sun drops behind the cape at that coast. And what I saw was unmistakably the corpse of the sun, hollow, just bones, the livid sun moored in the dark. It was the castle "nothingness" I had dreamed of. A castle of *néant* towering in a place that does not exist, the "mock" light that shines from the lamp of the imagination's power, the wind of irrationality. . . and when I looked closely I saw that the huge dead star was slowly rotating, illuminating the splinters of desolation. Like a mill that makes "time" flow backward. It must have become a dead star as far back in the past as my thoughts can reach. But then, the ordinary hot sun, what is it? Isn't it the "mock" sun? Nothing but a phantom sun whose orbit in the sky is created by our own mundane hopes.

A cool snake-tongue slipped between my eyelids. Staring at me out of a head of matted hair, huge eyes and a face covered with warts of moisture came at me. M sucked at me with her damp mouth, and in a stupidly anxious tone asked the most meaningless thing possible, *What were you thinking?* I answered, *I was asleep.* Then M lay down on her stomach on top of me, bent back from the waist and looked down at me. She went on, *What were you dreaming about? About the future,* I said playfully, and M, delighted, crammed those words into her own mouth, *Oh! About our future!* . . .

The wind suddenly strengthened. The coarse tongue of a long column of sand- and salt-saturated wind instantly stung our eyes. We felt millions of little scratches on our cheeks. *The typhoon's coming,* M said, and squatted down to put her things away. Just like a little child would after playing house. She had the hips of a cute little child. She stood up and said, *We've got to hurry back.* Her face had the composure of a flawless housewife.

Where the sand ended, there was a breakwater shaped like an upper lip. Beyond that, as far as the eye could see there was a grove of low pine trees. From the veranda of the villa it resembled the membrane of a bat's wing spread over the base of the cape. But as I approached, I could see a labyrinth of capillaries. The brush of wind combed the pine trees smooth at the height of my collarbone. M darted into the maze, and her head sank into the ocean of trees. As I chased her, M fled from mesh to mesh, pursuing me. During this teasing game of tag, the wind twisted at my neck and ripped my voice. Soon I lost sight of M. Over the ocean of trees that had swallowed her, drops of rain began to fall the way a shot bird drops.

M was already back. She was waiting, wrapped in a bath towel and sipping a cup of hot coffee. She was reading a deck of cards, playing fortuneteller, prophesying the assault of a storm, and seeing that she would spend the night at the villa. It was really ridiculous.

That afternoon there was rain and wind off and on, and from time to time a crack opened in the clouds. The bloodshot eye of sun peered maliciously through these sudden gaps. But we were already in the typhoon's lungs. The storm began at night in an eruption of furious breath. The lights simply disappeared.

That evening, M and I ate with the caretaker and his grandchild. At dinner we used long candles that reminded us of a Christmas feast. M went to her room early, and when I went to see her later, carrying a candle, she was already folded into a sound sleep, ignorant of the storm's clamor. After seeing the exasperatingly deep sleep she was in, my eyelids burned with anticipation, the great hand of the storm would crush or perhaps sink the world. I dropped off into a fitful sleep on a bed that was shuddering like a boat in the sea. But I had no reason to hope. In the morning, all would be as calm as a lie, the false sun's light would begin to repaint the world. The world would smile at me like the face of a woman who has just removed her make-up. It was a feeling of pure despair.

The storm ended at dawn. And in the morning light, I was able to see all the things that called for despair. M was prone on the bed, her apricot-colored legs and side exposed. For some reason she reminded me of an arrogant tiger. I saw instantly that even twenty years from now she would still sprawl out in exactly the same way. After I had carefully looked at her entire body, I pressed my lips against the desert of her ugly back, as if to jab needles of hatred one by one into her pores. That animal groaned with satisfaction.

We went out for an early morning walk along the beach that the typhoon had dragged its ragged hair over. The storm's trash littered the shore. The sand had been washed away, and the beach was all sea shells. As we walked, M squealed at everything she saw, pointing as she did at driftwood, bottles and strands of seaweed that were scattered around the beach like hairs. As far as M was concerned the world was only slightly damaged. It could never be destroyed. *Feels like a corpse or something has been washed up around here,* M was saying, in obviously forced high spirits. As she put her arm in mine, she closed her eyes and let her face fill up with sunlight like a bowl. She was trying to keep from spilling one drop of my "love." So charming and so seductive! I pulled her to the ground and kissed her to try to suck that "love" out of her face. Making no attempt to hold me, her arms just spread out like wings, and dug into the sand like roots up to her wrists. It was as if M were trying to keep me from flying away by holding on with her lips alone. I flapped. But there was no flight from the trap. (She didn't even close her eyes.) And the frustration raging in me only shoved me deeper into the futile battle. I became a soldier certain of defeat before the fight began. It was all so boring, this job of unfastening her, freeing her legs from the underwear, making my incision on her breasts. Yet, I was able to seem enthusiastic exactly because I did know that it was all futile. To make M understand this, I told her not to close her eyes. She put on her sunglasses. Otherwise she met my attack as naked as she was born.

　Someone is watching, M said in a deliberate voice. In a second, the sky became a blue eye. My weight still on her, I raised my eyes and scanned the rim of the dune. The seam of the sky and sea became a golden line and burst into flame. And, because of some fantasy that dozens of toadstools were about to poke their heads up out of the sand and flood me in barbaric screams, I could hardly move. While M was putting on her dress she told me that there was a reformatory on the terrace of the cape. I hadn't known. *Near here? You can't see it from here, but it might have been some guy from there, somebody was watching.* M crinkled her nose, sniffing for people. *What did you do with the dog?* I asked abruptly. M hushed me with her hand and said, *My nose is sharper than a dog's.* We went around the rim of the dune. And there we found it. A body washed up with the driftwood. *A nigger!* M screamed. It was a young Negro (or perhaps a mixed-blood). He had dropped there as softly as the larva of Satan, thrown up by the ocean, his yellowish palms and soles bared in the sunshine. *Where did he come from?* M pointed in the direction of the reformatory. *Then, he must have escaped during the storm last night. Is he alive? Touch him and find out,* M said. I refused to. It didn't matter to me whether he was alive or dead. As far as I was concerned, he was nothing but a fish that happened to look human, black outside, covered with a dark skin that would inhale sunlight. But my eyes made a scalpel-like, vertical slice through his body—peach-colored inside, fiery pulp. Then M pried a broken-oar lever under his stomach and flipped him over. We both gasped. A rose-colored knife of meat was pointed toward the sky.

　I saw by the wrecked boat and broken oar on the beach how foolhardy this Negro's escape had been. It seems he had tried to row around the cape in the middle of the storm. It was exactly what I had attempted over and over in my dreams. A little over-excited, I said, *The guy is stupid! And, the silly thing is he's still alive.* M lifted his damp coat, we saw an initial sewn on the inside pocket. Q. *Name must be Quincy or something,* I said, and M answered indifferently, *Let's go back and call the police.*

　The sun had already melted over the sky. The heat on the sand was so intense that I was sure this black ghost would evaporate like a slug. The very idea of police at a time like this just made me laugh. I knew that any policeman who might come would find nothing but a smudge of sweat on the sand. *We don't have to do that,* I told M, *either somebody from the reformatory will find this Q, or else he'll wander sheepishly back by himself, one or the other. What if he runs away?* M said anxiously. *They'd catch him in no time.* I don't know what else might have been on M's mind at that time. After lunch I went out onto the veranda to take a nap in the tickle of wind from the sea. I was dreaming about Q when M's short sharp cry woke me.

Q, his bare feet crammed into shaggy fur, came to my room. He came in and sat down, like a picture in a frame, and gave me a meaningless grin. It was all in dream sequence. But this reality was more diluted than a dream. Q, too, had lost some of his Negroid thickness. He looked faded. *You gonna tell the cops bout me?* Q said in an effeminate voice. (It had the luster of polished leather.) When I said I had no such intention, Q didn't register any concern. He said that I could report him or not, either way, it didn't make any difference to him. I asked why. And Q explained it didn't make any difference to him. Then he went to sleep on my bed. M left for town in a wild blast of the engine.

That was how Q came toward me, his rose-colored knife sticking out. It wasn't really a thing to stab me with, but a spear of meat for me to grasp, admire, fondle, and finally to tenderly melt. I soon understood that I was to be a paddle that was to steer this black canoe. When I recognized that, I knew that Q was a "mock" woman. I was in the bath washing Q. He was a furless animal, a rubber doll that would shrink and stretch obscenely, a bright piece of flesh wrapped in a skin of thin clay, or chocolate. In fact, this black Q had that grotesque darkness on the outside which women (including M) wrapped up with their white skins. Yet there couldn't be anything to attract me in this taut darkness covering the surface. I was able to look at him because there was no danger of my being sucked into his darkness. There was no "love" threat. I think it was a pure ritual of recognition. What Q taught me: that ritual which severs the dark epidermis, pours consciousness into the flesh like hot sulfur. I was totally clear. I made love to something that had no "love." Because I could see myself as well as the target as I attacked. Q's cry of pain verified the clarity of my consciousness.

During the few melon-sweet August days I spent this way, the talk I had with Q amounted to nothing but a few seeds in the pulp of silence. I wondered what in the world Q had been doing before he was put into the reformatory. *I don't do anything, he told me.* It may be that a delinquent is a boy who survives by not doing anything. Like me for example. Q didn't try to do anything but be the "mock" woman I had created.

One morning when another typhoon's approach was broadcast (the red sunrise glowing like a demon's face), M's arrival was announced by a senselessly long blast on the klaxon. M and I were alone during our dull swim in the inlet, but somehow M didn't say anything about Q, and I had no occasion to either. Q was hiding like an inconspicuous house pet in one of the rooms in the villa. That night, when the storm hit, M stayed at the villa. As the building first began to shriek in the beating wind, remembering that I had done exactly the same thing once before, I carried a candlestick toward M's room through the dark, low-pressure atmosphere that seemed to hover as flaccid as a jellyfish. Whether it was real or not, I don't know, but I felt I heard a scream. I rushed into M's room. An invisible wing flapped somewhere in the room, the candle flame flickered. M was not on her bed. But I saw a trace of something moving on the floor. When I moved the circle of light toward it, I saw M's face tossing in a ring of hair, her arm raised across it. And more amazing, a formless hulk of darkness was hovering over her naked body. It looked more like a chunk of darkness emerging from M's crotch than it did the Negro. The genie coming out of Aladdin's lamp. Now it does not seem to have been anything spontaneous, but rather a well-rehearsed play. I mean, perhaps that was because of the light glowing in M's eyes. They stared at me like a pair of full moons, commanding me to do something. I took a better grip on the candlestick and struck as hard as I could. It was difficult to distinguish the Negro's convulsions from those of the dark. Two, three, maybe four times, I beat on this thing. It felt like a broken eggshell.

Because of what happened that night, I realized I had no choice but to call this M, who had hung quivering to my neck like jelly, "wife." M managed to take Q away from me. And it was M's determination to possess me any way she could that I had feared the most. Yet it may be that her ceaseless trembling was caused by joy rather than fear. I had fallen into a well of despair. I couldn't read her face. I still can't. For twenty years, we have been a happy-looking, model couple.

Nothing happened, M said that night, *nothing does happen, not in this world.* This was M's incantation. It was true. The next day, the morning sun having repainted the world, we took a walk along the beach. The summer withered into a succession of indistinguishable days. Then one afternoon, near the end of the summer (I was seventeen and M turned seventeen that day), we were sitting on the sand under the cape as if we had already been married for twenty years. M scratched in the sand as if playing, she showed me a horrible thing she had uncovered. Under her hand, there were two pointed ears and two forelegs. I have no doubt they belonged to the dead collie.

FOUR POEMS

DOUGLAS BLAZEK

PROGRESS REPORT ON MANKIND
FOR INCLUSION IN HISTORY TEXTS OF HILARITY

Welcome year 1945
and Alamogordo

Now there is glue
to help fill in the atmosphere

A slow doodling
a blackening in of space

As we map our way
to the cloaca

Which is sure clumsy
making maps of mushrooms

Like these words
glue for your eyes to drink

As the space between
LIFE is blacked in

When refined it's called
technique

But black is black
as glue is black

As maps are glue
as words are maps

As we inch along the colon
to the cloaca

Babes, all of us.

WHAT I RETAIN AS MYSELF IS SEWN INTO LIFE

There it is, publicity to my birth:

blue
carbon
paper
        it was there
      before the garbage was emptied
it is there now
                afterwards as well.

Its color is a service
a harvest
a cyclone,
its gossip sops up my life:

            voyeur
        gelatin to dreams
a snare of my multi-realities.

Carbon paper, blue, #154–W, Codo,
PENCIL CARBON, kant-stik, 8½ x 11, 61104

I know all the magic code numbers
paper lodestones traced
          into my forehead
      maps leading to where the going is tough,
                articulation
            becoming an awl to silence.

The door bell might rip
      halfass discovery from my mouth
          but when it's just blue carbon paper
              and me
          all the earth
      in every plowed field
      clings with the blood
      of my mental flesh
as the earth is carved into enlightenment
    so that I may remain in my dark alone.

THINGS DECAY/REASON ARGUES

                  the day ends
in sunset streaked
with melted fire engines
                      & begins when
pale sharks slit open the dawn

the hand which works the puppets
absentmindedly holds the detonator
& people are left shattered like
                          pottery

    all of which is seen
if you walk at night
                  sniffing
loneliness & dusty doilies
in rooms without air
                  glass cases
displaying gnawed & fearful bones

              when fuses
blow
        all lights go out
                        unless
we move faster than light
                        which
is a danger
once the compass
is worked like a combination lock

running
          thru telescopes
toward the extremity of
                        crosshairs

targets are not depots
but signals along the track

            distance is not
very far, unless we have
                        the directions
prefigured

the closer we get
the slower we move
                    & we know
one huge rabbit jump
would do it
            our nerves
becoming rabbits chased
by crosshairs.

GARGOYLE OF THE CENTURY

for Don Cauble

my legs are uneasily
    connected to my body—
      not knowing what length to be.
if they are too long
    like railroad tracks
they'd not be able to see where
they started or where they're destined
      & if they are too short
      they might not go anywhere at all—
    green light on a deadend street.

at the laboratory of time
    I don't know where to start
      what to think first
learned a lot about rain
but there is something juggling inside me
twisting my muscles over my eyes
twisting my eyes down my throat
    I want to think about Hershey Bars,
that is easiest
    but when entangled in fiber
there's a better place to start
    & more places to walk
    after turning myself
   inside out.

each day I find myself
    more incapable of understanding
more naïve
    more unsure   of everything
   yet   strangely
not insecure
    if anything *more* secure
    as if this was meant
    as if it's natural for man to
    always be unsure.
I am growing & it feels good!

I am trying to express . . .
    trying for a word. . . .
my own word, a
word never heard before
my fishing pole dangling
not knowing if the water is polluted
if there is any bait
or anything to catch
AH, BUT I CAN MAKE LOVELY WORDS OF SEAWEED!
that is   if you can stand that green stuff—
    everyone around us
      tells us what to think,
    they tell us what to know—
but after their knowledge is handled
      again & again
    like wax candy   it becomes misshapen
& I don't know what it *really* looks like anymore—
    there remains just the contortions
      doughy like a boulder
ready for me to
push up a mountain.

ORPHEUS BELOW

A Verse Play in Four Scenes

EDWIN HONIG

CAST

ORPHEUS
EURYDICE
PLUTO
HERMES
CHORUS, *three men and three women*
ANTICHORUS, *three men and three women*

Scene I: On the way to Pluto's kingdom

ORPHEUS. While I live she lives.
She belongs to me.
  CHORUS. She belongs to no one.
She is with Pluto now,
lord of eternal sleep.
  ORPHEUS. She belongs to me.
In my breath she lives,
in my heart she sings,
in my eyes she walks
the earth still.

CHORUS. She who was dear to you
is a ghost of memory—
memory, the stage
where the dead walk,
seeming to belong
to someone briefly—
responding to our words
and to our bidding,
greeting the light
that seeks them out
until we who need them—
frightened, yearning,
hungry, shining—slip off,
and memory goes down
the same dark hole with us.
    ORPHEUS. She lives in me. She is not dead.
    CHORUS. Good—then she will live
in you a while.
Your striving now
will some day strangely help you
to relieve the pain of grief.
    ORPHEUS. I cannot abide your words:
empty, careless customary words,
words of no feeling.
    CHORUS. Our words bring you
no personal balm.
Death's custom does not change.
Words comfort the comforter.
The mourner goes uncomforted.
For him the death of one
becomes the death of all.
No one can break his grief
but the cherished one he seeks.
    ORPHEUS. Grief? I do not grieve. She lives.
I'll bring her back myself.
    CHORUS. How will you do it? Tell us.
    ORPHEUS. With my full voice,
with my whole body's voice.
    (*He begins a high vigorous chant as the scene shifts and the dead
appear: the Antichorus, male and female, half reclining as if being*

embraced by an absent lover. They may move slowly, though not mournfully, in response to his song.)

ORPHEUS. Life is the animal
of the world.
More than all
of us alive,
more than all
of us dead,
each of us
ever born
has only been
one eyeblink
of the animal
of the world.

(Chorus comes to the fore, dividing itself in half, male and female.)

FEMALE CHORUS. The end, the physical end:
the last days, beginning of absence.
Moving back to the last days you see
the tightening and loosening of body.
The body, the pressures, the hundred
delicate maneuverings, the sweat,
the pain, the flash and falling
of spirit, the failing.
Watching the body
fighting the self,
pressing, impressing
its own isolation.
Before the departure,
an absence already begun.

MALE CHORUS. Dogged by the need to rebound,
to measure, explain—some message
to lighten the brain—to tell
why the flagging body,
known to you for so long,
unravels, unhinges,
slips off its life,
to float away in the dark.

FEMALE CHORUS. Now her face finds your eyes
without moving her own;
sees you at last,

but sees you too steadily
to see you at all.
Behind the window of pain
you are left outside.

MALE CHORUS. Between living and dying
the gap slowly widens.

FEMALE CHORUS. Who comes between
to end the deceit?

MALE CHORUS. A dark shaping creature.

FEMALE CHORUS. The sole self moving,
unmoved, irreducible.

MALE CHORUS. Dark creature alone
each of us bears
from birth until death.

FEMALE CHORUS. Unclearly known,
barely acknowledged,
rarely engaged.

CHORUS. The still steady mover
of life's ongoingness.

MALE CHORUS. The end, and you see her
totally changed.
The end after hours
of furious breathing,
the color leaving her face,
a deep blood flush
creeping through her scalp,
the lowered breathing—
the animal rasp.

FEMALE CHORUS. One self-emptying gasp—
and you breathe in her mouth,
her mouth returning it twice
with breaths no longer her own,
before going still.

MALE CHORUS. Her thin loose arms
you try to rub.
They are cold.

FEMALE CHORUS. Her limp wet mouth,
her cheeks cold as meat,
the life pressed out.

MALE CHORUS. There is her head,
composed on the pillow:

your last look turning away
from the open door.

FEMALE CHORUS. No longer herself,
her quiet profile
strangely unchanged,
yet completely another.

MALE CHORUS. As someone asleep
who sleeps so fast
she is no longer herself.

FEMALE CHORUS. The delicate line
of the nose badly stretched,
making it seem almost hooked.

MALE CHORUS. Her wide mouth gaping
flabby, unbreathing.

FEMALE CHORUS. Her yellowing face.

MALE CHORUS. Her life—

FEMALE CHORUS.   —gone out.

MALE CHORUS. Gone out of life.

FEMALE CHORUS. What is the self, the sole self,
barely known, and rarely engaged?

MALE CHORUS. Our only being.
Without it we misunderstand
our love, our despair, our linked
belonging one to another.
Without it we miss knowing
we are who we are.
One life strikes up
in response to another's,
like music.
A singular weight
impresses the stream
of all consciousness
passing now
into forever,
passing forever.
Without it as we are nothing—
less than a carrot, a dog.

FEMALE CHORUS. Unburdened when known,
it moves freely,
touching all, of which
it is never a part.

MALE CHORUS. Subsisting in things
it has touched
as if saying, "I am
totally in but not of it."
FEMALE CHORUS. While shaping the form
it is making in order to be.
MALE CHORUS. One form still forming,
unknown till the end,
coming clear briefly.
FEMALE CHORUS. Seen and felt by another,
watching in terror, in love.
MALE CHORUS. As a tide washes in, washes out.
FEMALE CHORUS. As a sigh of spirit achieved.
MALE CHORUS. As a life momentarily fixed,
glimmering clear,
beyond life's urgencies.
FEMALE CHORUS. Finding its shape at last.
MALE CHORUS. Between living and dying,
the gap slowly widens.
Who comes between
to end the deceit?
FEMALE CHORUS. A dark shaping creature.
*(The voice of Orpheus breaks outs, repeating the song "Life is
the animal.")*
Life is the animal
of the world.
More than all
of us alive,
more than all
of us dead,
each of us
ever born
has only been
one eyeblink
of the animal
of the world.
I sing the animal
of the world.
*(Chorus reassembles, as before, while Antichorus, comprising the
dead, comes together opposite.)*

ANTICHORUS. Art is his weapon
against immortal death.

CHORUS. Art is his defense
of all life's beauty.

ANTICHORUS. Man wishes to forget
the life he lives.
So much of what he lives
is pain and groveling.

CHORUS. Pain is beauty's animal
and shares with him
all life's changes.

ANTICHORUS. If this were so,
death would not matter,
life would not matter.
Art would have no subject.

CHORUS. There is only life,
the only subject for song.

ANTICHORUS. His song denies the gods
and scorns eternal life.

CHORUS. Eternally his song
honors the life of man.

ANTICHORUS. A blasphemy that men
never will forgive him.

CHORUS. All women need him.
There is the wife he trusts
his art to resurrect.

ANTICHORUS. Through her his art is spent—
his final punishment.

CHORUS. Through her we see all women
rise up to worship him.

ANTICHORUS. Desiring him in body's madness,
as their husband,
their one common god,
they will tear his flesh,
they will break his limbs,
they will crush his manhood,
they will devour him.

(Antichorus divides, male and female, to sing this ballad.)

MALE ANTICHORUS. Let me take you in my arms.
Death must make love bloom.

I can quiet all your qualms.
    Death is life's bridegroom.
    ANTICHORUS. *Over and over the leaves of clover*
are plucked, again and again in vain.
    FEMALE ANTICHORUS. I let you come in one night,
    worm into my room.
Love died in the daily light.
    Death bulged in my womb.
    ANTICHORUS. *Over and over the leaves of clover*
are plucked, again and again in vain.
    MALE ANTICHORUS. I drop you, your taste is gall.
    Love has had its way.
Death dumps clutching lovers all
    into the light of day.
    ANTICHORUS. *Over and over the leaves of clover*
are plucked, again and again in vain.
    (*Enter Orpheus. Seeing Antichorus for the first time, he ap-*
proaches them curiously. As he addresses them, each successively
turns away slowly.)
    ORPHEUS. Who are you in that gown with drooping breasts,
like the painted mother of a woman I once knew?
She warned me against seduction of the senses
through music and poetry. Her daughter died.
The mother trailed me till she grew mad.
You're silent now. Why do you turn away?

And this one here, grinning for his pay,
I can remember him. He served me once.
He holds up his two stumps of arms
to show me where the hands were lopped
for stealing something from me once.
Strange, I can't remember what he stole.

Can this be the loose-lipped girl
with hollow eyes, the one who filled
my waking dreams when I was a boy,
who still trembles for her chastity?
She sways as though her great wet eyes
will drag her to the ground. She falls away.

And you—who are you with that face
so empty and immense that only
to approach you makes me want to drown?
Your silence deafens, like the traffic
of a city vanishing in time.
Who or what are you? How you stand your ground!
   (Antichorus fades away with his last words while Chorus replaces them at his side.)
   ORPHEUS. Why are they here?
They steal my breath!
   CHORUS. Your memory wakens them
when you are in despair.
They thrive in misery,
flooding your mind.
   ORPHEUS. I am done with ghosts.
My mind must light her image
till it sings Eurydice awake.
   CHORUS. You will have to go
where death walks endlessly.
He must let you enter freely.
No man has ever gone so far.
   ORPHEUS. I am that man—my song will do it!
   CHORUS. How? Do you know the way?
   ORPHEUS. Through me to her the way lies open.
This is what I know.
   (On upper stage Eurydice appears, loosely veiled, as a kind of promise. Light pours down on her.)
   ORPHEUS. See now, she lives! She's here!
Where I am she is with me, living!
   (Eurydice makes vague motions, as if to summon him; then in a burst of menacing and erotic music, she vanishes.)
   CHORUS. We are amazed. You are mortal,
yet you open the way to death,
which only those who die can know
and know once only—on their death.
What is it in you makes you know?
   ORPHEUS. I cannot tell you how I know.
Can I tell you how I breathe?
To sing I must know such things
and yet not know them overmuch.

Knowing the way is open, I
must bring her back, or I die.
   CHORUS. If she is not already dead,
then she will die. You too may die.
   ORPHEUS. You buzz like flies around
a honeypot. Leave me.
   CHORUS. Leave you? You keep us here.
Unless you die,
we cannot leave you
nor can we go beyond you.
If you know the way lies free,
go beyond us,
and there, alone,
find the stranger in the dark.
   (Chorus fades gradually away from Orpheus.)
   ORPHEUS. In the dark I know him.
He is darkness
filling silence
till he owns it all.
A wide opening of nothing
that devours everything.
Fear and joy together
lie down in his arm and die.

I alone am his undoing.
I shall be his undoing.

When he took Eurydice,
all night he breathed against my eyes.
His darkness almost swallowed me.
In his darkness I could drown.
He walled her off from me all night.
All night her cold sweat trickled
down my thighs.
I felt his weight move down on her,
I felt his black tongue move all night,
stoppering her mouth.
All night, all night
my body bruised, my bones were sore.
I turned to her, her breathing stopped.
The dark had swallowed her.

I alone am his undoing.
I shall be his undoing.

I awoke. Eurydice was gone.
I awoke alone. A welling up
of blood rocked my body still.
My sex became a stone.
I saw the door half open—
through the doorway
sunlight bursting.
Sunlight sang me back alive.
Whoever left the door ajar
had let the sunlight in.
Now the song the sunlight sang
is this song I sing.
It will be his undoing.

I alone am his undoing.
I shall be his undoing.

(*In a dazzling light and at the same burst of erotic music as*
before, Eurydice reappears, descending, smiling, toward Orpheus,
who remains fixed, concentrated, his back toward her.)

BLACKOUT

Scene II: In Pluto's kingdom

PLUTO. I say put him through this thing the hard way.
Let him drag along on wounded legs,
his guts torn open like a crippled dog,
all the way downhill on his belly.
    HERMES. Come on. He's a magician: Orpheus,
poet-musician, darling of the gods.
For him it has to be a special lark.
Sweating's only for heavyweights like Hercules.
    PLUTO. I don't see it. If he doesn't suffer,
what good is it to him—being in hell?
Tear him apart is what the thing must do.
    HERMES. You're fond of bloody messes. I'm not.
You're talking of religion. Me, I love
the living; apparently you don't or can't.

PLUTO. Somebody's got to draw the line between
the living and the dead . . .

HERMES.   Why? Why not
let souls spill over so the living can
come down and get to know the place they fear
or bring the dead back for a holiday?

PLUTO. Blasphemer! Only gods are glorious
and powerful forever; man himself
is muck, up in a flash, out in a fizzle.
Only a god comes down here and gets back.

HERMES. It's true, the gods delight to see men wriggle
like worms; it makes them feel superior.
Why else would you have let the poet come
down here to take his wife back? Do you care?
Were you showing off? What if he makes it?

PLUTO. Makes it? Isn't that your job to see
he doesn't?

HERMES. No, it's yours. You're boss. You asked him.

PLUTO. His music got me. A weak moment. I still
can't say just why I promised.—To stop his music!
Unbearable! It made me want to die!

HERMES. That's amusing—so awfully human! You're undead—
I mean, Lord of the Dead, a god, eternal!
Just think, you've got to live with you forever!

PLUTO. It gets a little fierce here—all the silence.
Then music filled my ears. I went weak,
I guess, and so my head nodded to him.
"Come take her, yes, but only stop the music!"
Silence again. I roared, "But if you look
at her before you reach the light—she's gone!"

HERMES. Wanting to be alive—meaning undead.
When gods get bored they play at being human,
and right away the pleasure's too much for them.
They call it weakness and impose the law.
You own the place and keep the score, so tell me,
landlord, isn't that what hell's about?

PLUTO. Also, you must make sure that he stays put.
You're responsible for him.

HERMES.   But not for you!

PLUTO. You've got to understand the way things are.
I can't allow these madmen, poets, prophets,
to hop down here and back. It breaks the law,
and it could kill morale, starting them all
to dreaming the old dream—to live forever!
The dead exceed the living now something
like two million to one. Think of the mischief
if some little man like Orpheus should start
hauling them all back again to earth!
Give him an inch and there's no stopping him.

HERMES. And who was it, tell me, gave him that inch?

PLUTO. But I admit a little weakness. I'm only—

HERMES. Immortal, yes. Also a statistician,
a bigot, prude, and lowest lowdown member
of the establishment. Like me you're cursed
enough with single-mindedness. At least
I know how huge one human wish can be.
I can perambulate among the spheres.

PLUTO. Then you'll take care of Orpheus for me?

HERMES. I like wild music and the passions. Listen.

(*Music bursts through, and Orpheus descends; Pluto immediately retreats.*)

NO CURTAIN OR BLACKOUT

Scene III: The same as Scene II

(*As Orpheus slowly descends, his way ahead is marked by a sharp narrow blue light. This gradually gives just enough illumination to bring the Chorus and the Antichorus out of the darkness on opposite sides. Stage center the figure of Hermes emerges, waiting. Orpheus stops when he becomes aware of Hermes.*)

HERMES. Welcome to Death's kingdom.

ORPHEUS. (*beginning to approach*)
I do not know you.

HERMES. I am Hermes. I come to guide you.

ORPHEUS. (*confronting him*)
I do not need you.

HERMES. Perhaps not. We'll see.

ORPHEUS. *(passing him)*
I do not want you.
  (The blue light dims and goes out. Orpheus stops.)
  HERMES. Have you been here before?
You insist you know the way.
Consider, this is not earth,
no halfway place, but hell,
where everything is total.
Darkness is pitch darkness.
Death is stony death.
  ORPHEUS. Until this point my way was lit.
A blue light led me like a hand.
  HERMES. Yes, human consciousness
deserves to be displayed here.
You're living and full-blooded,
a man carrying full tilt a mind,
a soul, and an immense idea.
These need to be lit up.
But you reach beyond a certain point,
and, as you see, that point is here.
Here's where Pluto reigns,
fanatic keeper of the dead.
He rules beyond the limit
where life contains itself no more,
where breath and all the faculties
no longer function. Except in certain
special cases, they usually stop.
That's why I've been sent to you,
to help you on the way from here,
and lead you living to your dream.
  ORPHEUS. I do not need your guidance.
I go the way I am
through darkness and through death.
My song will give me breath.
  *(A female member of the Antichorus rushes to embrace Orpheus
excitedly. Again the erotic music. Orpheus looks closely, as if she
might be Eurydice, then turns away. Hermes has not noticed the
interruption. The blue light comes on and sharpens with the first
word of Hermes' reply.)*
  HERMES. Then go ahead, I'll follow—
leading from behind.

ORPHEUS. My mouth wells up with song,
yet song won't lead me to her.
The breath in silence leaving
and re-entering my body
yearns toward her body,
making a song of nothing,
making breath itself enough.
I am a stone against a tree
aching to be that tree—
to grow, to shed its leaves
and sleep, yet never dream
what was or what will be.
In sleep I am that girl I seek,
cradled in our bodies' love.
Come, love, take away my breath!
   (*Another female member of the Antichorus breaks loose, as be-
fore, and with a cry embraces Orpheus. The same music and word-
less action follow.*)
   CHORUS. You are the harvest of the earth beginning.
Think that alone, in yearning and in growing,
and the fruit drops from the tree.

You are the hard ground over deep earth's longings.
Be that alone, in sleep's long burrowings,
till the fruit drops from the tree.

You are the seed through frozen winter burning
with root love, and with the worm still turning
when the fruit drops from the tree.
   ANTICHORUS. We taste the ripened pips,
and sweetness bursts our lips.
We crunch the crisp thighbone,
our teeth glinting like stone.
   CHORUS. What lives must feed on what's alive.
What's dead feeds on itself.
If the dead cannot live again,
the still-living may not die.
Yet they do—both things occur.
The dead live frozen in the mind.
The living, though still standing, die
feeding on grief, the dead belief,
bloated with wild memory,
in past beauty die.

ANTICHORUS. Spend yourself, give self away
to death, then think no more, and die.
    (echo) and die.
Living for you is past, praise death.
Becoming what you dread, so die.
    (echo) so die.
The tree you were became a stone,
believing in stone, though standing, dead.
    (echo) standing dead.
    (Erotic music mounts, a crashing light, and Orpheus falls; Eury-
dice appears at once behind him, glowing.)
HERMES. Orpheus, stand up, she is here.
You must lead her back.
This is what you came to do.
    (Orpheus rises, lightly supported by Hermes, who faces him
sideways, where he can see Orpheus and also look toward, though
not at, Eurydice.)
Poised behind you now,
she lights up emptiness
like the Venus star.
She is all you thought,
answering your thought,
telling how she came here.
    (A silence, then an increasing, heaving, rolling sound—like waves
of death.)
EURYDICE. I rode the waves to shore
where I was deposited.
Then I saw the tide withdraw,
the beating roar subside.
I was alone again as when,
ripped from my mother's blood,
I fell into the breathing world.
Why do I stand waiting again
to learn which way to go,
wondering how to go?
Does the body live or die?
ORPHEUS. You are all voices filing my mind
when it pleases and is pleased,
yet not one voice I yearn to hear.
CHORUS. She is your nature mirrored in a gift.
She is your passion spent and hovering.
She returns herself faithfully to you.

ORPHEUS. She returns faithfully,
but not herself to me.
Her voice is all voices
cherished by memory,
but not one of them
comes alive to me.
Although I may not see her,
her speech denies her presence.
She is far away, though near.
　　HERMES. You must not question what
is different or the same.
In your way you have found her,
now lead her away.
　　ORPHEUS. What Eurydice is this,
speaking to what I was,
not to what I am?
　　CHORUS. In asking for her
you asked for what
had died in you.
　　ANTICHORUS. Now die with her.
This is what you sought.
This is why you came.
　　CHORUS. Leave her now.
You no longer
need to have her back.
　　HERMES. You came for her.
Now lead her back.
　　ORPHEUS. First she must speak
in her own voice,
the voice I know as hers,
as voice I can recall.
Until I hear that voice
I sense her presence only,
not her life, behind me.
I did not come to find
a faithful loving ghost.
I came to bring her back,
my fully living wife.
　　HERMES. Until you speak to her,
she has no present life.
Until you lead her back,

her voice is in the past,
remaining all it was
when you saw her last.
 ORPHEUS. I do not want her ghost.
 HERMES. Then win her back to life.
Move, and she follows you.
Speak, and she will answer.
 (Orpheus moves and starts back, ascending, the blue light point-
ing the way ahead. Behind him, slightly to the left, is Hermes, and
last, directly behind, is Eurydice.)
 ORPHEUS. Eurydice, I feel your soundless steps,
your breathless mouth, behind me.
 EURYDICE. Yes, Orpheus. I follow where you go.
 ORPHEUS. I lead you back to life.
 EURYDICE. Yes, Orpheus, I know.
 ORPHEUS. Do you want to live?
 EURYDICE. I do not know how to want.
 ORPHEUS. Do not be afraid.
I will teach you how to want
and how to live again.
 EURYDICE. If I had fear, it would be for you.
If I had love, it would be for you.
I do not know what feelings are.
I have no sense of pain or sorrow.
Only some memory of knowledge.
I know you called me and I follow.
 ORPHEUS. First and last learn joy again
for all things living in their being.
I bring them back—the taste
of fruit, the leap of animals,
bird-glide and fish-turn,
where water is deep fire,
where all the air embraces earth.
I praise man and the creatures,
I praise the trees, the plants,
I praise the stones,
I praise the farthest star
pulsing in the eye.
Now the night listening
to the word is shriveling.

EURYDICE. Won't the day shrivel too?
Won't the day, listening
to the word, shrivel back
into the night already
shriveling into day?
  ORPHEUS. As I listen, a silence dies
and the word rises, rising
out of my hand to speak.
Where is the silence that lives
on this world, listening?
What listens beyond me?
Eurydice, come follow me!
   (As they continue to move, the blue light intensifies.)
   EURYDICE. I follow you, Orpheus.
   ORPHEUS. *(half turning)*
Eurydice, I know your voice,
it is your own voice I hear again.
   HERMES. Orpheus, take care; turn like that
again, and she is lost to you.
   (Shadows begin to appear, moving.)
   ORPHEUS. Eurydice, I know the way
is past these shadows
moving here beyond us.
They are and they are not,
and yet move endlessly.
   EURYDICE. It is the moving of other people
thinking beyond you,
creating and destroying,
doing the people-things.
You cannot even watch them.
They walk through you.
To them you are invisible.
To them only they move,
they who without knowing it
are invisible too.
   ORPHEUS. Tomorrow we will appear.
Tomorrow for the first time
there will be the sequence
of the living and the dead united.
Together there will be

only the instant meeting
of thought with thought.
Living and dead will be one.
Nothingness will disappear.

EURYDICE. Yesterday I remember I was yours.

ORPHEUS. So you will be again tomorrow
when we rise from this cold night.

EURYDICE. Will I remember what I was today
tomorrow? Will this sense
of being nothing, which is all
I am now, except the voice you give me,
return to cover up my mouth?

ORPHEUS. Eurydice, the voice you say
I give you is yours, not mine.
You will know that in your blood
before you face the light again.

CHORUS. Her blood is sluggish, scarcely moves.
Her limbs follow his but only
as if wired to his words.
He knows this wall but is too fond
of the remembered flesh she gave his words
to go back to doubting her again.

ORPHEUS. The light falters. I cannot see.
(Blue light dims.)

HERMES. It is still your light, remember—
your own, to bring you and return.

CHORUS. Her new fatigue has wearied him.
Look how his arms fall to his sides.
His drooping head searches the ground
for signs. Sink! say his halted feet.

ORPHEUS. (straining not to turn)
Eurydice, my wife,
take on my present life!

EURYDICE. My body yearns to be dissolved.
Now held together only by
your wish, it washes on my mind
and tugs it down like crumbled stone.
Believe me, Orpheus, each fiber in me
cries out to my blood to stop,
be still, become invisible!

(Female Antichorus moves in a group to block Orpheus, in attitudes half appealing and half menacing, as if he were their glittering prey. Orpheus turns away from them.)

ORPHEUS. I must free her of the past.
Eurydice, my wife,
I give you all my breath!

(Turning back completely, he lunges past Hermes to embrace Eurydice, and comes away holding her shroudlike garment, empty, in his hand.)

EURYDICE'S VOICE. Orpheus, rejoice, for I am dead.
I no longer need to rest in you.
Voiceless now I am myself,
the emptiness held in your hand
no longer burdens memory.
Orpheus, you are free to be
the voice you sought in me.
Thank you for my life, my death.

(As Orpheus begins to tear her garment to shreds, female Antichorus surrounds him, singing.)

FEMALE ANTICHORUS. Life is the animal
of the world.
More than all
of us dead,
each of us
ever born
has only been
one eyeblink
of the animal
of the world.

(Orpheus manages to break loose from them, going upward, where the light pours forth, but they follow intently, already holding in their hands parts of his dress: a sandal, his belt, and so forth.)

BLACKOUT

Scene IV: The same as Scene II

PLUTO. You think he escaped?
HERMES.   You mean she didn't.
PLUTO. Who ever said she would?
HERMES.   You pretend,
now that it's over, you weren't scared
she would—with your permission too.
PLUTO. I swear it won't happen again.
HERMES. I don't know. Mortals have a way
of coming back for more once they
have tasted the impossible.

PLUTO. Ah, just plain greediness. What else?

HERMES. No, it's passion leading them astray,
but passion brings on something more
abiding: a growing itch to transcend
empty time and circumstance.

PLUTO. Ach, there you go again, blaspheming.
Only the gods transcend. Everyone
knows that. Men are flies. They live
and die between a yawn and sleep.
They just don't have the grip we do.

HERMES. Pluto, tell me, what brought him here?
—Yes, Orpheus. To this hell hole?

PLUTO. Some insane notion that he was
better than the gods, I guess.

HERMES. Oh, use your head. The impulsion's
got to be a lot more personal
to drive a man down here. Think again.

PLUTO. All right: the gods themselves, his music.
You said he was their darling. Well,
it was a trick to put me down.

HERMES. Come, come, Pluto. We all know you're
tone-deaf. Besides, since when have men
needed the gods except as means
toward a special end? You think
he'd go through hell just to put down
a minor deity like you?
For God's sake, try to see it his way!

PLUTO. What are you getting at? I think
I see your meaning—a woman! You mean
the woman, Eurydice? For her sake?
The maddest thing I ever heard!
Sure, men have got to procreate—
that's how they keep alive enough
to not mind dying. But with a dead one?
Aren't there enough live women
up there he could jump on without
killing himself to get a dead one?

HERMES. All right, you're getting warm—if I
dare use the word about you. Hasn't
it ever struck you that love and sex
are man's way to transcend himself?

PLUTO. You must be joking. Love and sex?
For bulls and horses! *(laughing)* No? Yes!

HERMES. Yes, laugh yourself sick over it.
Most gods do. They have no choice.
Thinking yourself immortal you find
the urge to love is just the fault
that makes man mortal, like an animal,
or else the sadly childish way
he has of finding comfort in the dark.
But there's more to it than that.

PLUTO. *(still laughing)*
More to it than what? What else
but lovely sex? Or sex and love!

HERMES. It's the end of the gods. Orpheus
will ring the curtain on the gods
because even if he failed to take
his wife back from the dead, he has
opened the way to conquer death.
With love. With art. With life itself.
He's shown men what's inside them, what they
can be through what they feel and think,
despite the gods. Men following him
displace the gods, become eternal.

PLUTO. *(stops laughing, though still shaking)*
Displace the gods, will he? And where
d'ye think your little man is now?
*(Displaying long swatches of Orpheus' torn-out hair, with bloody
skin still attached.)*

HERMES. Pluto, where did that come from?

PLUTO. The women chasing him. They did
a job on him—tore him apart!
You know, and some who missed out on
his feel while he was still alive,
they got to eating him—his rump,
his face, his big male thing, even
his eyes and nails taste good to them.

HERMES. Just sound and fury, a new religion!
Still, how disagreeable!
Devour him, then puff his image
up, and raise him to the skies!

They'll forget he was a man who used
his brain to undermine the static
hell of dying gods. Now women
make *him* a god—an antihuman
floating abstract thing, an iceberg
stuck way up in some heaven they
must go down on their knees to worship,
guiltily, of course, since they've thrown
their brains away to do it. Sinful,
agh! Do you suppose men love death
more than they love their own lives?

    PLUTO. Well, he's dead anyway. You know from what? *(laughing)*
What did you call it? Lovely sex?
Oh, love and sex! Well, what does that
lead to, tell me, if not to death?

    *(Hermes turns away; Pluto goes down on all fours, laughing un-
controllably.)*

BLACKOUT

FOUR POEMS

ELIO PAGLIARANI

Translated by Fausta Segrè

INTRODUCTORY NOTE: *Elio Pagliarani was born in Viserba, Italy, in 1927. He holds a Ph.D. in political science, has taught at professional and night schools in Milan, and has also served as an editor of a political daily. He now lives in Rome, where he is the theater critic for* Paese Sera. *His work began to attract widespread interest in 1960, when his long narrative poem "La Ragazza Carla" was printed in the second issue of* Il Menabò, *an annual publication edited by Italo Calvino and Elio Vittorini. The following year a large selection of his poetry was included in the anthology* I novissimi, *together with the work of Edoardo Sanguineti, Nanni Balestrini, Alfredo Giuliani, and Antonio Porta. The collection, soon recognized as a landmark in Italian neo-avant-garde literature and the development of the so-called "Gruppo 63," was reprinted by Einaudi in 1965.*

Although at the outset some critics preferred not to consider Pagliarani, strictly speaking, an experimental poet, little more than a year later a different opinion began to prevail. "La ragazza Carla" was reissued in 1962, along with a group of poems from earlier books; but most important, "Lezione di fisica" ("Physics Lesson") appeared (1964), and with it a new phase of Pagliarani's development. People began to see that alongside the narrative trend there existed in his poetry another more informal aspect, distinct from

ELIO PAGLIARANI 99

*naturalistic messages; that an upsetting, ironic schizomorphism
moved within it as well, shattering chronistic elements, and working
a dissociation with the outside world.*

*Pagliarani is presently working on a new long poem whose tem-
porary title is La* ballata di Rudy. *Other recent works by him in-
clude:* Pella d'asino *(with Alfredo Giulani), 1964;* I maestri del
racconto italiano *(with Walter Pedullà), 1964;* Manuale di poesia
sperimentale *(with Guido Guglielmi), 1966;* Fecaloro *(together with
a new edition of "Lezione de fisica"), 1969.*

—LUIGI BALLERINI

physics lesson

to Elena

He started by studying the blackbody
Max Planck at the beginning of the century
            (arguments whether it was the beginning or the end
of the century), the radiations of the blackbody in the memory
of December 14, 1900
    one had to suppose that quanta of action were at the foundation
of energy multiplied by time
                        Oh Elena the well-worn pages' light
is a shower of quanta, I try to tell you there is opposition
between macrophysics and microphysics that the atomic world
                            of elementary particles
is studied by quantum mechanics—school of Copenhagen—
and by the wave school of the Prince of Broglie
                        that quite soon physicists
noticed how the two new mechanics though based
                        on different algorhythms
are basically equivalent: they both deny
deny the existence of precise relationships between cause
                            and effect
affirm that one cannot study an object
without modifying it
            light that falls on the electron to illuminate it

And I am here
and I am here Elena in a cage waiting
for the sound of an object communication of the effect
on you, of the modifications
                              It is not I
who betrays you, who is at your throat it is your friend
life
     After all as long as the cardiac muscle holds up
by now it is proved that I am a tough old bird,
                                   I'll dye my hair then Einstein
and his mane, just imagine him taking pen in hand
compelled to write Roosevelt "Dear President, let's make it
the A-bomb, otherwise the Nazis" the action of energy
of energy multiplied by time the epistaxis
in fact the nosebleed, Pasquina used to say at your age,
                                   the nosebleed that frees you

If one wants to know if A is the cause of B
if in itself the micro-object is unknowable
if the de Broglie wave for Copenhagen physicists
is none other than the physical expression of probability
                                        contained in
the particle to be in one place rather than another
                              a wave generated that is
by the lack of a rigorous causal microphysical connection
                              Therefore the A-bomb
because of the law of large numbers
     probability tends toward certainty
                              Therefore the A-bomb

Then the theory of the pilot wave and the one, so dear now
of the double solution, and if the micro-object exists in itself,
                              if matter
can reply with statistical behavior
                         Does God play dice
with the universe? And if earth were to display
fear of the game?

Don't shout don't shout they can hear you it's nothing
                              while I scratch an armchair
Herman Kahn already made the table
of possible postwar conditions, such that 160 million deceased
                                        at home
would not be the end of civilization, the economic recovery period
would be 100 years; it's clear, he writes, that there is
                              a further problem
that is, will the survivors have good reason
to envy the dead
                      What joy you give me when you're fed up
with me, when you tell me if you write about me you'll speak of joy
and be it active joy, triumphant, or a joke
dirty, maybe
                The fragrance of country greens in your dish
                              at Cesaretto's watercress
pimpernel a salad of earth's tender herbs easing our moods
the horizontal sky present here intercedes on people
and you and you everyone you ask to dance lights
your eyes and becomes handsome and grows
                          red wine
                              capers throwing pillows
in my room

                But don't you think I'm fed up too of living together
with myself my face my belly
                          we also have a craving for
joy, to readjust to joy, affirm life with song

and instead saying no is not enough it only saves the soul
we must live that no assess it involve it in action and temptation
so that opposition will act as opposition and have its witnesses.

from negations

to Giò Pomodoro

No to Michelangelo if blood flowed over form every bodily
channel no to redemption of usury in terms of space and volume
no to the idea that an image is a pattern
                    Of the two either we lost the measure of
each relationship between man and his death or if our fate
remains in our own image it is to fate
that we must turn
            for each description of ourselves
                            They're very in
wigs for dogs plastic fever, even Khrushchev according to Mao
                            is a paper
tiger, antinuclear boom in central California in the sense that
—Pope John let's leave him alone since he said that man
                            in these times
can love, burning while proving, Pope John is pertinent
to the subject, it has been shown Fortini told me
                        that Khrushchev cried
at length over Kennedy's assassination, and how much light
                            on Kennedy
reflected in his fate
                They don't count at all you see

wigs for dogs plastic fever
                    but yes certainly that disagreement those fates
and nutrition being equal
it is undoubtedly harder to live today
            no one ever had the certainty we do now a possible
            universal fate is actual
                        a scab
            that no surgery can remove from us

            Pharisees, you advertise savings
            We require further opening of credit
            Deflation favors only ex-electricians.

But one should also mention
      thank you for the applause
            and the cat calls at the Treasurer, thanks, thanks
one should also shout it is easier nowadays to cheat
        there isn't a racist or fool or coward
                without a perfect alibi.
Moi, je have nothing
        against cheaters
oui, je le sais what
        hell is paved with
et moi attending churches
        meditate on the variable

    Not a measure that varies or a concept that varies
    because concepts, measures, numbers, properties
    cannot vary (although as it is obvious something
    could have different properties at different times)
                A variable
  is instead a symbol with a given property
            But which property
  if the change in significance of a symbol is not possible
          within a language
  since that would represent the passage
  from one language to another
      If "Q" is a constant pr one can derive from "Q(x)"
  the propositions "Q(Prague)," "Q(a)" and "Q(b)" which cannot
  however be derived from "Q(a)." This shows that while x is
          a variable, "a" though indetermined
  is a constant: in other words "a" designates a (certain) thing
  only, for the moment, one doesn't know what.

        To endure living I mean to carry out
again an act that is an affirmation
      Già strong and clear: but you cannot guarantee
anything other than your intention
  objectively nothing distinguishes us cheaters from noncheaters

No, no it's true but it's only a premise, it is true and yet
　　　　　　　　　　　　　　　　there is a distinction
you don't notice and there isn't necessary intemperance
　　　　　　　　　　　　　　　　　in one's twenties
but then one learns from the pulse that discrimination
　　　　　　　　　　　　　　　is in the obtuse patience
of the artisan, in the prompt folly of an artisan without a customer
and one can exhibit with certainty this and only this certificate
　　　　　　　　　　　　　　　　　　Your exhibit
in the name of the constructors (Matrix One, Matrix Three,
　　　　　　　　　　　　　　　　　　Large Flag
for Vladimir, Crowd, Crowd, Rupture, Large Rupture—in bronze
generators)
　　　　　　the epic grammar of Achilles
　　　　　　　　　　　　　　the calculated risk
of rhetoric in recitatives
　　　　　　　　　　not precepts
　　　　　　　　　　　　　is the material
of the times
　　　　　　　against time as a bet on a structure
　　　　　　　　　　　　　banal because every project is banal
because each time it is said which
　　　　　　　　　　　banal with an x.

No to Michelangelo if he had administered to himself
profits and loss of blood.

merchandise diptych: I. the excluded item

　　　　　　　　　　　　　　to Ferrucio Rossi-Landi

Linguistic use and exchanges b) Equation with linguistic value
　　　　　　　　　Let us consider the equation x item A =
y item B
　　　　　and let us apply it to language
　　　　　　　　　　　God is the almighty being

Here the quantity (x, y) for both terms is reduced to one
there is only one God and He is the only almighty being
It would be easy
to quantify, saying for example that gods
are almighty beings
following Marxist analysis
he ended up with A's, a hair from magna cum laude, medicine classes
a well-planned choice: it is worldly and social
that relationship with the body
physical consciousness is not enough
it is not yet knowledge
new honors in law
if the relationships obscured things
violated the essence if the science of merchandising were
too empirical, the value in use of the expression almighty being
id est corporeity of language, is made equivalent to
the expression God
God takes on the value in exchange
with reference to almighty being
and can be inserted in linguistic circulation
as a carrier of such value In terms of work
Problem: a boy sees some rabbits
and some chickens in a yard He counts
18 heads and 56 legs
how many chickens and rabbits are in the yard?
Let us consider a kind of animal
with six legs and two heads: the chickenrabbit;
there are in the yard 56 legs: 6 legs = 9 chickenrabbits
Nine chickenrabbits that require 9 x 2 = 18 heads
there remain therefore 18 − 18 = 0 heads in the yard
degree in philosophy then they kicked him out
not that he violated laws it's that they said enough
family friends examples from texts his head
could have very clearly, actually it was he who did not want to
he entrusted to life
the measure of human linguistic generic average work
But these animals have 9 x 6 = 54 legs then 56 − 54 = 2
Two legs are left in the yard

Now consider another kind of animal that could be
                                a dechickened rabbit Subtracting
one chicken from one rabbit the remaining animal is
                                a dechickened rabbit that has
1 head − 1 head = o head, 4 legs − 2 legs = 2 legs:
                                the two legs left in the yard
the measure of human linguistic generic average work
            not that life was not to be found in classrooms
                                in his twenties and thirties
he had not yet been recalled for military service
      perhaps because they did not know exactly where to place him
so in the yard we have 9 chickenrabbits + 1 dechickened rabbit
                                In other words
9 rabbits + 9 chickens + 1 rabbit − 1 chicken
And now rabbits with rabbits and chickens with chickens we'll have
9 + 1 = 10 rabbits, 9 − 1 = 8 chickens
                    We find eight chickens and ten rabbits in the yard
and it can be inserted in linguistic circulation
                                as a carrier of such value in terms of work
the measure of human linguistic generic average work
                        with which one measures God
                        with which one measures God in terms of work
girls laugh, undulating on heels of cork
through the form of total or displayed value that Marx expresses
                                with the multiple equation
let us turn to the general form of value in which
                                a certain quantity of items
expresses the individual value by excluding one item
                                        girls laugh
undulating on heels of cork
        Non me rinvengo ben, pensa e ripensa
        che barzelletta è questa; io non l'ho 'ntesa
        se non confusamente.
        Questa si chiama 'l Pettine. E perché?
        Perché le rime paion fatte a denti,
        e mostra pettinar vari costumi.
                                He was gay and cheerful
        and began telling one of his stories. He always had new ones
        and then laughed with his belly jiggling.

The excluded item
in which to derive the value in use one measures the value
in exchange
the one with three degrees they caught him in the fall of '43
he explained the jokes in San Vittore
they didn't believe immediately
that scribbling in the notebook
was to impress
bosses and women
The excluded item
in which to derive the value in use one measures the value
in exchange
of all the other items considered as objectivized production time
corresponds linguistically to the known factor
in a definitive series.

merchandise diptych: II. survival certificate

to Toti Scialoja

They're right those who accuse you
I also caught you in the act
you were biting your lips till they bled
because someone was saying that art
Now from Milan they're buying property in Los Angeles
Here they invent parallel recessions and they immediately
become an example
of the functioning of communication
To me too, art seems to matter little
but it's our job

and our job now
is to hop to hop to hop
or they'll salt our tails
Don't you tell me too that art has nothing to do with time
when it is one of the ways for time
to be, when there are
more ways for time not to be
I loved so much

those who change with the seminal rhythm
                    of the world
                                        now they are bothering me
A lot of matured history, I said
            searching for signs in the body
                        now I search for other things in people
search for permanent traits
                I search for permanence in the present
                    (Not that, of course, etcetera)
                                    It must be that our growth
has been over, for a while, and we would like to stop
                    not to sway in the
                                        mobility of mutation
            Let's also take this into account
            It's not a question of closing, although
                            I'm also ready for this risk
            It's a question of saying I do this
                    and I haven't yet finished doing it
                    and besides these people exasperate me
            I am certainly the people
                            and I must fight with them
Little heart big hole
            the washing machine ad at the movies
                        and it's fine   Likewise love, is it right
to spare one's heart
            it's for your health and the children grow
                                but are we crazy
to doubt it?
            It's that I don't know how to love different
                                    except to stake
also in the heart an impulse
                soon I will not know how to love
                                    assuming I ever knew
        Neoromantics, gothics stone by stone bricklayers on scaffolding,
                not mystics or mystical like those who are in cages
and elaborate theoretical proofs of the nonexistence
                                    of every evasion
knights in tarnished armor semi-ideal knights
                    a message entrusted to a newspaper, my heart
            of shit and final outlet.

SUPERFICTION

ALAIN ARIAS-MISSON

To Nela

The Old Man and the Wood

Hello, says the old man, what are you doing? I was looking out over the deep valley to the neighbouring mountain. I don't really know, I answer. You see, I have been here all morning, watching the pines rustling across the valley and the big birds rise out of the tips and float between the mountains. I have been waiting here all morning without thinking of anything gazing out across the milky amosphere to the black pines; I remember the morning now, and the vacuity of it, I mean I have the sense of this morning stretching backwards into a sort of forgetfulness, and my existence has taken rise from a point in that nothingness. In answering you, I feel that the sense of your question has crystallized my meanings and relations, and that I bind myself with every phrase I add. I wonder if that answer will satisfy him; I still feel the call of the white space, and I want to lose myself in the solitude once again. But the old man busied himself about the feet of the trees picking up branches of wood. Why are you picking up those branches, I say. He does not answer and I look on wondering why he is picking up the branches of wood. He is picking up the wood busily, certainly. I am surprised because I realize that the emptiness of the view has lost its appeal for me, now I am preoccupied by this busy local activity. I wish I could describe it in some way, but my de-

scription would interfere with his actual activity. He is picking up
sticks of wood, mostly small ones, and gathering them in one arm.
Why are you picking up the sticks, I ask him again. You're inter-
fering in the structure of meaning, I say. You're a fool, he says.
You are involved in interpreting this experience, and you pretend
that I am destroying your so-called structures. I think for a moment
or so about what he has just said. Is it possible that the set of
meanings which I felt to be mine at the outset were disrupted by
my own musings? I can see his point. There was that statement of
mine about my description interfering with his activity. Although I
appeared to be taking my precautions, hadn't I in reality already
interfered with the make-up of the real? There is no doubt that I
felt unhappy with the whole business of the sticks, and had turned
an excessive attention to it. If my mind had remained quiet, if I
hadn't been so busy myself with his occupation, the actions would
no doubt have simply happened, pure and outside my meanings.
I look at the old man, amused by my confusion and the directness
of his remarks. I look out again across the valley, and I realize
now that this view, uplifting and serene as it was, was another in-
terpretation of experience. The silence before, which I tried to
recapture in words, was that emptiness—if it is still possible to talk
about silence and emptiness in the midst of this language. In other
words, in the very act of looking out over the deep valley I was
involved in a restructuring of experience, a splintering of aware-
ness. What was his role, then? Was I really mistaken when I
blamed him with interference? No, I don't think I was right, be-
cause his appearance was his affair, pure, opaque, and it was my
consciousness which disrupted the peace of this morning. This is a
point I can't make my mind up about entirely, because after all,
his consciousness is also involved, isn't it? You say that I am at
fault in constructing my own experience, I ask the old man. But
your consciousness is just as involved as my own. He looked at me,
and smiled. By now he had a large pile of wood stacked on the
ground, and was binding it with string. I am using my own eyes; I
mean, I am watching him in these actions, the trees are standing
cool and dark on every side, yet I cannot shake off the feeling of in-
terference. I continue to watch him: he tied the strings around the
load of wood, making a firm bundle. What is the matter with me,
I ask him. I was happy this morning, well quiet, looking out over
the mountains, and now there is a kind of double image in my mind

regarding the simplest actions. I accept the purity, the simplicity of
your actions, but there seems to be a meaning behind everything
you do. I don't mean of course that you are signifying anything to
me by what you do. And I suspect my own intellectual role. May-
be if we could speak a bit it would be possible to eliminate this
sense. Speaking will do you no good, he answers. You tie yourself
up in every phrase. I look at him, a little disconcerted. I am not
sure of the weight of what he says. I think that my consciousness is
implicated even in his words. I mean that if I construct on his
actions, why not on his words. I sense a familiarity about what he
says, and it makes me uneasy. I understand what you say, I say to
him, but it doesn't satisfy me. He shrugged and heaved the load
of wood up on his shoulders. I watch him, intrigued by my in-
tellectual sight, if I can call it that. I feel a certain well-being, even
a vitality. There is nevertheless a remainder of anxiety in me about
what is actually happening, and about what has been said. I take a
step towards him on the thick crackling undergrowth. This gesture
of mine impresses me. I am acutely aware of it, as if it were a self-
affirmation. He turned and trudged off into the forest. I watch him
until he disappears, and return to my post looking out over the
valley.

Silence

Two of them entered the room and looked about. It is the purely
physical, the observable, without a trace of the conscious, which is
fascinating. They looked around the room, and sat down at the
table. After they had sat for a while and discussed their affairs, they
left and closed the door behind them. They walked through the
streets quickly, hardly glancing at the surroundings. There were
many people in the streets at that time. Soon they reached the out-
skirts of the town. They walked on for about a mile and a half.
Well, here we are, said one of them. Yes, said the other, it's taken
time. The grass was feathery and swaying in the breeze, the ground
was dry and stony. I'm going to rest for a while, said the first,
we've had a long day, and we still have a lot ahead of us. The
other one said nothing, but also sat down on the grass. They both
felt a precariousness in their relations, just because of the purely
physical outline of their activities. The first one said, even if you

recall every event of the day, and every word that we have said, you will not be able to inject any significance into our relationship. The other got up without answering, and walked over to a tree. He leaned against the tree, and ran his fingers across the bark. The bark was dusty and crumbling under his fingertips. He gazed off into the darkening day. The touch of the rough surface on his skin was comforting, the physical evidence of it relieved the lineality of the day's experience. Why does he always question the reality of what we do, he thought to himself, he paralyzes the effectiveness of our action. The other got up, and walked across the clearing, and then back again. He looked up as if listening for something, then took off his jacket and put it on the ground. Every gesture is exhausting, he thought to himself, aimless and repetitive. The physical sucks out our souls. Yet for him also action was an indispensable minimum, a safety valve. What intrigues me, said the first, walking into the middle of the clearing, is the diagrammatic nature of the physical. I mean all the richness and music of life seem to be contained in the conversations and reflections we have. The other walked out of the clearing a short way into the woods. He looked about him in the cool gloaming of the woods, and knelt on one knee to dig his fingers into the rich earth. The caress of the earth in his fingers and the solitude of the woods were vaguely inebriating. He was disturbed by the fragmented character of the phrases, by the disjointed experience of reality. The touch of the earth, the rotting leaves, he thought to himself, have a sensuousness, but everything we do seems so removed, so hypothetical. What is it that actually brought us out here? Oh, we had a project, and we've been occupied with it all day, but that's the abstract. What has actually moved us? He stood up and walked back into the clearing. His companion hadn't moved from the spot he had been standing in. He hasn't moved a step, he thought to himself, but he might just as well have left. He might as well be a figment of my consciousness. Oh I know his subjectivity is as full and overflowing as my own, but it is something in the nature of these propositions which encloses and separates us. However clearly they wanted to communicate and to cooperate, they were acutely aware of a shell, an impediment which at times seemed to be of the nature of physical reality and at times of language. You know, said the other, we have always been aware of a lack of communication, of a disjunction in our activities and our thinking. In fact, their relationship was like the alternations of white and black. They both refined experience until it was schematic, even their immediate, sensuous experience was reduced to an appreciation. I know it, I know it more clearly than he does, thought the first one. I struggle against this abstraction of our experience, of our lives. This language sheathes our every day in a smoothness, there is no way to get a grip on our reality. It's not that I don't know where the real is; I hold it in my hands, I can breathe it, every word I speak is clothed in it. It's the abstracting nature of the language which destroys the hold we have on reality, the sense and smell of the world. He was stirred by these thoughts, and it seemed that by their violence he could get through to the concrete, to what was at the bottom of both their minds. Communication is not really the problem, thought the other. Or communication as a total, world process, I mean as involvement in the world, communication of ourselves, of the trees, the streets, the city, nature. But I feel that in every word I speak this communication is self-defeating. But I know what I'm saying, where I am, he thought as he looked around at the darkening surroundings. The first one was also plunged in self-reflection. The evening was gathering. Both of them were fully self-conscious, yet unable to communicate with each other, with the woods and the darkening sky. Clearly, their thoughts and emotions were close, their consciousness almost pooled, but they were unable to pass through to self-communication, and they sank now each into silence.

I'm Going Out

He looked about him and said: it's strange how we are put into a situation and become only articulations of that situation. You mean that we are involved because of the Mother's womb malady, I said to him, because of her neuroses, because of her narcissistic fixations perhaps? Yes he answered, that is what I meant, in a way— I'm not really interested in a Freudian analysis, what intrigues me is our helplessness in the throes of her coming to consciousness, that we are particles thrown about and colliding in the Mother's convulsions. Yes, I think, he is right. We are nonentities, the flux

of this prose is itself only a manifestation of her menstrual irregu-
larities, of the unpredictability of the tide. And what, I say to him,
do you think we can do about it, I mean what can we do to direct
our destinies in this storm of the menstruum, of the womb's convul-
sions. Nothing at all, he replied, looking down at his feet, we are
given birth to and destroyed in the same wave, cast up and thrown
down in her clutchings and heaving. I look about me a little wildly,
as if the walls of our compartment were even now shaking and
contracting. You are involving me in a fantasy that really doesn't
interest me one bit, I said to him, why don't we move on to some
subject, I would rather contemplate the sea or the woods moving
in the wind. You cannot escape the Mother's trauma wherever you
go, you see, he answered, you reproduce in those outside images
the painful throes, however you alleviate the immediate memory by
the esthetic distance, by contemplation as you like to call it. No
you are mistaken and lost indeed, he continued, your consciousness
goes prattling on and it's only bad blood. You can't frighten me, I
said, I know who I am and where I am. You are carried along by a
flow of blood and there's not a damn thing you can do about it,
he said. Damn her, I burst out, did we ask to come into this world,
that she has to lay the curse of her blood on our heads, that we
have to carry her load of sickness for aeons? I knew, mind you,
that every one of these statements, which were uncontrollable, was
pure cliché, but they were running away with themselves. The in-
terest which I had was purely in the esthetic and anomalous qual-
ity of this flatness, I knew the source of inspiration, if that ghastly
throbbing could be called such, and the flat language were strictly
related, and it wasn't my intention to interrupt the current. So, I
said to him, beginning to enjoy the conversation in a gruesome
way, because I can assure you that it was hurting my esthetic and
personal feelings, and it was only by putting it at arm's length that
there was any way to keep it up, you really feel involved in this
mother complex, you feel yourself an articulation of it. We are such
an articulation, he said to me, there's no way out of that one, we
are linguistic particles so to speak, in as far as our exchange, our
speech here is fixed, manifesting the uterus conflict. Oh no, I said
to him, I don't like that, I don't accept that at all. You see, I knew
deep down when I began this exchange with you that it wasn't so,
I mean I looked on it as an esthetic experience, and I said to my-
self, well what the hell, let it roll, but I want you to know right

here and now that I won't let it reach any more significant level than this. I spoke to him in this way, because I was worried about it all by now, and I really did feel myself more deeply involved than I liked to admit. Everything was rasping on my nerves, you see, I can't even control my metaphors, I'm not interested in controlling my language, it's the need for references to it, something has to take me outside this murderous maternal context, some kind of balance of sanity. Look, I said to him, I have you before me, that is enough, let's get into this more directly, our implication in the crime of the Mother, I laughed, the blood on our heads, what is all this, I don't accept it and I don't believe it, but we have become somehow involved in this story. As I spoke these words I realized what the nature of the involvement was, do you see, at least I saw this was my first mistake in an argument where I wanted to prove myself outside. How absurd! How could I be outside any more than you yourself! We are all caught up in the entrails or the intestines of the Mother, there's no getting out of that. Yes, he said, you have said it now. You know what I mean now, don't you? I am speaking to you, you who are every bit as involved as we are, he continued, I am looking out as it were towards you, but there is no out and there is no in, that is the horror of it. I don't like the dramatic fantasy of this, this whole conversation was becoming extremely distasteful to me, it was I thought, exactly the reverse of those mystic monologues we had become used to, this must be the bloody inside I thought to that calm and resigned exterior. I didn't like and don't like the turn things are taking, I said to him, I don't want any kind of part in this murderous game, I don't like the language and I don't like the context. You can do nothing about it, he answered, you, you are sunk into this over your head. You are a fool, I said, and I walked over to the window. I gazed through, the horizon stretched away to the mountains, some were capped with snow, there I thought is some promise, some freshness. This turmoil, this maternal blood and cliché is too messy, too confusing to live with, it's unnecessary in fact, I said to him. He just looked at me, and walked over to the window I had been gazing out. What is the point of that, he asked smiling, is that necessary. No, I suppose not, it is completely unnecessary, I answered, but—I looked out the window again. I looked out the window and gazed towards the mountains. I knew there was some relief that way. I looked out the window and nodded at him, don't you see, I said to him, you can breathe—I don't say it's necessary, I know the flood rages within, but that's totally unnecessary, the air that rides icily off those slopes and sweeps down to the city cooling us and filling our lungs, that is something we can live in. He shrugged his shoulders, and touched the walls. I knew what he meant, that eloquently silent gesture revulsed me, I thought of the veins and muscles of a womb. I am going to sit down here in perfect peace, he said. I knew what he meant but why accept it? I won't sit down at that table and eat with you, I said. He turned to me and opened his eyes. Why, he said, why? I pointed out the window, I'm going outside I said. You can't he said, it's not possible. I looked at him again curiously, why not, I asked. He just looked around him, and put his hands on the table. Why not, I ask you? I looked out the window again, the crystal air on the slopes, I thought I could feel it! I'm going out, I said.

The Shadow and the Flame

Look, he said. He thought: will she realize what I mean by these words. Of course she looked up, but it didn't correspond yet to what he intended. Why, he wondered. What is the difference between the shadow and the flame? I can almost hear myself thinking, I can hear my voice resounding in this room. Look, I said to her. What is it I actually meant. But as soon as I speak the words they are rough, in the air. She looked up when I spoke, a light in her eyes. It is the light I was watching for. Even now I can hear my voice echoing. I am almost afraid to speak again, to make another move. I am frozen for a moment in these reflections. Even to think costs me, spends me. I would like to hold to this moment, the moment of my speech and her looking. I know nothing could unfold out of this crystal, but silence. And only silence can keep alive, while I think. Her voice broke into his thoughts. Listen, he said to her, why are you here. I have been watching you, I didn't know what to say. It is difficult to say anything. I don't feel myself. Sometimes I feel as if I were in my own skin, sometimes I feel as if I were transposed outside of myself. Sometimes it is as if my words were carrying myself. I do not want to speak, often not to think. Do you understand what I mean. But it is necessary to say something, to address you here. He gestured nervously. She looked at

him. Why should he be nervous, she thought. He seems like a
pleasant person. I understand him better than he thinks. The ex-
istence of each one of us shifts in and out of these words. We are
really playing a life and death game. It seems simple enough in
these conversations. Why did you speak to me, she asked. I was
quiet alone. Now I have this tug of war with you. I don't like to
speak. I know every sentence I say is artificial. I don't feel it to be
myself, but what else am I. You are a fool to have begun this. He
looked at her with surprise. Why surprise, he thought to himself.
It's like a dance of light and shadow—one dances in and the other
dances out. We can't really say anything. Look he said, it's time
for us to say something, I know what we are involved in, these ex-
hausting platitudes of exchange, can't you see that I wanted to
experience something of life with you, and instead we are being
wasted in this language. Yes, I realize that she said, but why
couldn't you speak out sooner. Let's go out, maybe we can speak
with greater ease out there. So they went out and walked in the
sunshine talking for several minutes. They held hands as they
walked, and felt the sunshine glowing in them. I watched them
from the window, moved and at the same time estranged. Why did
they leave the room, I wondered, and their reflections. Were they
"happier" out there. That is what he had meant when he spoke of
himself as other, and when she had spoken of being happy. But
who are we really? I myself tend to identify with them, and they
speak with the same voice as myself. Now they are two persons
walking together in the yellow sunshine out there. Their exchange
was wasting you, I thought. Now they had precipitated themselves
into this otherness, annihilation. I walked to the door and looked
out. Maybe I should join them, I thought. It is almost too much to
bear the weight of this language alone. The phrases are lopsided
and awkward, and don't fit us. We weren't born to speak. I think
we left the garden of Eden too soon. They look like creatures of
light out there. I am not interested, I thought, in developing this
language. I do not want to carry my weight any longer. I'll just
look out the window to keep this scene alive in my mind. They are
walking away now. I can see nothing beyond except some trees
blowing in the wind. I would like to speak to them for a few mo-
ments. It's too bad they've gone. They were consumed by their own
speech from the beginning. That is what he said really, that they
were being used by their words. I'm tired, I think I'll join them.

I walked out the door into the open air. I was not convinced by my own words, I knew that I was also being used by them. I hurried across to them.

Moonlight

I walked out into the place alone. It was late, and the moon was full. The night wind, and so on. Do you understand, I said to him. Yes, he answered, looking up. I thought you were coming. Yes, she said, I said to him: look at the moon, by now he should be coming. I thought: should it really be the time already? I don't remember anything in particular. I wonder what they agreed. He looked at me expectantly, you might say. Yes, he answered, I think this is the place; the moon is full. This was made clear at the beginning. I was a little puzzled. Why should they have chosen this time and this place. What was really intended by these remarks. I couldn't remember having really agreed on anything special. He said, it's time certainly. I'm sorry, I suppose that was a stupid remark. Really it's in order to determine the circumstances with clarity. She laughed at that. I don't think that's necessary, I think we were all fairly intent on this meeting last week. I wondered, do they realize it. The whole matter is relatively unimportant. But we did decide to come together. We have come together in any case, I said. I think we should come around to the matter. You think it is easy, she answered. I have been aware of how this came about from the beginning, and I am not so sure as you seem of our chances of success. I thought to myself, do they realize what they are about. They speak of coming together as if it were nothing. To me it is already clear that we risk being destroyed. She looked up at the moon. Why? What was she thinking? She said: I am anxious. I feel such a dispersion. There's no difficulty in speaking. There never is. But there is a danger of losing all relationship. When I first came out here, I breathed in deep the night air. You could smell the night. But now I don't know. We could so easily be lost in it. I looked at her surprised. But why do you say that, I asked. I felt such a peace myself in this air. I confess, when I first came out I felt a suspicion. But I knew of course there was nothing malign in the air. I mean I was not concerned with any fiction. He thought: maybe this is our problem. We form no fiction. The night air is so clear. She looked up, and said, I almost feel the urge of touching the ground to assure myself of being here, I was looking at the shadows on the grass, our shadows. I asked him, do you hear the resonance of our words tonight. He just laughed and thought: it's true. With the brilliance of the moon and the empty night. I looked at them both: don't you understand what is happening. I said: we are losing ourselves in our words. She looked down at the shadows. She reached down to touch one of them. Look, she said. I know I am substance, I'm flesh and blood. But we have been talking for a few minutes about nothing. I don't know what we are involved in, but my voice is so free. I know what it is, he said, and looked up at the moon. I think there is no way of extricating ourselves. I hold my hand out in the light of the moon. Listen, I said; what is vital here is the words we use. He looked at her. What you say means nothing, she said. The open place was bathed in moonlight. We three looked at each other. I would like to say something to fix this uncertainty—I feel at a loss. I walked away a few yards into the shadows, and looked at my two companions. Say something, I thought to myself. I am so aware of my immobility. I know very little is preserving us. I know the reality supporting us is as tenuous as the moonlight. I looked up at the moon and held out my arms. The light splashed about them. I looked out towards them again, they were almost lost in the shadows. I wonder, why is it. We came out tonight with a purpose. Why are we unable to materialize it. I knelt in the dust, breathing its powdery dry scent. I understand what you mean, she said.

The Richness of Experience

I had no idea what they were doing there. But I knew that it would quickly develop with the text. I mean I knew that they were fully incorporated, flesh and bone. I did not know who they were. She walked over to him in the light of the falling day and touched him on the shoulder. He turned around and looked at her. It was likely that they were deeply involved, as it's said, because of the intensity of their looks. They walked away in the dusk. I looked about myself. I wondered where they had gone. I wondered if the question could even be put, because wasn't their leaving simply a silence, what was their leaving. I looked after them for some time, I could see nothing. I knew that my own involvement was doubtful, uncertain, but I felt bonds with them, there were bonds between us. After they returned I talked about the matter with them. I mean my isolation in terms of the text, as I called it. I think we've gone through this before, he said, so that a remark will be enough. The text is your fiction. Actually the fullness of life is here, at the threshhold of language. I am convinced of this myself. I mean the richness of a so-called textual experience. We walked for a while along the edge of the woods in the twilight. She bent down now and then to pick up a flower or a bit of bark. The moon was just beginning to appear on the horizon. I was wrapped in the coolness of the air and the quiet of the evening, the tree, the long fields. I breathed the air consciously, I mean I was conscious of the breathing, of the words I used. I knew every footstep I took. One of the most remarkable things is the acute awareness of such moments, and the floating consciousness at other times. I asked her if she knew what I meant. She said: don't you realize even now, as I was bending down picking flowers and bark, that I was experiencing this floating consciousness? There isn't really any need to talk about these things as if we weren't able to experience in reality. This is what disturbs me so deeply. I was happy walking in these woods with you. I felt the cool glow of the moon, and the wetness of the grass on my fingers. When you speak of floating experience it's so obvious that all that is removed. That would be the anguish of fictive experience. I looked at her. There was no way to keep up the tension of that moment. I looked at him with curiosity. I understood what he meant to convey to me, but it was doubtful. I suggested that we go for a walk in the city, and he accepted. We walked for an hour or so in the streets talking about these things, and looking at the sights. We both knew where we were, that was quite clear, but it did not interfere with our walk. Why should it? I suggested to him we walk towards a nearby café and he thought it was a good idea. I pointed at the buildings as we passed them and he nodded. It did not seem necessary to talk of a floating consciousness anymore. When we arrived at the café there were a few people. We took a table and ordered beers. I was perplexed by his manner. He seemed distant for example. I asked him, and he said no, I hardly feel touched by this walk, etc. I don't know if we were trying to get away from the concept of a floating consciousness, but it seems to me that we are fully in it. In any case it takes me a little while, just talking, to get my feet on the ground. I looked around the room a little desperately. I knew why he spoke about this now, I knew that he felt I was again assuming the text. And in fact that was so. The fiction was mine! Excuse me a second, I said to him, and got up. I walked over to the other side of the café and asked the bartender if I could use the phone. Of course I didn't really want to use the phone, it was a pretext, it was in fact a fiction, I was even sorry that I had used that whole set of phrases. I was feeling a little ill at ease, because everything I said seemed to be catching me up. I wondered why I had got involved in this conversation. I walked about a little nervously. I decided to leave without saying anything to him. The air outside was cool and I hurried along, holding my collar shut. I knew really there was no need for any of these pretexts. Actually I was tired of becoming involved, not in the conversation, but in this kind of language. The point is to know what you are doing, what you are saying every moment. The floating experience is an illusion, the illusion of life. It is the distance between the language and the fullness of life, as we have called it. It is in this vacuum, this remove that we had seemed to float. I know that when this is clearly recognized, then it is possible to live in the richness of experience. There was no need to go through all that; I mean the walk in the woods, and then the walk through the city, and stopping at the café, all these were props, it became so obvious. I was relieved now that I had cleared a few of these things up. The fictions had weighed heavily on my tongue, the irritation of them. Yes, and I was perfectly aware that these fictions began with myself. Now it was clear that anything could be said. I could speculate about them, or I could go for a walk, or anything else, a thousand things that can be done.

FOUR POEMS

DANIEL HALPERN

WOMEN

She dreams
Smooth green snakes
On rainy nights

It seems
He read her
Rough copies of great poems

She would fake
Understanding so he
Could go to bed happy

She thought it right
Things went on this way
For he brought home

Beautiful things from the city

TWO LAMENTS

I

The walls of her house are dark
Where rain has turned to wine.
The Cherokee neighbor grumbles cactus
Into the ground and salutes her.

Tamed by static
The laundry clings to her like children.

He only springs for sadness

Is her thought as she roams the house
Gathering errands in her arms.

In the citrus light,
Her hair tied tight in a snood,
She puts a sponge to water
And shines the cedar of her house with lemon
Wax.

The antique clock sleeps in iron, drumming
A progression of fingers to her head
Where the number for her love
Waits . . .

For sadness

She sighs,
But it shines the stainless,
Wanders in and out of rooms beneath her hair
And paces in her eyes.

When the bell rings,
And she goes running for the phone,

There is only sadness for a tone.

II

The rain in the garden is not gentle;
Rather, it is rough with bark
Gathered from the high tree:
Sweet mimosa, leaves
Like his open hand.

Like moss
His red tracks are tacked
To the ground
Where they gather
Surface.

On the pock-marked patio
The water pools itself
And sways
As the clear Brandy burns the lawn
And the hydrangeas revive.

He only springs for sadness

And spring moves in from the cold
With light rain
Dripping from burgundy shingles,

A dropping of sad feet into mud.

THE IMPORTANCE OF RITUAL

"This pillow's nothing," she thinks
All night. "To get your head
Off the bed you have to fold it
In threes."

And the black drops her

In the morning
She throws the urine
Out the window and applies
Florida Water to her cramps,
Which fade—
Waves to ripples.

   Garbage trucks grind up
   The silence around her coffee

She opens the door
And the postman falls through the porch.
"I could stamp straight through it
Too," she thinks.

   "The violence, the violence
   Is terrible," she thinks.

Someone told her:
"Put sweet basil behind your ear
And quick, turn on it,"
Catching the pocket of scent
Hanging like hair.

She placed the herb on her ear
And turned to it, catching
It, loosing it,
The wind
Eating it.

The pillow,
The cramps,
The coffee next door,
The postman descending.

   Florida Water and basil

In a heavy chair time for her
Is the growth of nails
Through her clenched fist.

FIRST DATE

By number
I find her house haunching
On a minor street:
A tired circus of old wood
With windows caught
In a perpetual blink;
A trapezoid of memory
Tucked in by grass
That rolls in remembering
Decades of
Watering and clipping.

Two storied
The upper leans on the lower
Like a squared elbow.

She comes,
A foot-fall of sound,
Opening the door
Onto the intricate nature
Her living has sewn
Into the broken silence.

CORNADA

E. M. BEEKMAN

Two inches above the slight, brown nipple aureoled with down, the curved bone drove through the smooth olive skin, through the flesh, the tissue, passing by the heart.

"Cornada in the chest."

I know. I am the one lying here begging my shredded flesh to grow solid and smooth and olive again for another mishap on a late afternoon. Don't even bother. I will not open my eyes. A coma is fine with me. Contracts, money, the season: they can wait. Wait for me. I have to search for that treacherous horn lurking down below, foiled in the folds of the muleta. The faker faked. The animal has his revenge when you cross. The right hand feigns and the left deals death or is dealt with. Never trust the left La Lola told him. Death comes from the left. Bring the horns by the lee of your right and cross over with your left for the kill. Left is the heart. Left is death.

It was the wind. I tell you it was the wind. You stupid clown. Peón. Keep your lids shut. Ah, how brave he is now, telling the babblers behind the exploding bulbs that it was the vision of the animal which was at fault. A film over the eyeball. Your balls are filmed. Celluloid balls: they shrivel at a touch of the flame. I'll fire you when I choose to get well again. You can wait, all of you. You can wait for me for a change. The circles of howling morons betting on my blood. Impresario, you can go in there and fight yourself. With the cigar between your teeth and with that ridiculous Stetson you got from a tourist you pimped for. His wife you left at my table that night mooning over my hands who killed so much. So much, she sighed and stroked them with fascination. No sex. Fascination. And I was forced to look at my hands and admire them with her. Those mirrors of beauty. You know that's bad luck. Strong fingers—tendons taut as the cables of El Songo's boat—

capable of guiding the curved sword inch by inch down into the hand's width of death between the churning pistons of the black shoulder blades. Back of my hands olive and smooth. As hairless as hoofs. It's the wrist that counts lady, the wrist. If it goes you go. Yes, you turn, you go fight and have fear shred your cigar and swallow it lit down your guts and you'll run, battened by their laughter, run for the barrera.

"The bull was bad. We're going to make a formal complaint. Nowadays they'll throw anything on four legs into the ring and make them fight it."

"He's got no statements to make?"

"You must be crazy. Look at him. He hasn't opened his eyes yet."

"Will El Loro fight at Burgos next week?"

Andrés, the senior banderillero of Paco Morelos, looked at the reporter in utter amazement.

"My matador lies dying here with three pints of blood pumped into him. A chest cornada. In a coma. Hasn't opened his mouth yet to say blah and this imbecile, dunked in ink until it clogged up his brain, is asking if he'll fight next week."

Paco smiled. Drew his lips taut again. No one had noticed. I won't fire you, you old bastard. Give it to him, that used ink ribbon. No I won't fight at Burgos. No I won't make a statement. No it wasn't the bull's fault. The wind. It was the wind. My curse is the wind. Befits the son of a fisherman. The chill of the wind offshore flapped the wet shirt against his chest. His father saw him holding his teeth with the palm of his hand. Smiled and threw a cut of old sail over his shoulders.

"Get in the lee. If you can find any. Hold on tight, son. Always watch the wind. She brings us money or disaster. You wanna be a fisherman, you better make good with her, Lady Wind."

"God, he's shivering to death. Where the hell is the doctor?" Andrés ran out of the room. The reporter from *ABC* exploded a bulb right in his face, leaning his rancid body over the edge of the bed for a close-up, pulled the dressing down a bit to get the blood oozing for a nice gory picture for the delightedly horrified aficionados. He would like to be able to rise, slowly, eyes sewn shut, stuff the man's gaping mouth with the soaking bandage, take his pants down and shove the flash up his ass and pop it for a real inside look of a reporter. A grateful world would grant him his retirement at a very tender age. Andrés, dragging the doctor by his sleeve, foiled his dream.

"What you're trying to do," shouted his man, "kill my patrón? Your mother left your brains in the afterbirth."

"All right, all right," the doctor calmed.

Scalpel the vulture. You can put it on my bill. But the surgeon's command was silence and it swaddled him in muffs of drawn breath. Expertise fingered his chest, checked his pulse, listened to his heart below the left nipple where the horn had wanted to get to, to rummage and murmur death. Beads of sweat were sponged from his forehead. Could you but sponge the beats of fear from where your ear listens.

"Chills are common when they're in a coma. If it is a coma. Can't be sure yet. We must wait. I got all the splinters out. But you never can tell. Was an astillado did you say? Their horns make the worst wounds. Sometimes a bit of horn wanders. Astillados. They make things very difficult for me."

Again he shivered. A tiny horn murdering him slowly and carefully beneath the skin. Carving itself a path toward a vein it would drift lazily upstream, bank and short-circuit the brain. Andrés felt spooked by the sweating body shivering on the hospital bed which did not look like a man he could pass a sword for the kill.

"El Loro lies dying with a cornada de caballo and *ABC* would help it along just for exclusive pictures," he muttered to keep his spirits up.

"Well, I've seen worse ones fight a week later," the surgeon said. "Everybody out. Nurse. No one permitted in here unless cleared with me. Understand? Astillados. The least they can do for me is get a clean wound from a sharp, solid horn."

And they put the lights out on the young novillero and left him alone to open his eyes to the dark room where a subtle black beast hid to splinter his mind. He had been very lucky. Bulls had thrown him, ripped his satin breeches, knocked the wind out of him with the flat of their horns—but they could not gore him. It was rumored that he was charmed. Magazines like *ABC*, oiled by his pesetas, had milked several cover stories about the fisherman's son from southern Andulacía, whose mother had Gypsy blood and who had drunk charmed milk from her breasts. Paco paid no attention to rumor, tongued or printed. Because he did not speak very often they had nicknamed him "The Parrot" as a kid, and it had stuck as his professional apodo. Soon his mother would hear the stories and, hearing the worst, La Lola would keen and pray to their local idol, The Virgin of the Waves. The surf rustled round the room, thrust-

ing its luminous curve into the darkened sand. His eyes got drunk
on the dizzying shimmer of liquid pewter undulating gently like
miles of uncut suits of light. The nightbeach, emptied of alien
noise, purred under the constant strokes of the sea. The two boys
ran the sand to place the gay harpoons into the limp morillo of the
foaming bulls the sea cast onto the shore. Gently they roared and
the trick was to place the banderillas before the rush of shimmering
silver was sucked into the sand. Their targets were innumerable.
Panting and sweating they would rest on a rock and calculate their
runs towards the ever-charging herd. He cut himself a suit of
lights from the endless rolls of liquid cloth. His naked body cast in
silver he fought the silver salt on the sand of the enormous arena
which curved out of sight beyond the breakwater where the ships
moored. A bull from the surf is by no means an easy kill. Slowly the
green hump of muscle swelled, crested, lowered the horns and
rushed at him from the left, crossed and rose from the right,
abated, and when he looked for it, issued between his feet, foam
torrent and glistening white jabbing at his thighs eager for the
femoral artery which would squirt his life into the vast meadow
where myriad moonlit heads swayed, snorted, crashed and gored.
Even so they could not catch him for he fought silver against silver,
and he could laugh up at the furious cusps ripping into the sky.
The cloth was drawn away from the hooking horns and the enor-
mous spangled chest would expand, indifferent to the danger of the
horn, and unfurl another cape. Paco laughed. He fought like the
sky at night. What could be braver than that broad chest flecked
with light contemptuous of the waxing fury which waned before
his vast courage. Calmly he stepped out of the marine suit and,
covered by nothing but the sky, fought the most gigantic bravos
the sea could raise. To keep the muleta at arm's length hurt his
chest. Cornada. Why, said the muzzle, moist and black, why didn't
you stick to fishing? You could have made a fine fisherman. Maybe
owned a boat and get the good catches off the Canaries. The wide
grin of bone lurked in the corner next to the door. No bull had
ever talked to him like that. Never keep your eyes on the horns.
Look past them. The huge black canvas rippling with muscle.
Magician. You think. A faker. Fake the pass of the muleta at the
end of the faena de la muerte, keep my head down and in the
folds. Then between my horns, empoque, you cross with your left
hand to keep my death away from your body and shove the sword
in with the right. You won't be able to do that again because you'll
never know when I will raise my head, hook with my left horn

and catch you in the thigh. In that triangle of flesh all of you fear so much, where the femoral pulses.

"But it was the wind that fooled me. Not you. I had you right where I wanted you."

"So you thought until you woke up on the hule with a cornada in your chest. Look, I was kind to you. I am warning you. Men from the sea have no business with bulls and sand. Fishermen make lousy matadors."

Paco raised himself from the soaked pillow and sheet. The bone crescent was snaking through the dark of his room, slithering with laughter. Hornéd snake. Snaking bull. The sweat was drenching the dressing of his wound. Bulging black, the animal muscled toward his bed and threw his stiff, wide hat on the bed. Paco drew himself up against the headboard. Disregarding him as would the wind, the bull whisked past him, flanks heavy with sweat and dung, humped horns razoring for his body. Stopped short, raining sand on the fighter. And Paco clearly saw the bull wink at him and the eye telling him that both of them knew the cape to be a trick for the public, but that in reality he was going to come after his thighs, paying no attention to the deception at all, no matter how still he'd stand. Paco rasped his tongue over his palate and called him a coward. The morillo tensed, the muscles bunched and spread and grew till the horns were curving outwards from the black hood of muscle and swayed to strike.

"All right. All right. Relax. Let's take a look."

Paco stole a glance between his lashes and saw the doctor and a nurse over him. The light was on. In the corner next to the door was a chair with his clothes. They changed the dressing.

"Leave the door open. It's too close in here," the doctor ordered.

"He was screaming," the nurse said, "he was afraid of something."

"Yes."

That one word classified him among the dubious fighters who, after a severe goring, no longer are able to stand the danger in the ring and lose their nerve. The doctor knew. He had seen many sewn men become cowards. El Songo spoke calmly to his son above the wood, water and wind. The fishing boat was being chopped by broncos as bad as those in the ring.

"With a wind like this the waves see no need for mercy."

The father was mending the nets which had been ripped the day before. The churning boat in the tossing sea didn't seem to bother him. Paco sat with silent admiration for this man who so often was jailed for months in the ill-calked hull to make a few

thousand pesetas. From that money he had to buy his gear, feed
his family, and pay the two men who worked under him as menders
of nets. El Songo did not like to be voluble. Tough and strong and
thin as a weathered cable he kept on fighting the harsh inequities
of his craft and his existence. So seldom did he have a bonus—
when the weather was calm, the schools large and lazy, the nets
holding, the wind benign and the price of fish booming—so seldom
that it was a miracle of Nuestra Señora de las Olas and extra candles
were burned then every day of her fiesta. In Barbate, La Lola and
the other wives would curse everything marine when their men
came home in their battered boats after many weeks with no
money and a great thirst for vino y casera. Songo loved his son
very deeply and silently. Both man and wife looked a decade or
so older when, in their early thirties, after four gory miscarriages,
they had their first and final child. Like a bonus, it was a miracle
and the Virgin stared past many candles for many days. To see him
grow strong and tall, Lola worked as often as the whistle of the
cannery would invite her. Worked thirteen hours a day gutting
fish for ten pesetas a box. The whistle didn't blow very often.
Barbate had nothing else. Tourists didn't know of its beach and no
one had seriously considered it because of the Levante, the wind
that hurls from the mountain ridges surrounding the bay and drives
people, weather, and the sea crazy. A few miles inland were the
blond plains and arid hills of parched Andalucía. Perhaps it was the
Levante which made the fighting bulls, raised on two large ranches
by the river, so fiercely defiant and dangerous. Perhaps mad? Paco
Morelos was brought up between sea and hills, boats and bulls,
sombra y sol.

"Why fight the bulls? If you need to be brave there is enough
of it here," Songo said nodding at the sea, not looking at his son,
threading the net. Paco had never mentioned his nights on the
beach fighting the bulls, nor that he knew that the rings of Spain
had nothing to offer him as fearful as the broncos he was riding
now. When Songo smiled, the broken stumps of brown rotting
teeth formed a friendly grotto.

"If you and I work hard for some years we could maybe buy a
small boat ourselves."

A faint light, about the strength of a flickering wick, straddled
the top of the mast.

"La Luz de San Termo," shouted one of the men, and all hands
struggled to get the boat to the nearest harbor. Those faint flames

are followed by very dangerous weather and no one stays out at sea if he can help it.

"Your mother is scared of the bulls," Songo said looking at the florescent mast.

"Why not of this?," Paco asked.

"She knows the sea. She doesn't know the bulls."

It was the only conversation father and son had had on the subject. Paco felt unable to explain to his mother that the bulls and the waves were not different and the hazards as great. He had left and been very lucky. The ranchera who owned one of the two big farms had helped him and introduced him to the man who raised the bulls who were fought in the ring. Whenever unsure or when too many people bothered him, the wiry, taciturn youth would go to the beach of Barbate and watch the sea cast its nets on the sand. She cast them better than his father, overlapping them so they spread like fans, held down by the weight of the foam until they were blotted by the sand. She casts them well indeed, he thought, and learned to wave his cape and muleta like the water cast by the surf. Watching the sea for so many years, and from listening to his father's sober narrations of his troubles, Paco had learned that the wind was the most treacherous element. El Levante swooping down from the mountains scared the people of Barbate more than anything else. Without it the men could always return home empty-handed; but when it lashed the sea to fury they found corpses on their hands. He had drunk luck at his mother's breast. He had no fear. He wanted to buy his father a boat. He wanted an art, not a trade. So Paco Morelos, El Loro, fought bulls in the rings of sand. And when in his first big fight in Cádiz his parents watched him perform from box seats and couldn't applaud from fear, he had told them that he hated nothing so much as the circles of howling mob and the treachery of the wind with his capa and muleta. And his mother had answered that there was nothing to fear but black bulls who were now grazing in the hospital, swatting the flies from their flanks with their long tails with silken tassels, telling him with their eyes that they would toss and gore him the next time he dared play the artist with them. When he raised himself on his damp bed, their humps swelled and the cusps of death darted like tongues of snakes through the doorway. He whimpered. They made him moan. No balls. He held his groin with his right hand and moaned for the black bulls were tossing their hats on his bed and the stiff headgear had almost covered him with darkness. And when they took to their wings and lanced him with their blades of horn, ripped at his flesh, lapped his face with the tongues hanging from the side of their muzzles, he shrieked. No one stirred. But the beat of their wings. He ripped a strip from the sheet on his legs, tied it into a knot twice and threw it under his bed mumbling between his clenched teeth very rapidly over and over again: "San Cojonato si no encuentro mi valor, los cojones te ato." The winged bulls dove for him, crescent bone searing the night of his room. Fear had put him to the horn. "San Cojonato si no encuentro mi valor, los cojones te ato." The nets of the sea caught the sand from under his feet and the hooved surf clawed at the land. His father was mending a worn net of black rope in which his mother wrapped his body which was cast into the sea down to where even blind fishes couldn't live. The waters sooted over the blaze of the sky at noon while a freezing gale howled at the bottom of the sea.

A week later Paco was waiting for his first bull to come out of the puerta de arrastre in the arena of Burgos. He had entered the ring through this doorway which was also the last passage for the dead bulls. His adversary tossed his black head, horns curving up to the circles of blaring mouths and went for the cape Andrés was waving. When Paco had placed his pair of banderillas in the black neck engorged with maddened muscles he stood still, caught by the fast bulk shearing past his body. The flank scuffed by his suited belly and the thin wings of colored paper darted in the slight breeze. Sculpturing man and beast with his cape into arrested motion, he told the bull that he understood. Strange how we both need each other's death. Strange that both of us are scared, cunning, desperate, furious and valiant. You taught me failure and coupled fear. To fail you. The bull grunted and took the fake again and again. The mob felt he was working too languidly while he talked. "¡Me cago en la Hostia!" one enraged drunkard yelled at him when he returned to the barrera. Paco drew the sword from its sheath, took it by the blade, and handed the pommel up to the screeching mouth. When the sword sank inch by inch and could go no further, when the knees gave and the massive head jerked to the ground, he stood immobile and watched impartially with interest. He nodded to the corpse and bid it a fair journey. When he turned and kept his eyes from the praising crowd he knew what scared him. He never won. For behind him he saw the dead animal stick its tongue out.

TEN POEMS

CARLOS BOUSOÑO

Translated by Louis M. Bourne

TRANSLATOR'S NOTE: Carlos Bousoño, renowned both as a critic and poet in his native Spain, was born in 1923 in Boal (Asturias). He received his early schooling in Oviedo, and later obtained his B.A. and Ph.D. in Romance philology from the University of Madrid, where he now teaches. From 1946 to 1948, however, he gave a course at Wellesley College on Spanish literature and lectured at Harvard and in Mexico on contemporary Spanish poetry.

His first book of poems, Subida al amor (Ascent to Love), *appeared in 1945. This was followed by* Primavera de la muerte (Spring of Death, 1946), Hacia otra luz (Towards Another Light, 1953), Noche del sentido (Night of the Senses, 1957), Invasión de la realidad (Invasion of Reality, 1962), *and* Oda en la ceniza (Ode in the Ashes, 1967; second edition, 1968), *which was awarded the* Premio de la crítica. *It is from this last collection that the translations appearing here were made.*

Bousoño's early poetry, rhetorical, melancholy and generally formal, deals with the theme of religious doubt from a somewhat orthodox standpoint, as well as the morbid silence and waste that characterized post-Civil War Spain, and tentative experiences of love and memories of childhood. With the poem "la Plaza"—in the 1957 collection, Noche del sentido—*Bousoño seems to have discovered his mature free verse style and the depth of his philosophical concerns.*

His present use of irrational imagery, paradox and antithesis are directly related to the existential arguments of his poems. Indeed, the desperate energy of Bousoño's best poetry is based on the tension of opposites—the understanding of life as a mixture of tragedy and comedy—and on the feeling that love and friendship, in the dramatic and frightening circumstances of being, are the means through which one can prevail.

ODE IN THE ASHES

for Francisco Brines

Once more. The waves, the events,
The tiny insistence that pierces
Granite reality, the immobile
Block where time
Circles like a sad
Eagle.
      Every minute the world changes,
Death changes,
And scorn, the daily appearance of eagerness,
The radical meaning.
             We lose our grip,
Firm contact, handle of shadows. Give me
Your hand, lift me up, I would touch
Perhaps the sublime
Handle without ash, the majestic
Rock, the lofty seat
Of splendour, the door that doesn't turn
Nor open, nor close, the ultimate
Source of water, thirst, diaphanous
Winds,
From the wretched clay where zeal burns
Like a hot coal. Oh temptation of being
In the wondrous truth,
In the radiant space, burst open with reverence
Beyond shadowy
Respect. Oh hardening
Sacred ideality that neither flames nor burns
In the dazzling invisibility, in the incredible
Force of the world. Oh iceberg of oceanic passion

Where weariness
Can shine and complaint
Burn and change, and man crave and be satiated
With continuous nourishment.
                              Oh discouragement
Of forgetting, craving, being consumed,
Centre of man.
                    You, my companion,
Sad with being,
You, who fret as I do about what you don't know and perhaps don't
      know what you have,
Give me your hand in desolation,
Give me your hand in incredulity and in the wind,
Give me your hand in the ruinous sob, in the gloomy chant.
Give me your hand to believe, though you don't know,
Give me your hand to exist, since you are shadow and ash,
Hold out your hand to me till the heights, till the vertical pass,
      till the sudden peak.
Help me to rise, since the arrival is impossible,
The advent, the encounter.
Help me to rise since you fall, since perhaps
Everything is possible in impossibility,
Since perhaps very little is needed to acquire thirst,
Very little to top the abyss,
The slope towards thunder,
The vertical wall of doubt,
The embankment of fear.
                        Oh give me
Your hand because very little is needed
To leap to joy,
Very little for absolute laughter and rest,
Very little for everlasting friendship.
                              Give me your hand,
You who fret as I do about what you don't know and perhaps don't
      know what you have,
Give me your hand till the huge flower that turns in happiness,
Give me your hand till the fragrant happiness enraptures,
Give me your hand and don't let me fall
As you do,
As I do,
Into the horrible void of shadows.

ANALYSIS OF SUFFERING

for José Olivio Jiménez

The cruel man is an investigator of life,
A patient reconstructor, an objective watchmaker, an expert
That would like to know existence,
The secret of life which one explores in suffering.

The lover of learning is ready
For his delicate operation.
And the material of analysis remains
At his mercy: a man suffers.

It is horrible to know the truth, and the miserable discovery
Destroys the one who achieves it,
As no one has or ever will be able to know fully
In its palpable truth,
The life itself revealed in another, without dying.

However, it is very certain
That suffering expresses
Man, though it ruins him,
Because after the painful experience
There is another man who is born, on knowing himself,
And knowing the world.

Not always, certainly,
Can the one who has suffered
Endure the weight of his knowledge.
Some never return
To life, as it is difficult to exist
After the shame of having so known.

Others live, their dignity
More broken, in the infamy
Which all sorrow is,
Meanly
Continue, and a grimace
Is their gesture, their habit.

There is the man who wears
Distress in another fashion,
The concentrated reflexion which all sorrow is.
After the dreadful meditation, man can hear,
Touch and see,
And know himself and be among men.

And this is how the cruel man blunders
In his philosophic labour, because only he who suffers,
If perhaps he merits it,
Gains the knowledge which the cruel man seeks in vain.

The one who suffers knows and not the one who causes suffering,
This man doesn't survive his knowledge,
And though neither can the sufferer many times
Undergo that terrible experience,
He succeeds at other times
In listening with surprise
To the purest concert,
The immortal melody of the inaudible light,
There, in the very centre of human misery.

THE DANCE

for Pierre Darmangeat

Being and nothingness are made to dance together.
They are made to dance and stay embraced.
With heads together, with love and tenderness
The constant pair perform an eternal dance
In the endless dawn. In the whirlwind the hills,
The cities, the hours appear discontinuous.
Villages and towers, castles,
Rise up in the plain. Settlements
Are born and die with the speed of a flame
And the courtier whispers
Flattering words while
The centuries pass by and the dawn vanishes.

Dust has renewed its nativity. Swallows
That never return to the nest,
Sepulchral doves, torn banners,
Distant bells, chirpings.
It's here that the great dance has begun.
Joy and despair walk arm in arm,
And everything springs to light and everything is as if it
    hadn't begun.
A mountain begins with its highest peak,
Rises to its slopes and above is the valley.
Dry yourself in the midst of the cold water of October,
Lorenzo, plunge yourself into the plethora of nothing.
We are glutted with necessity and the hunger's a surfeit
    as beautiful
As an emerald. Tell me,
Travellers who erase your footprints with such care
    and attention and vanish into the night,
Tell me where you are, to what strange splendour you return,
Invisible,
Where, dancers who question the mystery,
Where to find you.
              The dead,
Killed, assassinated: the living,
A mountain of sudden injury. Pale
Obscene cities, inhabited by bones,
Lofty urgent cathedrals,
Violins.
         Oh beauty, oh meaning,
Oh terrible living at the edge of a sob
And night where hope dies.

IN ASH THERE IS A MIRACLE

for Guillermo Carnero

In ash there is a miracle.
There the world breathes.

In ash there is an awakening and a hearing and lightning
    and a rapturous possession and a resurgence.
In ash there is daylight and the future sun
Gleams.
In ash there is fear.
Everything begins again.

In ash there are men.
There is love, there is misery.
In ash there is night and a rustle in the night,
And there is a breath among the shadows and there are sighs.
In ash there are tears.

Why doesn't one hear within the ash
The breathing of that world that breathes
The stifling air,
The breathless force that must arise? Be silent.

There is a wind in ash that no one hears.
And a dove flies beneath the sun.

BEYOND THIS ROSE (A Meditation on Last Moments)

for Pedro Gimferrer

I
A rose springs up.
You meditate. Reality
Swells, and expands, contracts, closes up.
When you look, you bury. Oh funereal
Pomp. Lily: dreadful
Neigh, dark complaint, miracle. You that have listened to
The melody of a rose, blood-coloured
In the dawn like a call
From a tiny reality,
You see behind it the deep
Stirring of another life, the slender
Speed with which something hastily moves
Through the night, as if it wanted to reach an insatiable
Goal. There is beyond this rose, whose stem
Stands smoothly erect, a germination become nausea,
A horrible panting,
A frantic anxiety, a fetid existence which declares itself.
A trumpet shoots
Its light, its sonorous zeal
Into the excrement. What do you say,
What do you whisper, what do you whistle
In the dark, beyond this rose,
Reality lying hidden? What melody
Do you compose and understand and deny and stifle,
What rustle of footsteps
Do you destroy, what sound
Do you contradict and deny? The cadence is stated,
The sigh realized.
The rustle is silence,
The hope, the ruin. Everything whistles and waits,
Silent, haughty,
Beyond this rose.

II
Beyond this rose, beyond this hand
That writes and this brow
That meditates, there is a world.
There is a dreadful world, luminous and contrary
To the light, to life.
Beyond this rose and causing its dream,
Parallel, inverted,
There is a world, and a man
Who meditates, like I, at the window.
And on this night, with stars in the background,
As I move my hand,
Someone moves his hand like mine, with stars in the background,
And writes my words
In reverse and erases them.

BUT HOW WILL I TELL YOU

But how will I tell you if you are
As light and silent
As a flower. How will I tell you
When you are water,
When you are a fountain, spring, smile,
An ear of corn, wind,
When you, love, are air.

How will I tell you,
You, young lightning,
Early light, dawn,
That you must die one day
Like one who isn't so.

Your eternal form,
Like light and sea, by chance demands
The lasting majesty
Of matter. Beautiful
As the ocean's permanence
Just before dusk, your flesh is more
Ephemeral than a flower. But if you are
Comparable to light, you are the light,
The light that might speak,
That might say "I love you,"
That might sleep in my arms,
Have zeal, eyes, weariness
And an endless desire
To cry, when you see
The roses in the garden
Bud, once more.

HUMAN QUESTIONS CONCERNING THE EYE OF A NEEDLE

for Claudio Rodríguez

Is that possible?
Is a space expanding
Terribly at each instant possible,
At each wave of humanity that victoriously
Enters the light, at each stroke
Of glorious misery, fraught
With love and sadness and become light,
And suddenly become light,
Light that swiftly
Penetrates in the light,
In the only light?

Is it possible that suddenly
The deep human sea, the miserable
Surging
Of calamity and patience,
Enters by pushing, by sudden shoving,
Brutally, we would say,
Through the simple cracks of mystery?

Does the eye of a needle always await
The wondrous threading
Of the terrible brutish wave
Of atrocious suffering,
And will whole fish there
From the green human sea
Of sorrow, and everything
That happens and is
And befalls man,
And all the rest,
Penetrate wisely like
A huge wave
Through the impossibility of a little hole?

Can the tiny hole,
The break, the seam
Purposefully torn,
The large unseen hole,
The invisible duct,
The thread hole
Finer than a dream
And than the pallor with which we struggle,
Terribly
Bear us?

Will the enchanting pressure
Of human suffering,
The power of grief,
The irresistible force
That takes us there,
Break down the gloomy walls,
And in agony, scrape away
The sorrow, the wall?

Who can say!
The silence is sealed and I hear the murmur of the sea
Which the silence pounds
Once and again.
. . . Once and again, as if the silence
Had an opening,
Only just one tiny hole.

THE SALVATION OF LOVE

for José Hierro

Persist.
Snatch a piece of wood, save it from the flames,
From devastations, from fears.

Our name is erased, our works disappear, they are misunderstood,
    stifled,
But may the whistle of propagation remain without a doubt,
The religion of the permanence of something
Doubtful, ambiguous, incredible:
That which the child does when he plays, that
Which has the name of fire and doesn't burn
Nor glow in the night. Save a sound,
Only just a warm number,
Only but an attitude whispered
Between two lights,
The pale expression of a lone gentleman,
Later buried among jasmine. Put
This flower in the buttonhole of someone sad,
Pick up the fallen man in his dream
Of love, the sombre man,
Hardly afflicted.
There is a tear in the depth of the well,
A tear large as a child,
A lament, a lasting love for someone
Long since dead. Save it for the love
Of life. Save it for the love of love's continuity.
Save it for the love
Of man.
            What is coming has to be man,
Has to be love and generating love,
And has to be a practice of love
Without hope nor reward of other love.

You are those called, those chosen
To decide if the generous deed will last,
The act of living vitally beyond life itself,
Of modestly accepting to be only but
A bridge in the road,
A gloomy bridge, ennobled
Only by love. . .

TO A SERENE POET

The immobility of your being, which doesn't exclude
    the weariness of life
But which expresses peace and hallucination
Of a rendered knowledge;
The immobility in which you know how to live and
    breathe naturally and be within the shadow,
The speed of your personal calm,
Of your full and entire being.
Your tranquillity has always surprised me when, paralyzed,
    you move,
When, paralyzed, you venture
Out of yourself, cast
Towards your dizzy outskirts from a placid exposure,
There where you arise suddenly future
And where you make yourself intelligible,
Suddenly.

What is it that your eyes see in that meaningless surrounding,
From which only you can return,
What is it that you see, what impossible forms do you recognize
    and notice
In the shadow? Your hands scratch at signs,
Grope at the forms
Of things,
At a reality which isn't,
Which absurdly exists there where you reign.
Grope, knock, insist and tell us
The truth, the insatiable
Rancour with which that deep and horrid
Mountain watches us
Which will replace us.
There that bulk awaits
Horribly alive and throbbing,
Obscene and alive,
Atrocious, because it breathes,
Obscene, since it exists.
And you watch with your eyes
The blasphemous existence
Which now replaces us,
Replaces you.

But perhaps what you look at
May be something else.
Perhaps there is hidden in that deep silence,
In that tragic space of universal quiet,
An order of beings perfectly lucid,
An intelligent meeting of realities which systematically
    exclude us
From the globe, ah,
Without malice.
Perhaps your look
Has been able to return from that kingdom
With that serenity so propitious
For men, because you know
More. Perhaps you have reached
A deeper, incomprehensible
Knowledge.
        Perhaps renewed by your wisdom,
Leavened by that knowledge of yours which blossomed
Beneath this foam
Where we live ignorant and float uncertain,
Deep in the sea of your knowledge,
Sunk there, in the rocky sand
Secure in the depth, but extracted and pure here for us,
You may divine us in a better
Way, know us more
Deeply,
And deeply gaze at us with a serene smile.

THE PRICE OF TRUTH

for Angel González

In the old garret of frayed memory,
Behind the spoon of dry-rotted wood,
Behind the old wardrobe, it will be found or next to the flaking
Wall in the dust
Of centuries. Perhaps it will be found beyond the pale gesture
    of an old
Hand of some beggar, or in the ruin of the soul
When everything has ceased.
I ask myself if the dusty road
Of tenacious doubt is necessary, the sudden fatigue
In the sterile plain beneath the sun of justice,
The ruin of all hope, the worn rag of fear, the invincible
    disquiet halfway along the path that leads to the ruined tower.
I ask myself if it is necessary to leave the high road
And take a left by the short cut and footpath,
As if nothing had remained behind in the deserted house.
I ask myself if it is necessary to go without wavering into
    the horror of the night,
To penetrate the abyss, the wolf's mouth,
To journey back, backwards to negation,
Or reverse the truth, on the desolate road.
Or rather if the sob of dust in the confusion of a terrible
    summer is necessary,
Or in the confused alcoholic awakening with trumpets of sleep
To know oneself suddenly deserted completely, or rather,
If it is perhaps necessary to have been lost in the foul
    commerce of love,
To have contracted in the shadow an ideal
Bought for a price, a memory of light, a spell
Of daybreak behind the hill, towards the river.
I admit the possibility that it may be completely necessary
To have descended, at least sometime, to the depth of the
    dark building,
To have gone down uncertainly through the danger of the rickety
    stairs which threaten to collapse at our every step,
And to have penetrated finally with valour in the indignity,
    to the dark cellar.

To have visited the place of shadow,
The territory of the ash, where all vileness rests
Beside the patient cobweb. To have settled in the dust,
To have chewed it tenaciously in the long hours of thirst
Or of sleep. To have answered the silence
Or the final question
With courage or fear and there to have realized and rallied.
It is necessary to have understood by means
        of the offending truth
That assaults us in the middle of the night and suddenly
        keeps us awake and robs us
To the last cent. To have afterwards begged long days
Through the lowest areas of oneself, without hope
        of recuperating the loss,
And finally, dispossessed, to have followed the right road and
        entered the absolute night with valour still.

THE TAILOR WHO TOLD THE TRUTH

NANCY WILLARD

In Germantown, New York, on Cherry Street, there lived a tailor named Morgon Axel who, out of long habit, could not tell the truth. As a child he told small lies to put a bright surface on a drab life: as a young man he told bigger lies to get what he wanted. He got what he wanted and went on lying until now when he talked about himself, he did not know the truth from what he wanted the truth to be. The stories he told were often more plausible to him than his own life.

What was the first lie?

That his father was rich. The richest man in Germany.

Told to whom?

Ingeborg Schonberg, the parson's daughter he loved in Potsdam, where he grew up. Yes, a lie, because his father was not rich. Karl Axel owned a secondhand shop in one of the shabbier quarters of the city. The family lived behind the shop: Hans the oldest brother and after him Heinrich, who were tall and blond and loved practical jokes and wanted to go to sea. Johanna Axel, nee Schweber, daughter of the widow Schweber who cooked for a doctor and his family in Potsdam. Johanna Schweber made good money till she married Karl. Morgon Axel, born in 1896, when Hans was seven and Heinrich was six. Yes, that's the one: Morgon, who from the beginning was dark-haired and short like his father. He was five years old when he told his first lie. No, not his first lie. Let us call five the age of discretion here: therefore, the first lie on record. Told to the parson's daughter, age five and a half. The second lie does not concern us. Because then we would have to deal with the third and fourth also.

Look at him now, seven going on eight, a pack of lies behind him, reading at a cherry-wood table in his father's shop, among busts of Kaiser Wilhelm II and Frederick the Great, who lour at him like schoolmasters. Morgon has made himself a little place for his books behind a barrier of cut-glass bowls, stags' heads, stuffed owls, and nutcrackers carved like the heads of dogs. And don't forget the cuckoo clocks and the shields and visors and guns of the hunters who have gone down at last with the stags and the owls that they killed. Morgon has befriended the guns and named them: Ernst, Dieter, Barbarossa.

Sometimes Saturday and always Sunday (on Sunday Johanna Axel is singing in church), Karl takes his three sons hunting in the forest beyond the city. In the forest live woodcocks, partridges, wild boars, and deer with antlers that branch out like coral. Morgon's brothers knock partridges out of the air as easily as winking. His father shoots hares and saves the paws for luck. He has hundreds of paws stacked away in a cupboard. Morgon hits nothing, but that's because he's so new at it. In his sleep he dreams of shooting so straight and so far that he knocks the sun out of the sky.

Is there anything more monotonous than shooting partridges and hares every Sunday of your life? It is the fourth Sunday of his tenth year, and he's been hunting with his father ever since he told his first lie at the age of five. The creatures they've shot, he says to himself, would fill the Nymphenburg Palace. Has Morgon seen the Nymphenburg Palace? Never in his life. But he has read about it. He has tried to read every book in his father's shop and all the books in his father's house, though he understands very little of them: *The Memoirs of the Margrave of Augsburg, History of the Imperial Army, The Court of Karl-Eugen, Prince of Württemburg.* Morgon has told himself that if he can read them all, his brothers will come back.

They come back before he has accomplished this. One clear July afternoon there they are, standing in the middle of Johanna Axel's kitchen, both of them shining like the family silver. Trim blue jackets buttoned high at the throat, gold epaulettes, gold buttons where eagles sleep, a spiked helmet where an eagle is spreading its wings. The iron cross nestled in ropes of gold braid that glitter like icicles across their chests. Boots so tall their legs look slim and graceful as a girl's. Johanna Axel nearly goes out of her mind with joy.

"I have a son in the Academy at Kiel and another doing us proud in Berlin: I couldn't possibly ask for more."

It is Saturday. Have they forgotten?

"Tomorrow we'll go hunting," says Hans, slapping Morgon on the back. "It'll be like old times."

That afternoon they all go visiting, all except Morgon who stays home to mind the shop. That's how he happened to be there when the bell tinkled and in hobbled a wild boar which lifted its head over the counter.

Morgon jumped: the cut-glass bowls and nutcrackers jumped with him. The boar's face slipped away and he saw an old white-bearded Jew in a skullcap and a black coat.

"I wonder," said the Jew, "if you'd be interested in buying a few items I have here."

Morgon eyed him suspiciously, for hairs stuck out of his nose like tusks. From the box he had set on the floor, the man brought up a clockcase, carved to resemble a country church.

"A few repairs, and you can sell it for a fortune. It belonged to the fourth Duke of Württemburg. When the clock strikes, twelve angels rush out to beat the hours. The Crucifixion takes place in the upper window, and the twelve Apostles come out of the lower door two by two, bow to the Saviour, and return. All the while it plays *Ein' feste Burg ist unser Gott.*"

"But it doesn't keep time," said Morgon, staring at the motionless hands.

"No. But if it did, you could sell it for a fortune."

"Then my father won't want to buy it. What else have you got?"

The Jew sighed.

"I have here a fine collection of masks, at least two hundred years old. They come from the castle of Grafeneck. The Duke's guests wore them at a masked ball. Here you see the mask that the Archbishop was forced to wear in order to have an audience with the Duke—"

He pulled out the face of the boar, carved in wood and painted bright blue. Gold rings hung in its ears. The old man laid it on the counter.

"And here's the mask ordered by Baron Wimpffen. A great joker, I've heard."

A red hyena with pearls in its snout joined the boar.

"And of course, for the Baroness d'Oberkirch, this lovely brown doe wearing a tiny crucifix in a golden crown. The others, well, I'm not sure who wore them—"

He laid them out in a row across the counter for Morgon's approval. An emerald green dog with roses curled on its cheeks. A black bear wearing a mitre, and an animal that looked rather like a goat, though Morgon couldn't be sure. Under the jeweled eyes of each face were slits for the wearer to see out.

"Six masks in all, young sir. They're absolutely priceless."

Morgon lifted the bear to his face, the Jew lifted the dog, and they looked at each other, then each set his mask aside.

"Well, I don't know," said Morgon. "Can you come back Monday? My father does all the buying. I only wait on people."

The Jew's expression passed from polite reserve to polite terror.

"Can't you give me something toward them now? They're worth at least four hundred marks."

"I'm sorry, I can't. You'll have to come back."

When Karl Axel returned and saw the masks, he was delighted.

"They're superb," he exclaimed. He was in excellent spirits: they had gone to see his brother Ernst who ran a butchershop and whose wife had given him nothing but daughters. Business would never be better than in the next few days: Rabbi Mendel's grandmother had gone mad, fled out of her house, and plunged a knife into Ander Krüller's only son. Yes, that same Krüller who sat on the city council, and all the cousins of Rabbi Mendel and his wife, who numbered in the hundreds, were selling their possessions and fleeing the city.

"If he comes back, we'll give him two hundred marks. But it's likely he's on his way to Berlin by this time."

Is there anything more monotonous than hunting partridges and hares every Sunday? Is there anything more exciting than an animal who might, at the edge of enchantment, turn itself into a human being? The next morning Heinrich and Hans and Morgon packed up the masks, shouldered air guns, and traveled to the forest beyond the city. Morgon carried the masks on his back. The forester let the brothers take the horses they always rode with their father. When they reached a clearing they dismounted. Morgon threw the masks on the ground.

"The rule is," said Hans, "that whoever plays an animal will try to avoid the hunter for one hour. If he succeeds, the animal wins.

If the hunter shoots him, the animal loses. Who wants to be what?"

"I'll be the bear," said Heinrich. He stopped, picked up the bear's face and slipped it over his own. Morgon gasped. Before him stood a bear in Prussian uniform, cruelly raised to the tenth power.

"Morgon, your turn."

"The dog," said Morgon. He put on the mask. Its features pressed against his face. He felt hot inside and the eye-slits did not fit him properly. He could hardly see.

"Go and hide yourself," said Hans.

"But the animals should be allowed to take their guns," exclaimed Heinrich. "In case we meet the boars and bears who do not turn into humans."

Hans played the hunter, and Morgon had never known such excitement. To lie in the bushes and hear his brother stalking him, to hear him cocking his gun, that was much better than watching woodcocks drop out of the sky. Furthermore, in the role of the animal Morgon excelled both his brothers, because he was smaller, and as he was unhampered by a uniform he could move faster.

"The hunter has the worst of it," said Hans. "He knows it's just a game and there's not a chance of hurting anybody when you're protected by a mask. We ought to play without masks."

"Without masks?" repeated Morgon.

"Why not? Once you've played the animal, you don't need a mask to turn you into a dog. Then you're as vulnerable as an animal really is. It makes you play harder."

That's how Morgon Axel, at the age of ten, crawled out of a bush in the forest outside Potsdam and lost his right eye to the gun of his brother. The hunting came to an end, the brothers went back to their regiments, and Morgon Axel got fitted with a blue-glass eyeball.

"Don't be bitter," his mother told him. "It was a game that turned out badly."

On his eighteenth birthday, he went to enlist in the Imperial Army, but no lie was big enough to cover the blue-glass eyeball he wore in his head. So he went to Berlin and applied as assistant to Otto Strauss, a tailor who specialized in uniforms, on whose door you could read in bold Gothic script:

O. Strauss, kgl. preuss. Hoflieferant

Inside you could find all those decorations which so warm the heart of your Prussian officers. Drawers of epaulettes, gloves, and

buttons for every rank. Yes, and the shelves of spiked helmets em-
bossed with shining eagles, like the blessed instruments of a holy
sacrifice. Yes, and the bolts of blue wool and spools of gold braid;
tasseled swords and riding whips and slim black boots. On the
walls, O. Strauss had kept several large photographs of the Kaiser
and his family and many smaller ones of high-ranking officers wear-
ing the uniforms he made for them. And look, over here's the most
recent one: a fine photograph of General von Kluck's First Army
entering Brussels, with horses and caissons. (Did Otto Strauss
know General von Kluck? No.) It was August, 1914, and uniforms
were greatly in demand. O. Strauss marched up and down the shop
and surveyed his prospective assistant.

"What I need," he said, "is somebody who knows as much about
the military as he knows about fitting and altering clothes. Tell me:
how many centimeters should you leave between the cuff buttons
on the uniform of a captain in the reserves?"

"Herr Strauss, you insult me," exclaimed Morgon Axel, waving
his hand grandly. "I come from a long line of tailors. My ancestors
were the royal tailors to Frederick the Great. A dressmaker on my
mother's side designed the wedding gown of Wilhelmina von Grä-
venitz."

O. Strauss leaned against his counter and stared, but Morgon
Axel continued unabashed.

"And as for the military! I have two brothers. The oldest is a
lieutenant in the Imperial Navy. The other is the captain of the
division of the Prussian Guard recently cited by General Luden-
dorff. I am related by marriage to Colonel von Lettow-Vorbeck and
my oldest brother has the ear of Admiral von Holtzendorf."

O. Strauss touched his ear nervously.

"My father won the *Pour le mérite* in the last war." And as he
spoke, Morgon saw his father dashing through Ypres on a black
horse, shouting to the soldiers lounging in the courtyard: *Attack!
We are being attacked from the west!*

"Why, may I ask—"

"I had the misfortune to lose my right eye in a hunting accident.
But the left one is as sound as yours."

"Well, well," murmured O. Strauss. "I'll be glad to try you out.
We have all sorts of men coming in here. You'll find most of them
are hard to please."

From that lie forward, Morgon Axel acted as O. Strauss's as-
sistant. By day he helped him lay the patterns for cloaks and jackets

on long fields of blue wool, and he pinned sleeves and collars on the stocky bodies of officers who made appointments to be fitted. After work he hurried to his room high up in Frau Nolke's house at the other end of town, lugging the shop's manuals on the regulations for military dress which he read far into the night. When he had memorized the fundamentals, he began borrowing uniforms, every night a different rank, so that he could examine how they were made.

In the house next door, the West Bavarian Singing Society met twice a week, and on those evenings Morgon Axel could not study. Rich joyful voices flooded his silence, and he opened his window to hear them.

Über's Jahr, über's Jahr, wenn me Träubele schneid't,
Stell' i hier mi wied'rum ein;
Bin i dann, bin i dann dein Schätzele noch,
So soll die. Hochzeit sein.

He leaned on the sill and looked out. Across the street on the sixth floor of a tottering building, an aged dancing master was teaching young women in bloomers and tights the intricacies of the *pirouette* and the *entrechat*. From his window, Morgon Axel could plainly see into theirs. A war is going on, he thought, and people are still dancing as if Germany meant nothing to them.

Sitting down at his table once more, he tried to consider the width of the collar on Captain Hess's uniform but found himself staring vacantly at his own face on the mirror of the wardrobe. It was a warm September night. Under the linden trees, the officers were walking, yes, those officers over whose flesh his fingers had walked miles and miles, gathering pleats and folds on the way. He got up and slipped into the uniform of Captain Hess. Slipped into the sleek trousers and longed-for boots. Buttoned the blue jacket across his chest, fastened the belt, and stood barefoot in front of the mirror. And then stepping out of the bar reserved exclusively for commissioned officers, he leaned on the windowsill and looked up at the figure of a single girl dancing by herself. Perhaps she knew that Morgon Axel was watching. What was the good of military regulations, of drills and marches, if it couldn't protect you against longing to be free? Captain Morgon Axel would send someone to fetch her, but that wasn't the way. The next night, another would take her place.

One evening Morgon noticed the studio was dark; no one ever danced there again, and shortly afterward the singers, too, disap-

peared. For the next three years he lived on Frau Nolke's turnips
and O. Strauss's chocolates (courtesy of his customers), which the
old gentleman hoarded shamefully. A young lieutenant, being fitted
for a cloak, told Morgon that he had bought all his Christmas and
birthday presents for the next year, though it was only March, so
that if he were killed in action, his family and friends would know
he hadn't forgotten them. A captain from Bremen, who lisped in
honor of the Kaiser and wore a monocle, ordered six pairs of Hes-
sian boots, because, he explained, a soldier should live at all times
in his boots. He was modeling his conduct on Frederick the Great
who kept his hat and his boots on even when he was ill, rose at
four every morning, and in the evening played the flute for recre-
ation. Both the captain and the lieutenant left their photographs for
O. Strauss to hang on his wall and both were killed at Soissons.

But one clear night in November, Kaiser Wilhelm fled into Hol-
land. What was to be done? The Imperial Army marched grimly
back to Berlin, passing through the Brandenburger Tor. Wreaths
crowned their helmets, and they carried a new banner: "Peace and
Freedom." Morgon Axel wept and applied for passage to America,
taking with him one fur-lined cape (Army surplus), one suit (much
worn), and seven animal masks which his father had willed him;
there was nothing else left, and Morgon Axel was the sole heir.

Now look at him, middle-aged, still short and rather stocky, a
square figure, in a tweed hunting jacket with absurd shoulder pads,
standing in the doorway of his tailorshop on Cherry Street, Ger-
mantown, New York.

Wait. You must give an account of the years in between.

*The evidence for those years has been lost, except for some brief
scenes* undated, by which we may only surmise that he worked as
a tailor in New York City and married Ursula Rincetti, daughter of
an Italian cabinetmaker and restorer of styles past.

Now Morgon is sitting in the tiny apartment where he lives with
his wife and his son, Amyas, aged twelve. Christened Hans Federi-
co but nicknamed Amyas by a young English girl who worked in
the Germantown bank auditing accounts and occasionally babysat
with Amyas and held him in her arms and sang him to sleep with
an old song:

You and I and Amyas
Amyas and you and I.
To the greenwood must we go, alas!
You and I, my life and Amyas.

It is spring. Or summer. Or any season. What you will. Morgon is sitting in front of the television set, watching the "Ed Sullivan Show." Morgon Axel has the only color television on the block. He is admiring the red sequin suits of the dancing couple, "who have recently played at the Copacabana." There is a Copacabana in Los Angeles, you may have heard of it; but it is another Copacabana which concerns us here, just as it is another Sunset Strip, another Hollywood, another Las Vegas and Broadway that we are speaking of, rather than the ones generally known. Long hours of watching television and films have built these streets in Morgon Axel's head, like a stage setting, deficient in details, but peopled with a cast of thousands. Captain Hess and General Ludendorff and Colonel von Lettow-Vorbeck have given way to Roy Rogers and Gene Autrey and Fred Astaire. Sometimes Morgon watches the talent show on the Albany station, "Stairway to the Stars," and as the young people sing, tap-dance, and play the piano, it is Amyas he imagines, leaping on a trampolin and being discovered.

For Amyas is talented that way, no doubt about it. He has that grace which Morgon so marveled at when he shouldered the weight of Captain Hess's uniform one night in Berlin and saw, in the opposite window, a young girl dancing. Once a week Amyas studies gymnastics and trapeze acrobatics with Taft Toshiho in Yonkers, who also teaches judo to secretaries and housewives. Amyas and the six other boys in his class have already performed in high schools and Kiwanis Clubs around the state and at the Ulster County Fair. It's only a matter of months, says Morgon to his friends, till you'll be seeing Amyas on television. On Broadway.

"Tell me about how it was when you worked in the theater," says Amyas. He is five years old and his father sits on the edge of his bed, waiting for his son to go to sleep.

"Well," says Morgon Axel, "the shows are not worth mentioning compared to the *fêtes*. Before the war, such *fêtes*! I remember one *fête* I designed for the Count of Ansbach-Schwedt.

And as he speaks, he sees himself very clearly standing on a balcony in the castle of the Count, surveying the garden and the woods beyond, brilliant with thousands of lanterns.

"All the guests came in hunting costumes. I designed over a hundred masks like the faces of animals, no two exactly alike. The women put on the masks and the men had to hunt for their partners in the forest."

The next morning there is no forest, only the shop, which is small and untidy. The front room contains two mirrors, a few chairs, bolts of wool and gaberdine, catalogues and swatches spread open on a table, and a rack of finished garments which barely hides a dressmaker's dummy. In the window Morgon drapes remnants of silk over a truncated plaster column. On the walls hang his masks and his guns. That's the front room, where the tailor receives his customers.

But there's another room behind it, separated from the first by a red curtain. Sybil, the tailor's golden retriever, lopes back and forth between them like a messenger. Customers waiting for their packages can hear the tailor's wife stitching and sighing behind the curtain. Also, the clicking of Sybil's toenails against the bare floor; they have grown long from lack of exercise, for though the tailor dreams of hunting and has his dog and his guns all ready, he seldom finds the time.

Why do you say nothing of Ursula, the tailor's wife?

Searching the tailor's memory, we find that up till now she passed through it as through water, leaving no footprints. A dead civilization which shapes what we are though we will never know what it is.

Nevertheless, give us a picture of the tailor's wife.

Why, when the customers slipped through the curtains for their fittings—the tailor had built a tiny dressing room here—they saw sitting under the naked bulb that dangled from the ceiling a slender woman with dark hair clouded around her face as if she wanted to hide herself. She was always bending over a piece of work and treading the sewing machine with her heel. In front of her on the pegboard wall, which was no more than a foot from her nose, hung spools of thread in every size and color, and this was her horizon from eight in the morning till six at night.

Behind her the table was heaped with dresses to be mended, zippers to be put in, skirts to be hemmed, trousers with ill-fitting cuffs, and suits cut and basted, which had to be finished. The tailor's wife never looked back for fear she couldn't go on. She had told this to the priest one Sunday when she went for confession, for she was a devout Catholic, though her husband, raised Lutheran, attended no church now.

"Sometimes I think I'll die of despair, Father. I look back and see that the pile never runs out, for just when I think I'm near the end, Morgon heaps on more work. What's the use, I say to myself, of working my way through a pile that's got no bottom? And then my fingers just stop, Father, they won't turn the wheel one more time."

"Then you mustn't look back, my daughter," whispers the voice behind the grille. "Reach behind you and pick up one piece at a time. One at a time. Then you'll be able to get through the day. Not to finish the pile; that's not a thing any of us could do in a lifetime. But to get yourself safely across to the next day. God Himself doesn't ask more of you."

"If only He'd give me a vision to help me through the bad times, Father. Just a small one, so I don't forget what's under the pile." *An angel dancing on the point of her needle. A wheel within the wheel of her machine.*

Having no visions, she settled her love on her son. If he was not an angel, he at least came close to flying like one. When she sewed costumes for Amyas and the six boys in his troupe, the needle leaped for joy like a dolphin in the sea of nylon and satin, and the stitches unwound themselves in love. And all the while Morgon Axel walked up and down in the front room and graciously accepted an order for yellow jodhpurs from William Harris, the fiery-haired riding master of High Stepping Stables outside of town.

"Can I make jodhpurs? My dear Mr. Harris, I can make anything. You should have seen the silver jodhpurs I made for Gene Autrey when I worked in the city. Why, I could make jodhpurs to fit a spider! I remember the first riding outfit I ever made—it was for the Duke of Augsburg who was giving a ball at his castle in Westphalia." (A self-indulgent laugh.) "All the guests came in hunting costume. Well, I made the Duke a splendid habit in russet velvet, and when it was done, what do you think? I'd cut the trousers with the nap going up one leg and down the other and when the light struck him he seemed to divide himself like a pair of scissors. But he was very kind about it. 'I've invited so many beautiful women,' he said, 'that no one will notice.'"

Mr. Harris pulled off his gloves, a finger at a time, hung his camel's hair overcoat on the rack, and stood stiffly in the middle of the room while the tailor crawled around him on the floor, puffing a little as he took the measurements of the riding master's trim figure.

"Ah, the life I've seen," sighed Morgon Axel, pulling pins out of the cushion that dangled next to his heart. "When I worked in the city, I had my own place right over the Stork Club kitchen, bathroom, shower. I had the whole floor to myself, just for work space. Did I ever tell you about the time I had dinner with Jimmy Durante and an English housewife who was flown over because she'd won something in a soap contest? The company gave me a Lincoln—turn, Mr. Harris."

Mr. Harris turns and looks straight ahead at the curtain. Behind the tailor's story, he hears the chugging accompaniment of a sewing machine.

"You ought to give your wife a vacation," he says suddenly. "Every time I come in here—"

The tailor hears and does not hear.

"A Lincoln, Mr. Harris. It had a built-in bar where most cars have the back seat. But I'm glad to leave it all behind. Here in the country, I'm happy. I go hunting when I want to, I take off a week here and there when the weather's nice. I'm nobody's slave."

A sigh floats out from behind the curtain, as from a dark well. The tailor has unwittingly spoken the truth.

What did Mrs. Shore, the banker's wife, size 18, coming to have her new coat lengthened, tell the tailor?

"I've been hearing so much about that boy of yours! My husband saw him and his group at the county fair."

"Oh, you'll be hearing from him one of these days, Mrs. Shore. Any day now, you'll be seeing him on television."

One day the letter from Albany arrives. Now the boast has come true, Morgon is as nervous as a flea, and he appraises the most casual movements of his son.

What does the tailor see when he looks at his son?

Himself. Younger. Morgon, yes, but he has lost all the heaviness of a Prussian upbringing. Amyas ambles into the shop after school and throws his books on the chair. He is fourteen.

"Did you practice today?" asks the tailor.

"Yes," says Amyas, pulling a candy bar out of his pocket. He is tall, nearly six feet already, and has an enormous appetite which worries his father.

"Don't eat that," says the tailor, slapping it out of his son's hand. "You don't want to get fat."

"I burn it up fast enough, don't I?"

On the television screen, he moves like a flame. Morgon Axel has called all his friends. He brings the portable down to the shop, and Tuesday morning they come by to watch. His wife wanted to go to the studio and watch it live but then they would never know how it looked to everyone else. Here they are, the butcher who works in the grocery shop next door, the fellow from the gas station across the street, Amyas's classmates and teachers, and Kris Kristofferson, the old violinist who lives upstairs and doesn't have a color TV. They stand around the set, which Morgon has perched on one of the shelves, having removed the heavy bolts of cloth in honor of the occasion. After a tap-dancing girl and two young boys who play an accordion duet, the master of ceremonies appears on a corrugated pedestal studded with stars. He says something which the tailor barely hears, about the seven members of an acrobatic troupe, led by Amyas Axel. And then suddenly it is he, the fulfillment of all Morgon's dreams, flying like an angel, like an eagle, from intricate trapezes, hanging from the ankles of one boy, jackknifing to another, like a squirrel jumping from tree to tree.

Without fear.

Then all at once the screen goes black.

"Oh!" cries the tailor's wife.

Across the darkened screen appears the words:

Power failure. Please stay tuned.

But though they hover around the set for a quarter of an hour, Amyas does not return, and when the image flashes on, a young girl in a tutu is spinning around on her toes.

In the evening when he's watching television, the tailor sees out of the corner of his eye another performance going on, less important than the one he's watching only because he's not a part of it and it goes on all the time. Amyas on a stool, his legs crooked around the rungs; his mother shelling peas, nodding, listening; the window open, the warm spring air coming through—

You have told us about the tailor and the tailor's wife but very little about Amyas. Who is he?

It is impossible to say for certain, because he's always moving, and his mother's testimony is so different from his father's memories that they might well be describing two different people. Parents seize an image of what they want their children to be, behind which the child moves, trying to fit his body to the shadow-child or hold it up as a shield which lets him grow in secret.

But when Amyas was sixteen, he had nothing in common with this shadow-child. He became a new person. And that is always terrible for the parents, who have chosen someone else.

That is to say, having grown tall he began to grow wide. Enormous. From slim acrobat to a man pregnant with the acrobat that had been himself, for you could see the old Amyas still, in the eyes, in the gestures, and you could hear it in his speech. At the age of sixteen he weighed four hundred pounds, through some imbalance of his body which had been waiting all those years to take away his grace.

The tailor knew nothing of glands and imbalances. He began to loathe the very sight of his son, who seemed to give himself up to the slovenly spirit that had gotten hold of him. Amyas grew a scraggy beard and let his mother trim his hair only around his ears.

It was his mother who made his clothes now—acres of tweed, of gaberdine, which heaped the pile behind her like a mountain. The sick or deformed child cries out for love. At dinner she saved the best pieces of meat for Amyas, the extra piece of pie. These acts of favoritism enraged the tailor.

"Amyas, you look like a pig. Don't eat like one."

(Amyas has just dragged his sleeves into his soup. He is not used to his new body.)

"You just want the rest of the blueberry pie for yourself. Be glad you don't have a big belly to fill," snapped his mother.

She set the piece of pie in front of Amyas. But shame overcame him. He pushed it toward his father. The tailor found that he did not want it either, yet having asked for it, he pretended to eat it with relish.

He knows Amyas is always hungry, and he takes great delight in keeping him that way. Didn't he bring Amyas up in the paths of righteousness and didn't Amyas fail to bloom? In the back of the tailor's mind is a lurking suspicion that his son *could* turn into the old Amyas if he really wanted to, that he's done this to humiliate his father in front of his friends and customers, to whom he has boasted over and over:

"One day you'll be seeing him on Broadway."

You can't spank a child for taking this way to get back at you but you can humiliate him back to his senses. Amyas sits in back of the shop with his mother, helping her ease the weight of that unfinished pile on her soul. The tailor struts around in the front room—yes, he is prouder than ever now—joking with his customers.

"Well, if I can't have an acrobat for a son, I'll have the male Mae West. Sometimes I feel like I'm running a side show in here!"

He whispers it into Mrs. Shore's ear, or into Mr. Harris's ear, or into the ears of the young girls who come to have their skirts shortened, and they giggle, for they don't know that it has gone into Amyas' ear also.

There is another voice that only Amyas hears. It tells him to go away, it marshals his father's words and looks together. His mother worries about him, of course, but when she sees he is determined to go, she gives him the names of relatives in the city and a few old friends.

"I'll write," promises Amyas.

But he never does. And when, after two weeks, his mother writes her friends and her relatives, she finds that Amyas has never stopped there at all. And that's awkward to the tailor, almost as awkward as having his son home, because people are always asking:

"How's Amyas doing in the big city?"

"Oh, you can't imagine the tales he writes us. He's doing impersonations now. He has a huge apartment over the club where he works—the Cobra, I think it's called. People come up to his place all hours of the day and night. He told us that one night all the Rockettes showed up in his room with a case of champagne."

It gave Morgon the fright that comes over a man who discovers he's a prophet, when nearly a year after Amyas left home, Mr. Harris came in one morning to order a tuxedo and remarked to Morgon, who was fitting a sleeve,

"I think I saw your son yesterday."

"Amyas?" squeaked the tailor. "Where?"

The sewing machine in the backroom came to a dead halt.

"In a little restaurant on MacDougal Street. I don't remember the name of it—I'd gone there with some friends, and we were having dinner, when suddenly a man came out and announced there would be a floor show. And the act he introduced—well, there was this very large man" (he avoided the word fat) "who came out in pink rompers and played a mandolin and sang. I don't remember what he sang. But he was awfully funny."

"Amyas doesn't play a mandolin," said the tailor, trying to calm himself.

"Well, perhaps it wasn't Amyas. But it looked like him. I asked the waiter to tell me the name of the man we were watching. 'Pretty Baby,' said the waiter, 'he doesn't call himself anything else. The manager makes his check out to Pretty Baby.' I asked if he played here often, and the waiter shrugged. 'He comes and goes like the wind. We have people who drop by every night, hoping he'll show up. Sometimes he'll stay away for months.' They say he's turned down a couple of movie contracts."

When Mr. Harris left, the tailor hurried into the back room. His wife sat at her machine and looked past her husband as if she were trying to focus on a point just short of infinity.

"You think I don't feel it, too, Ursula? You think you're the only one who feels it?"

But inside he was afraid. How could the news of Amyas so change the shape and color of his wife's face?

"Why don't you go upstairs and lie down? I'll take care of the shop."

She went without a word. By the machine lay the little date book where he noted the work to be done; Morgon picked it up. At ten o'clock the Fitz girls were coming to pick up the skirts they had left to be shortened and that Miss Johnson who handled trouble calls for the telephone company wanted three zippers repaired in the dresses she'd brought in last week.

At eight o'clock, Morgon stood in the back room and surveyed the pile. Dresses. Trousers. Jackets. Skirts. Seams to be let out, hems to be taken up; buttonholes to be moved over, he had counted on Ursula finishing them today. He sat down and picked up the first skirt, which was already pinned, and started slowly around the hem. Yellow flowered cotton. Like stitching bees into a meadow. When Mrs. Shore came at a quarter of nine to call for her coat, he had hardly fenced in half the pasture.

"I don't hear the machine," said Mrs. Shore as she tried on the coat before the mirror.

"Ah, my wife's not well. I think she's got a little attack of sinus."

Saying it almost took away the dull fear in his stomach. Nobody he knew had ever stayed in bed with a sinus infection for more than a few days. After Mrs. Shore left, he hurried back to finish the skirt. But every time he looked at the pile to be done, a panic came over him. He locked the front door, hung out his sign: *closed,* and worked all morning in silence. At noon his eyes ached and he went upstairs to find his wife.

He found her in bed. Her face over the top of the bedclothes looked pinched and craven. The old fairy tale: the wolf grinning in grandmother's nightgown. Morgon stood at the foot of the bed and stared at her helplessly.

"You should drink something. Shall I make you some tea?"

Silence.

"What can I do for you? Does anything hurt?"

"Here."

She pointed to her heart.

All afternoon they sat in the waiting room of the emergency clinic, among crying children and a few old women bent nearly double with age. When the receptionist finally called *Mrs. Axel,* she rose from her chair and trudged into the doctor's office without looking back. It hurt Morgon that she had nothing to say to him.

Morgon waited. He picked up the *Reader's Digest.* The elevator to the right of him opened and closed; flocks of young doctors hurried in and out, white-coated like geese. Presently he heard his name. Everyone in the room watched him go.

The doctor's office with its certificates and abstract paintings and cabinets of instruments made Morgon feel shoddy and stupid. The doctor was younger and taller than Morgon. Wearing his white coat and the casual emblems of his profession, the stethoscope and head mirror, he introduced himself and peered over his glasses at the tailor.

"You're Mr. Axel? Please sit down."

Morgon pulled up a chair and faced the doctor at his desk like a student waiting for a reprimand.

"I'm sending your wife to St. Joseph's for a rest. You are familiar with St. Joseph's, I presume?"

"I thought," stammered the tailor, "that St. Joseph's was for people who—"

He stopped. Waited. He didn't want to give the wrong answer.

"Your wife hasn't had a heart attack, as you both feared. Rather, it's a case of severe depression. A mild nervous breakdown, you could call it. I think that with a month of rest she'll be able to come home."

What did the tailor do on his first night alone?

He rambled aimlessly from one room to the next, feeling as if a burden had been lifted from him: *the moment before you savor your freedom.* He fed the dog, washed a few dirty dishes and put them away. He had no desire to cook anything for himself and decided to eat at a Hungarian restaurant on the other side of town which had always intrigued him. Mr. Harris told him that a family ran the restaurant in an old house and he praised it for "local color."

When he entered the front hall of Czerny's and hung his jacket on the rack, he felt as if he were coming to visit an old friend. The first room he saw contained nothing but a pool table where several young men in leather shorts were shooting a game. Morgon passed quickly into the spacious dining room; it was completely deserted though each table was elaborately set, as if for a banquet of ghosts. Fifty napkins, folded like mitres. perched between the knives and forks and water glasses; a nesting ground of strange birds.

The tailor found a seat in the corner. To his distress he found that he could look right into the kitchen, where three women were eating at a little table. It would be awkward to move now, he decided. After all, they were paying no attention to him. A baby crawled over to the largest woman, dragging a long rope behind it, which seemed to be tied to one of the table legs.

But an old man in a white apron was standing in front of him, his pencil poised on his pad.

"Will you have wine?"

Morgon nodded and looked around for the wine list; there was none.

"For dinner we're having skewered meat and noodles stuffed with red cabbage."

It was an announcement rather than a menu, for the old man whisked out of sight and reappeared a moment later with a bottle of wine: *Schwartz Katz.* Morgon felt he ought to say something.

"Is it good?"

"Everyone likes it," said the old man, shrugging as he yanked out the cork and poured the tailor a glass.

In the tiny kitchen, the youngest of the three women got up and hurried to the stove. His order had set them all in motion. He avoided glancing at them, but he could hear them chattering in their own tongue as they stirred and scraped and shifted the dishes about. They had interrupted their dinner to serve his.

The tailor ate slowly, aware at last the women had sat down again and that they were, perhaps, eating what he was eating, only without the amenities of clean linen and good service. Suddenly he imagined that they saw him as an eccentric, a crank, and he longed to go and sit down with them. The light outside was falling away; the woman with the child rose from the table and stood at the window, and suddenly everything flared up gold under the last look of the sun. Then the darkness dropped; the old man turned on the lights in the dining room, and the oldest woman began scrubbing a large kettle at the sink.

When did the tailor first miss his wife?

Not until he saw a strange woman washing dishes in a strange kitchen. So it had always been, so it would always be. The man out in front, the woman in the kitchen with the child—ah, that was where the real life started. Amyas, ten years old, sits on a stool in the kitchen and talks to his mother, who is shelling peas, nodding, and listening; the window open, the warm spring air blowing through.

Morgon paid his bill and left. He did not want to go home. He walked over to Main Street and peered in the windows of the shops. It was Saturday night, it was summer, and the young people parading up and down the street gave it the air of a carnival. Standing in front of Pearlmutter's pawnshop, Morgon examined, with great interest, guns, suitcases, rings, boots, electric fans, cameras, and hair-dryers. By the time his bus arrived, he felt sated. Pressing his face to the window he tried in vain to separate his own image from the passing world outside. He got off the bus and felt the first drops of a warm rain and hurried toward his building. As he passed the butcher's door he saw a little boy, barefoot, hugging himself on the stoop, smiling at him. The tailor hardly realized what he had seen until he was inside his own door and it was too late to smile back.

What were the tailor's thoughts as he lay in bed?

The room is still and nothing is lonelier than the dark.

What did the tailor see when he entered his shop on Monday?

A pile of unfinished garments in the back room. How was he going to finish everything? No kindly priest had told him the trick of reaching behind and taking one at a time, the trick of not looking back. Furthermore, he couldn't very well sit and sew while customers were knocking at the door, demanding to be fitted or to pick up their packages, or simply wanting to pass the time of day. The front room faced the world, resounded with courtesy and opinion; light flooded it from the outside and everything appeared to be under control. But now the tailor found that all this depended on the state of things in the back room, where a deep paralysis had set in. Overcome with anxiety, he closed shop on Thursday and Friday to catch up on back work. He sat in his wife's chair and lost himself in the tedious tasks that banded her life like a ring.

And what did the tailor say on Sunday when he visited his wife?

He stood at the foot of her bed, clutching his hat, staring at this woman who was almost a stranger to him. Her hospital gown gave her an antiseptic air. She seemed to have lost so much of her coarse dark hair that Morgon could almost see the outline of her skull. For the first time, he heard himself lie.

"You look pretty good, Ursula."

Silence. She gazed at him curiously, as if she had forgotten his name. To Morgon's relief, the patients whose medicine bottles cluttered the other three nightstands were gone.

"Are you comfortable here?" he asked.

"It's all right."

"You got nice neighbors?" He jerked his head toward the next bed.

"Margery Wilkes and Norma Tiedelbaum are nice. They're downstairs with their visitors. But Mrs. Shingleton—agh, she's disgusting. Saves all her toilet paper, keeps it in her pillowcase. She's supposed to move up to the sixth floor next week."

"Terrible," said Morgon. Then, hesitantly. "Have you seen the doctor? Has he told you when you'll be ready to come home?"

"I will come home," said Ursula slowly and distinctly, "when I can find someone to take my place here."

"What!" exclaimed Morgon. "Why, there are plenty of people waiting for hospital beds."

"Yes. But nobody willing to take my place."

The tailor felt a little frightened, for it dawned on him that his wife was really losing her mind.

"Do you mean to say that when you're well, you can't leave the hospital? Did the doctor tell you that?"

"No," said Ursula. She closed her eyes. "Amyas told me."

"Amyas!" cried the tailor.

"Every night he comes and stands at the foot of the bed. 'Amyas,' I say, 'when will you come home?' I plead with him, Morgon. I plead with him. 'It would take a thousand years of weeping,' he says, 'to pay a fraction of the grief I've had to bear since my father turned me out.'"

"That's not true!" shouted the tailor. "I never turned him out. He left of his own free will."

Ursula opened her eyes, as empty of feeling as those of a fish.

What was the vision of Amyas's mother?

Amyas, dressed in a doublet of green taffeta cut like oak leaves, on a cloth of gold. He hangs like a lantern on the trees outside, his white face shining through the window.

A full moon tonight, says Margery Wilkes in the next bed.

Amyas, whispers his mother, when are you coming home?

What was the vision of Amyas's father?

Gaberdine in a heap; bills to be paid; a dress form with a hole in its belly and no head or arms or legs; the orders streaming in;

his wife's face. Himself dancing on a treadmill, fed by days pointed like spikes. Without undressing he lies down on his bed, closes his eyes, and sees, brilliant and strange, the mask of sickness that has come over his wife's face.

"The animal always tries to avoid the hunter. If the hunter shoots you, you lose. If you avoid him, you win."

Ursula shakes her head but already Morgon is counting for her to hide.

"Eight! nine! ten!"

Shouldering his gun, he sets out. Trim blue jacket buttoned high at the throat, gold epaulettes, gold buttons where eagles sleep, the iron cross nestled in ropes of gold braid. Every bush shelters a victim. Far ahead of him, Amyas is running for his life, and Ursula hobbles through the underbrush after him, dragging a trap on her foot.

"Ursula, wait! The game is over!"

But the gun springs back into his hand. He pulls off the epaulettes and the iron cross, he throws his jacket to the ground. His wife does not stop running; she knows he is the hunter who will never take her alive till he runs beside her as a creature of prey.

Darkness is rolling in; at the end of Market Street you may see Pearlmutter's pawnshop. Inside, Solomon Pearlmutter in pinstriped pants and a Hawaiian shirt, is standing at the till, counting his coins into a deerskin pouch.

Suddenly the shop bell tinkles and in limps a stocky man carrying a huge knapsack on his shoulder and a rifle in his hand. Solomon touches the pistol he keeps under the counter.

"I have here a number of things I'd like to get rid of," says the man.

And he begins to empty the bag on the counter with ritual precision. Masks carved like fabulous animals, photographs of acrobats, broken trophies, a box of military decorations. Solomon keeps his left hand on the pistol and shakes his head.

"If I can't sell 'em, I don't want 'em. You see the kind of things I got here. Watches, rings, guns."

His right hand waves toward a wall studded with electric guitars. Everything in Solomon's shop knows its place; the guitars stay on the wall, the pocket watches and diamond rings lie in a glass case by the cash register, the accordions huddle together in the front row, the guns hang high over the desk at the back of the store where he figures his earnings at night.

"You won't take any of them?"

The wild look that comes over the man's face makes Solomon uneasy.

"No. Sorry."

"What will you give me for this rifle?"

"Let's have a look," says Solomon and reaches for it.

Quick as a snake the tailor takes aim, but he does not shoot.

Long afterward, when the tailor's body had crumpled across his mind a thousand times, Solomon Pearlmutter wondered why his attacker had not taken the first shot.

When Morgon Axel awoke, he was lying in a strange bed. He tried to prop himself up on his elbows and felt as if a knife had cut and salted a deep crevice between his shoulders. Letting his head sink back to the pillow, he turned it slowly to the right and the left. An endless row of beds echoed each other in both directions, yes, and across the aisle as well, though someone had dimmed the light in this room and drawn the window shades. The only light that let him see all this came from the hall.

Those who cannot walk must fly. So Morgon Axel raised himself up until he saw his own body tucked under a blanket on the bed beneath him. But the real Morgon Axel was floating horizontally out of the ward and down the corridor, like a dandelion seed. Past closed doors. Past a green oxygen tank next to one of them. Past the vases of flowers which the nurses set outside the rooms every night.

Far ahead of him, he heard voices. A buzz, a confusion as of owls' wings, crickets' cries, pigs rooting for truffles in the woods, squirrels rolling acorns in attics. A murmur and cry of doves. Hovering six feet above the floor, Morgon grabbed the door—*Doctor's Lounge*, said the letters under his hand—and pushed himself through.

A forest was growing in the doctor's lounge. Yes, and there was a judge's bench where an old Jew sat, pounding a gavel and calling the quails to order, and a skeleton stood at one end of the bench and at the other end Amyas Axel, in green doublet and white stockings, was walking on his hands back and forth under the nose of the owlish clerk, who perched on the Jew's shoulder and saw everything. The woods were packed with spectators, rabbits and bears

and deer, who lifted their heads behind the witnesses in the front
row, blonde Ingeborg the parson's daughter and Hans who died
years ago and Heinrich who died with him; only their spiked
helmets survived. And here's Otto Strauss, and next to him Frau
Nolke, peeling a lapful of turnips.

When the last leaf stopped rustling, the Jew began to speak.
At his first words, Morgon sank to the ground like a dead balloon.

*Members of the jury, we are entering upon the last stages of this
trial.* You know that we have been trying to administer justice in
accord with the law. What is the administration of justice but this,
that a guilty man be found guilty and an innocent man be acquitted?

Let me remind you, members of the jury, that your role is very
different from mine. I sit here to see that this trial is conducted in
accord with the law and to clarify to you what the law is. You
have heard half a century of evidence and it is the task of each of
you to decide whether the facts presented to you support the
charge against this man: the failure to love. The punishment, if he
is convicted, is death by loneliness.

And now let me deal briefly with the evidence of the case. You
have heard the testimony of the prosecution—

(The skeleton bows; like a cardsharp, a bookie, a flimflam man,
his skull is always smiling)

—who has argued that Morgon Axel never knew what he saw
and never touched what he knew but hid it in lies and loved his
lies more than the naked face of truth. The face of truth is neither
steady nor kind. That is why we cannot subpoena the key witness
at this trial: we should have to summon everybody on earth.

(Amyas, in hobo clothes, is walking on a single strand of hair
that extends over the judge's head. From an inside pocket he pulls
a pair of white doves and sends them circling over the courtroom.)

The case rests on the testimony of Solomon Pearlmutter—

(Solomon Pearlmutter, subpoenaed during sleep, stands up in
the front row and bows. When his wife wakes him tomorrow, he
will tell her he dreamed an extraordinary dream. She will ask him
what it was, but he won't remember; already herds of rabbits and
quails are arming on the borders of his sleep, ready to drive his
broken dream into the pit.)

—who concedes that before he shot the accused, there was enough
time for the accused to take aim and fire. What you must decide,
creatures of the jury, is whether Morgon Axel did indeed wish to

shoot Solomon Pearlmutter or whether the accused wished Solomon Pearlmutter to shoot him, so that he might take his wife's place and put on the terrible eyesight of truth.

You have heard the defense, Amyas Axel, plead most eloquently on behalf of his father. Over the objections of the prosecution, I am admitting into this court a kind of testimony never before, I think, admitted into any court.

(Amyas, balancing on the strand of hair, takes an invisible loaf of bread from an invisible oven and slices it into baskets.

(The birds take the baskets in their beaks and fly down with them to the jury and to the spectators.

Morgon Axel reaches for an imaginary slice and pulls out a real one.)

Creatures of the jury, I have nothing more to say to you. I ask you to go out and consider your verdict and tell me whether you see before you (a rustle of leaves and collars; a thousand heads turn to look at Morgon Axel leaning against the door to the forest) a man who is guilty of loving nothing but his own lies or whether you see a man who has tried to patch himself together a good life out of a bad one, and who is capable not only of love but of change. Of giving himself up to put on another man's truth.

Morgon Axel sits up in bed. A young nurse is speaking to him, smiling pleasantly.

"You may go this morning, Mr. Axel. The X-rays of your shoulder show that the wound is superficial. If you take the elevator at the end of the hall down to the ground floor, you'll find yourself directly across from the front entrance. There's a taxi stand outside."

Morgon Axel climbs unsteadily out of bed. Someone has laid his clothes on a chair. He dresses and rides downstairs in a crowd of doctors and wheelchairs, and chooses a taxi. A nice green checkered one. When he leaves the cab, he hands the driver all the change in his pockets, which isn't a great deal. He travels lightly, this Morgon Axel, without any baggage to hold him down. The sky is clear, the air as sweet as forgiveness. He unlocks his shop, and bending over, he props the door open with an empty spool. The room smells stale and musty. Morgon Axel pulls a chair outside, sits down in the sunlight that dapples the front of his shop, closes his eyes, and waits for his wife to come home.

POEM

JAMES PURDY

My dear, this is a dreadful coming out of
    she lay like madonna in his arms
    he knew her and yet she was moonlight
    he felt her hardening nipples and called "dove" to her
    she screamed as he bent over her dimples
    there was no time for a negative
    he was gaining momentum before she knew he was
    how he robbed her of all she had! and yet she
        seemed to abet him on
well, give me my best time, she called.
He knew the end was near, as did she
        locked in their mutuals, they coughed,
            pleasure-barked, and tree-toed one another
my, it was delicious and fatiguing
as he fell again with alacrity on her best parts
she is said to have called, *alas,* to everybody,
there is no limit to all things.

175

SMOKEY THE BEAR AND THE PLATINUM BLONDE SPACE VIRGIN

WILLIAM WITHERUP

It was the first day of spring, and it was also only three days away from Gordon's birthday. The magnetism of the sun, the moon and the planets was very heavy, and he could feel the ram's horns pushing at his scalp. He had to restrain himself from butting the other suits and briefcases that passed him; from tucking his own briefcase under his arm and tearing down the sidewalk the way he used to rip around left end.

The bay smelled especially sharp, salty and sexual. Gordon breathed deeply and held the air in his lungs. Then he expelled it with a "huh!" from the pit of his stomach. The attack breath in karate. A middle-aged secretary was just passing on his right and almost jumped off the sidewalk.

No. He could *not*. He could *not* walk into that sterile office with its grey, uniform desks, its flat white walls, its buzzing neon and its stale air. He could not walk in, just as he did every other day, and open his briefcase and spread out his work. It was pointless. Endless. He would call in sick.

No. Even better, he would get drunk. He would stop in Spiro's and have about ten shots of whiskey. Then he would walk into the office, straight to Mr. Hughes's glass cubicle, get up on a chair and piss on his desk. Everyone in the office would look up. A state of shock. Then Rosalyn Sanchez would stand up and clap her hands and scream out, *Oh, you sweet gringo, what a beautiful piaba!* Then everyone would realize the import of his act and they would break into wild cheering. Rosalyn Sanchez would grab his piaba.

"But, Gordon," Mr. Hughes would exclaim, "what about your pretty little wife? What about your policies?"

Spiro's was crowded with early-morning drinkers. Drinkers mostly of Irish Coffees, Bloody Marys, Screwdrivers. So the bosses couldn't smell the liquor. Gordon took a seat at the far end of the bar and spread out the morning paper in the whiskey-colored light.

CHICAGO RIOTS SPREAD

"The usual?" said the bald-headed and very muscular Spiro, who always gripped the bar and confronted his customer as if across the scrimmage line. The usual was a cup of black coffee.

"No. This morning a shot of Jack Daniels with a beer chaser."

Spiro looked at Gordon suspiciously, as if Gordon's eyes would betray a plunge over right tackle rather than the expected end run.

"Really, Spiro. Jack Daniels and a glass of draft."

"Never thought I'd see it, kid. You were one of the great ones. One of the great ones. Never thought I'd see you come to this, this early morning drinking. What about your pretty little wife? What about your policies?"

ARMY TANKS IN THE STREETS OF CHICAGO

After his fourth boilermaker, Gordon began to feel good. He fingered his scalp and felt the two bumps. They had grown larger. Two years ago he had worn a helmet decorated with ram's horns. Galloping Gordon of the Los Angeles Rams.

Spiro was hurt. Gordon had been one of the great ones. He came and stood in front of Gordon and wiped a glass. His brown, Greek eyes were wet, as if he were about to cry.

"I see the niggers are at it again," he said angrily to cover what he was really thinking about.

"Why not, Spiro? Why not? Two hundred years of castration by whitey. They're growing back their piabas. Rebirth through ritual fire. Ritual fire, Spiro. That's what we all need. Rebirth through ritual fire. Rise up out of our old dead selves like the phoenix."

Now Gordon had really broken faith. First the drinking, and now siding with niggers. Spiro got mad.

"Yah, and I'm Smokey the Bear. Well, I'll tell you. If I had my way I'd put out their fire. I'd cut the balls off every one of those black mothers. Then we'd see who'd riot!"

"Here's to Smokey the Bear," said Gordon raising his eighth shot.

"Maybe you'd like one of those black bucks in bed with your wife, hah? That's what they want. They want all our women. What about your pretty little wife?"

"Here's to my wife. Here's to my policies." Gordon drained his eighth glass of beer. "My wife. A platinum blonde space virgin. She lives in a cold zone, a universe of ultraviolet light. We have sex by remote control, via the TV, the electric range, the electric toothbrush, the electric blanket, the ionized electric air-purifier, the FM radio, the stereo tape recorder and record player, the intercom, the atomic washing machine and the multidimensional self-flushing toilet. To put it simply, my wife and I have never touched. So today I am quitting my policies, quitting my wife and going off to become a hippy."

This was the last straw. Spiro's world completely collapsed. Crying, he swung on Gordon. "You dirty sonabitch. You used to be one of the great ones." But Gordon stepped back with the agility of a ram, took the man's drink next to him and toasted the bar.

"To everyone in the bar and to Smokey the Bear. Smokey, keeper and protector of the ritual fire. May he be with us all today as we go about our dull and endless routines."

When Smokey came in to cancel his fire insurance policy, he had a friendly smile for everyone in the office. Gordon didn't see him at first, but suddenly the office was filled with a heavy animal smell like around the cages at the zoo. When Gordon looked up, there was Smokey. Smokey went directly to Mr. Hughes's glass cubicle, cleared all the papers off his desk with one swipe of his paw, and then lumbered out right through one of the glass walls. Hughes turned purple above his starched white collar and then fainted. Simmons, junior executive to Hughes, came out of the next cubicle, tried to appear very important and masculine, *harumphed* a couple of times and laid his hand cautiously on Smokey's shoulder, but Smokey shrugged his shoulder and sent Simmons sprawling.

Smokey stopped in the aisle between the rows of grey desks and then stood on his hind legs. He was at least seven feet tall, and there seemed to be a faint aura of green light about him.

"I've come to cancel my fire insurance policy and to burn these silly green trousers and this silly little god damn green hat with my name on it."

This was a signal for wild cheering. The underwriters stomped

and whistled and beat on their desks and the secretaries screamed
and giggled. Smokey took his policy out of his back pocket and
put it on Gordon's desk. Then he sat down and rolled over on his
back with his feet in the air and tried to kick off his trousers. He
was having a difficult time, and Rosalyn Sanchez hopped up from
her small swivel chair, grabbed Smokey's cuffs and helped him off
with his pants. When the trousers came off, there was a sucking
of wind as all the secretaries caught their breaths.

"Thank you, Rosie," he said in his deep voice. He placed the
trousers and his hat on top of the insurance policy. "Anyway,
Smokey is not my real name. That's silly. I'm fed up with Walt
Disney and all those other faggots who have misused us animals
and make us walk around in silly human clothes and make us
speak in idiotic voices out of *Looney Tunes.*"

Gordon looked at the small pile of clothing on his desk. He felt
proud. His desk had been chosen for something special. He lis-
tened attentively and appreciatively as Smokey spoke. Everyone
was quiet and still. It was like a board meeting.

"And I am not the only one fed up with this plastic culture. I
can see most of you are, too." He looked around the room confi-
dentially, his small brown eyes piercing to the bone of every man
and woman there. "But I also see fear in your souls. Fear. You are
trapped in security, in new car payments, furniture payments, doc-
tor bills, house payments, club dues. You are frozen in fear and
trembling. You are like specimens pickled in plastic bottles. You
are cut off from nature. Men, your testicles have dried up. Girls,
your breasts have run out of sap." Smokey looked around the room
again. Everyone hung their heads at the truth of Smokey's words,
except Rosalyn Sanchez and Gordon. Gordon met and held
Smokey's gaze somewhat defiantly, sucked in his gut and shifted
his testicles around in his underwear. They were still there, though
he had woken up the previous night to find his wife trying to cut
them off with her manicuring scissors.

To Smokey's accusation, Rosalyn Sanchez said, "Fuck off, bruin."

"That's the spirit!" Smokey replied. And he looked around the
room again very significantly. "Except for Gordon and Rosie here,
the rest of you are as timid as church mice."

Both Gordon and Rosalyn stood up. Rosalyn curtsied sugges-
tively and Gordon bowed. The ram's horns had definitely come out
of his head now. They protruded two inches through his hair.

Smokey motioned them to sit down. It was still his show.

"As I was saying, most of you are frozen in fear and trembling. But I am going to release you from your fear. I am going to tell you my real, my secret name. This name is centuries old and was given to me by a Kwakiutl shaman. This name has great power, and it will impart to you strength and courage."

The tension in the office was almost painful. Hardly anyone dared even breathe. In the next instant they would be liberated, reborn.

"My true name"—and Smokey's voice dropped several octaves deeper, became gravelly and guttural like the grinding of a glacier —"is QWAXILA!"

At this, the aura surrounding him became brighter and the odors of pine and fern and wildflowers and springwater filled the office. Gordon felt a strange power flowing into him, through his ears and nostrils and eyes and fingers and toes, into his pores, his blood, his viscera, his testicles. The ram's horns fully sprouted.

The power soaked into everyone in the room. They began moving toward Gordon's desk carrying file folders and stacks of typewriter paper and carbon paper. "QWAXILA," they chanted. "QWAXILA," the women moaned. They brought more and more paper and piled it on the desk, the pulse of the chant quickening and their movements picking up speed until they were dancing frenziedly in the aisles. The men had removed their ties and unbuttoned their collars; the women had taken the bobby pins and clasps from their hair. Everyone had removed their shoes.

"QWAXILA! QWAXILA! QWAXILA! QWAXILA!" The light around Smokey grew brilliant green and then turned to flame. He touched his paw to the pile of clothing and papers on Gordon's desk and they went up like a dry forest. The other desks and chairs were moved back against the wall, and Gordon's flaming desk was pushed out into the center of the office. Everyone began dancing around in a large circle. "QWAXILA! QWAXILA! QWAXILA!" The men threw out their arms and the women twirled, exposing their pretty lace underwear.

Hughes woke up and climbed up on his desk.

"What are you doing?" he shouted. "What about your husbands and wives? What about our clients?"

Someone picked him off with a bottle of ink. Someone else took down the large framed picture of the company's founder and added it to the fire; someone else the American flag, and someone else the flag of California.

Rosalyn Sanchez came whirling by Gordon, her hands snaking out in the firelight, foam at the corners of her mouth, her long black hair whipping as if in a wind.

"Rebirth," Gordon said. "Purification by ritual fire. I love you. I have always loved you from across the eternal grey desks, the office steppes. I am being reborn as my true self." Gordon gave a toss of his horned head, snorted, and picked her up in his arms. He caught her smell, the woman smell and the smell of sweat, and it drove him wild. He carried her across the office to a desk near the window. Outside the moon had risen. The city was burning.

"QWAXILA," she whispered in his ear as he nuzzled her neck. The inside of her thighs were smooth against the palm of his hand.

The elevator door opened unexpectedly. A cold, ultraviolet light filled the office and snuffed out the fire. The dancers froze in position. They looked hopefully, desperately at Smokey, who was whimpering. And afraid. Frozen in fear and trembling.

Gordon's wife stepped out of the elevator. She was dressed in a mauve and silver space suit. Her platinum hair and her perfect steel teeth glowed in the ultraviolet light. She carried pruning shears, and behind her walked Spiro, clothed in a purple robe and gold sandals and bearing a quart jar of Peter Pan Peanut Butter that now contained the testicles of castrated Negroes. Spiro was still crying.

TWO POEMS

JOHN TAGGART

THE ROOM

> "So dense. The density. A reduced world.
> The room. . . .
>
> But better, nevertheless, the waking world,
> the object-poor, the edgeless."
> —William Bronk

It does not have to be
but let it be
a dream: the room

is made completely of wood
several kinds
of wood, planed

whole and nearly smooth
as the machines
used to lift and position stone

for pyramids
must have been.

There is nothing between
the angles of the wood. There
are no windows, no light or air.

Surely, it is wrong to want to be here
wrong not to choose the room's opposite
the sky

where everything is approximate
and large, the ocean
which is the same as the sky.

It is even brave to do this
to remain
in the relative

except
endlessly, endlessly

to feel the directions of grain
the faint edges
where the shapes are joined

everywhere a definiteness
everywhere density.

The dream is the shape—
pure, yet enlarging—
of sensation

a definition of sensation
that is more than that
the density of

—how would you say—
the self itself
expanded, to a world.

There are no windows.

LIVEFOREVER: OF ACTUAL THINGS IN EXPANSION

for Abraham Veinus

> *The music is in the flower,*
> *Leaf around leaf ranged around the center;*
> *Profuse but clear outer leaf breaking on space,*
> *There is space to step to the central heart:*
> *The music is in the flower,*
> *It is not the sea but hyaline cushions the flower—*
> *Liveforever, everlasting.*
>
> *Louis Zukofsky*

1
"One
must
not come to feel
that

he
has
a thousand threads
in his hands,

He
must
somehow
see the one thing."

One. . .
a meeting
assembly
one

as, leg
bolted on
this table
locked there

by hands
constant
the hands build constantly
to make

a pressure
a procession
something, simply, that
will stand up.

It
could
be
a poem

though
that—
inertia system—
is not what must be seen.

I
mean
the
one enduring object

made
from
all these
diagrams

having
what
to do
with one another

. . . the wife
in
photographs
beside her husband

their
red-
haired daughter
in the middle

so
that
looking at them
we say

there
is
something
between them

some
look
or extended to things
position:

I
drew
three right angles
to see

where the voices
parts
of a Bach fugue
were, being too much taken.

You
do not confuse
the photograph
for the actual family.

The diagram
not
the music, a figure
composed

of
lines, not
the music,
diagram

to hold
for sight
what the ear could not
hear

the
one
thing, which
is a process

2
              reduced, many voices
to
one question
one answer from

the
notes
of a few possible days,
a thousand threads

to
one,
having
what?

and one,
process
a matter
of community

to
all in common
a sort of
ownership

of
actual
things
in expansion

the
polyp
bud-foot, trees
bands of the eclipse's corona

our talk
making
everywhere
a nexus.

Think of it
as a
table
of multiplication.

This
is
the total possible
universe.

It's
the same universe
where
you live

—the
same
old stars—from,
to one

to
walk
on,
to see again.

ZUCKER

BENJAMIN HAIMOWITZ

Every time I went to camp, every bunk I was ever in, there was a patsy for everybody to push around. You wouldn't take Steve Zucker for a patsy at first. He was as tall as Big George, who'd been the biggest in our group summer after summer—tall, dark, lanky, with close blond hair. There was something small and funny about Zucker's face, and somebody, somewhere, must not have liked him, because his nose was kind of squashed in, but at first that gave the impression he was rugged. Everybody figured him for first baseman on the subsenior softball team. But at the tryouts three days after camp opened, Zucker missed almost every ball thrown to him. By then everybody had begun to wonder about him anyway. He seemed to choke up every time you looked at him.

Before long everybody was picking on him. Except me. Not that I'm bragging—I was just too much of an outcast myself. There was my father to begin with. My father was a truant officer who worked summers as a camp swimming counselor. He wasn't exactly the regular-guy type, and there were always wisecracks about my father to deal with. Then I was always having bad luck. I'd been coming to this camp for four years, ever since I was nine, and every summer something bad seemed to happen. One summer I slipped chasing some skinny, little jerk who'd said something about my father, and ended up with six stitches. Once I fell out of a tree. Once I was just fooling around and had a guy in a bear hug, and my braces got caught on his tee shirt—a thousand dollars' worth of bracework ripped out. If I didn't get hurt, I was always good for poison ivy or the flu or something. I'd never be in Zucker's place, but I'd never be too far from it either.

So after Zucker fouled up his tryout, I offered to help him with his fielding. I was one of the three or four best ballplayers in the division, and Zucker jumped at the offer. That night we hurried through supper and made it up to the empty softball diamonds. Zucker at first base threw grounders across to me at third, and I pegged them back.

At first I just lobbed them back, and he looked almost classy plucking them out of the air. Then I sped them up, and the throws started getting away from him. It was easy to see why: he was pulling back from the ball. He said it was just his timing, but it wasn't his timing, he was pulling back. To prove it I told him to throw a little soft grounder, so I could practice throwing on the run. I charged the ball and went through the motion of firing it with all my might without ever letting go of it. Zucker almost fell over from fright.

"You see?" I said. "You see?"

"But you were right on top of me, Noah. You were coming right at me."

"Steve, it's nothing to be ashamed of. Everybody's afraid a little at first. Just remember that it's only a softball. Just remember that."

He took my advice to some extent, because he did stay in front of at least one. Only the effort must have been too great, and he forgot to catch the ball. At the last minute he kind of stabbed at it and tried to jump out of the way, and the ball hit him in the chest. He collapsed to his knees.

"You all right, Steve?" I said, hurrying across to him. He was on his knees, his eyes squeezed shut, his hands clutched to his chest. "Where'd it get you, Steve, the heart?" He didn't answer.

After a while he got up slowly, and I walked him back to the bunk. I got him to take off his sweatshirt so I could take a look. There was a little pale, pink spot on the right side of his chest. "You see, I told you it was nothing, you old faker," I said. Zucker smiled weakly. I was relieved he hadn't been hit in the heart. I went into the bathroom to wash up, and when I came out, he was lying on his bed, still looking shaky. I asked him if he was all right, and he nodded doubtfully. I began to worry again.

"I've been meaning to give you something," I said. I went over to my cubby, and took out the copy of *Les Misérables* I'd borrowed from the library for the summer. I'd been meaning to offer him one of my books anyway. "*Les Misérables*," I said. "It's about a man who gets hounded his whole life for stealing a loaf of bread." He looked kind of bewildered. "There's a great chase through the Paris sewers. You can skip around if you want."

"I don't know," he murmured. But he began to leaf through it, so I left him alone and tried to read my own book. I was still a little afraid of Zucker dying of some freakish blood clot on the chest. Finally I ventured a look. He was lying on his back, staring at the ceiling, the book beside him. He wasn't reading, but at least he hadn't died.

A few days later I asked Zucker if he wanted to practice again. He thought about it a very long time, then finally said, yes, he did, if I'd take it easy. So I did. He rolled grounders to me as hard as he could, and I lobbed them back. That and not much more. Whenever I speeded things up, Zucker would get jittery and quit. And then he'd ask me about his progress, whether I thought he'd make the team. I'd tell him he was improving, slowly but surely.

Probably I would have told him he was getting nowhere at all, if I hadn't been so intent on convincing him about things. Every time Zucker would quit, we'd sit on the bench and talk. And always within five minutes I'd be trying to convince him about something. We must have covered about everything, but mostly it was politics and then maybe books and baseball. I never had so much to say in my life. Everything seemed clear, and Zucker was the perfect audience. He never had anything much to say, and, when he did, it was always the most obvious thing, the *Daily News–Daily Mirror* kind of thing, the lowest common denominator. His simple objections would only sharpen my appetite to argue, to plant the truth in his poor, weak mind, to straighten poor Steve out. He'd just sit there and smile and say he didn't know. What was he smiling about? Was he just being polite? Was I making a fool out of myself? He always seemed a little fearful, as if I'd hit him for one of his objections. But in the end he'd always exhaust me.

Then one night I was in a bad mood to begin with, because I'd had a run-in with Big George. We got up to the ballfield, and started in, and one of the first grounders Zucker threw took a bad hop and got me right where it hurts. There I was running around in agony, when suddenly I noticed Zucker. He wasn't sympathetic, and he wasn't laughing either. He wasn't even paying attention. He was standing on first base staring off to the mountains. "Zucker," I shouted. He turned, and I let one go as hard as I could right at him. Zucker dove out of the way, and the ball flew into the woods behind first.

I knew I'd never find it, but kicked around in the woods for a while anyway. Zucker was sitting on the bench when I came out.

"Shit. Well, that's that," I said.

"What's the difference?" said Zucker. "Hell, what's the difference." He stared dolefully off into the distance, seeming hardly to notice me.

"What do you mean?" I said.

"Hell, you said the other day I wouldn't make the team."

"I said probably."

"Probably then." He kept staring away, ignoring me.

I said, "If that's the way you feel, why'd you come today?"

Suddenly Zucker broke into that little smile of his. He looked at me. "I don't know," he said, "I don't know. You're always talking so much. You know. . . I'm not so dumb."

"Look, what the hell is this?" I said. "You're the one who's always quitting, not me. You're chicken. Sure you won't make the team, because you're chicken."

Zucker's smile vanished. Suddenly he buried his head in his hands. He just stayed that way, head in his hands.

"Steve? Steve?" I started shaking him. "Hey. Hey, Steve."

Zucker wrenched himself away from me. His eyes blazing, he began to pull furiously at his sweatshirt. He got the thing off, thrusting his arms at me. "Chicken, huh? Chicken, huh?" His arms were covered with black-and-blue marks. Everybody gets black-and-blue marks at camp, but I'd never seen anybody with that many.

"Who did it, Kurtz?" I said stupidly. Everyone had done it, but it was natural to think of Kurtz first. Kurtz had the bed next to Zucker's. He had a nasty temper and was always giving it to Zucker. "It's Kurtz, isn't it?" I said.

"Son of a bitch," Zucker muttered.

"Come with me, Steve. We're going to talk with Kurtz." He didn't seem to hear, his head remained buried in his hands, so I took off alone to find Kurtz. When I found him he was alone, and I told him he'd better keep his hands off Zucker. He had this lisp, and he was spluttering all over the place about how he wasn't the only one and how I'd hit Zucker too if I had to sleep next to that slob. I told him he'd just better keep his hands off Zucker. Never mind about anybody else, he'd just never better lay a hand on Steve Zucker again, if he knew what was good for him.

But in a way, too, he was right—he wasn't the only one. Somehow this wasn't enough. It suddenly seemed to me that in my own way, even I had been bullying Zucker, forcing myself upon him. After everything, I didn't know that I liked Zucker any more than Kurtz did. Certainly I wasn't helping him by cramming things down his throat, and I vowed to be a better friend or give the whole thing up.

When I told Steve what I'd done, he said something about, gosh, Noah, he appreciated it, but, gee, he'd better learn to fight his own battles. In appreciation, though, he asked me to come with him to meet his mother on visiting day that week end. Zucker's father was dead, and his mother and aunt were coming down to visit.

Zucker's mother looked like Zucker, tall, thin, and light-haired. Her hair was drawn into a pony tail, and it gave her a kind of timid, girlish look. Zucker's aunt, though, was short and fat and never shut up. She asked me a few questions about myself, then started telling me about Steve. "You should see the letters he wrote," she said, leaning into me, whispering. "Oy, he hates it, he can't stand it, he wants to come home. She was ready to bring him home. I told her she's crazy. What, he's no baby no more, right? You gotta learn sometime, right?"

"Sure," I said.

" 'What's he gonna do if he comes home?' I told her. 'No more candy store to hang around.' Twenty-five years they had that candy store. Sure, she sold the store, how do you think she's sending him to such an expensive place like this camp? Twenty-five years, and he's gonna come home? You want some advice, sonny? Be a teacher like your father. Don't run no candy store."

I left them at the bunk, thinking they'd want to be alone. When I got back later, they were all still there. Zucker and his aunt were sitting on Kurtz's bed. They'd been straightening up his cubby, because there was a huge improvement. Probably it wouldn't be that way for long. I'd helped him with his cubby once, and two days later it was a mess again. They were about to go, and Zucker said to come along.

"Well, this was very nice," Zucker's aunt said. "A day in the country. Only this really ain't the country, you know."

"The other boys seem very nice, Stevie," Mrs. Zucker said. She spoke softly and kind of coaxingly.

"I know that," Zucker said moodily.

"Who was that big boy?" the aunt said.

"Big George," Zucker said.

"Big is right," his aunt said laughing. "I bet you get along OK with him, huh Stevie?"

When we got to the front office, everybody had run out of things to say, even Zucker's aunt. Finally the taxi came. Mrs. Zucker took my hand and smiled. I don't know why, but suddenly I felt sorry for her.

"Your mother's nice," I said to Zucker as we walked back to the bunk. Zucker looked at me. We walked on, and suddenly he started getting chipper in a way he'd never been. "Nice?" he said. "Of course she's nice—sure she's nice—she's Zucker's mother." He danced around, poking at me awkwardly with jabs. I feinted, and he danced away giggling. Then suddenly he danced in again and took a pretty good swat at me. I just ducked away. I ran after him a few steps, but he was too fast for me, so I just stood in the middle of the road making believe I was angry. Down the road Zucker doubled over with laughter. When I caught up with him, though, he got serious. "You know what, Noah?" he said.

"What?"

"You're the best friend I've ever had."

"What?" I said, looking around, "me?"

"It's true, Noah, you're my best friend."

I laughed, embarrassed. "But you've only known me a few weeks."

"That's OK. You are, really." He looked at me with his soft blue eyes. "Am I your good friend, Noah?"

"Sure, sure you are," I said. "Hey, what is this? Get out of here." I pretended I was going to kick him, and he took off laughing.

Then we got back to the bunk, and something funny happened. I was in the shower room, about to turn on the water, when I heard Kurtz shout out for all to hear that he was going to change the blankets on his bed because Zucker's mother had sat on them. I was about to go and give it to Kurtz, but something held me back. I just wanted Zucker to do something first, say something, anything. In two days, Zucker was going to be the hero of the camp. But that day he never said a word.

The next couple of days it rained all the time, and everybody got bored. The second day the counselor wasn't around, and there was a free-for-all that left the place turned upside down. Everybody was still bored. Little Herbie Levine brought out his musk turtle. He'd caught the snapper a few days before and kept it in a can in the john. They poked around at it for a while, and then it stopped raining, and they took it outside. There was Little Herbie Levine and Big George and Kurtz and Sammy Nagler. Zucker wasn't around. I went out a few minutes later, and they were going to boil the musk alive. They had some newspaper, and they were getting dry wood from under the bunk.

"Hey, you can't boil that thing," I said.

"I wanna see if it's alive," Herbie Levine said.

"Hell, it sure isn't going to be alive if you boil him."

But there was nothing to do about it. In a way, I wanted to see it too. You could see the point of the musk's diamond-shaped snout protruding from under the shell, and even that looked wicked. Herbie Levine was good with fires, and in no time he had one going. Everybody was very intent on the musk and the fire. The musk didn't move.

"Shit, beats beatin' off, huh Herbert?" Big George said giggling. "Hey, Herbert, you think it's dead?"

But then the musk began to move. First just a little, but then it really came to life, swimming side to side, one dull and frantic motion, back, forth, back, forth, thudding around the can. At first you kind of enjoyed it, and in a way you even enjoyed it more when the musk wouldn't die. But it just kept going back and forth that way, not dying, and suddenly I found myself trying to kick the can off the fire. Afraid of being burned, I only grazed it.

"Leave it alone," Herbie Levine said, excited.

"Leave the fuckin' thing alone," said Big George, grabbing me.

"Don't tell me what to do, you tool." He was a tool too, Little Herbie Levine's tool. By now the musk was dead anyway, floating at the top of the can, its legs and head out full. The water boiled, tumbling it around.

Everybody stood around just watching that for a while, the shamefulness of the thing sinking in. Finally Herbie Levine kicked over the can, tumbling the musk out on the charred ground. He carried the musk over to the woods about 50 yards away, and just around that time Steve Zucker showed up. It just so happened that he was coming out the backdoor of the bunk as Kurtz was going in.

Kurtz slammed into him with his forearm. He'd been coming down an incline, and he caught Zucker by surprise, and Zucker collapsed against the bunk wall. Kurtz never turned his head. He went straight into the bunk as if nothing had happened. Zucker sagged against the wall as if he were dying.

"Whatsammatta Zuckahh?" Big George said.

There was a ditch a few inches deep along the bunk wall. Zucker struggled out of the ditch and started limping around.

"What'd you do Steve, hurt your ankle?" Herbie Levine said. "Really, Steve, you didn't break your ankle, did you?"

"It's all right," Zucker said weakly, limping around.

"Then what are you limping for?" I said. I don't know why, I just couldn't stand him limping around like that.

"Here, Steve, sit down," Herbie Levine said.

"C'mon, Zucker, don't walk on no broken ankle," said Big George.

Zucker sat on the ground, and Herbie Levine started feeling all around his ankle. "I don't feel any break," he said. Zucker stared straight ahead, his eyes starting out of his head. "Did you see what Kurtz did?" Little Herbie Levine said to Big George.

"Yeah, smacked right inna him."

"Kurtz has been bullying him all summer," Sammy Nagler said. "I mean we all do, but he does it most."

"He oughta kick Kurtz's fuckin' ass," Big George said.

Herbie Levine looked intently at Zucker. "You want to fight him, Steve?" Zucker just stared ahead.

"I'll tell you one thing, Sammy Nagler said in his high, piercing, girlish voice, "I'd respect him one whole lot more if he did."

"Take it easy. Let him make up his own mind," said Herbie Levine.

"No, I'm just saying. . ." Sammy Nagler's eyes came earnestly to mine. "That's the trouble with Steve, Noah. He doesn't stick up for his rights. Really." He should know: he was about half Zucker's size, and he'd hit him enough.

By now a crowd was starting to gather. Zucker sat in the middle, grimacing and staring off grimly. Finally they got him to test his ankle. He kept hobbling around.

"Getting better? Think you can fight him?" said Herbie Levine.

"I don't know. . ." Zucker said weakly.

"We'd respect you for it, really," said Sammy Nagler.

"Shit, you could beat Kurtz with a busted leg," Big George said.

"Yeah, if it was Kurtz's leg that was busted," I said.

Zucker stopped hobbling around. His lips started to work.

"What do you say, Steve?" Herbie Levine said.

Zucker stared grimly into the distance. He seemed to sway slightly.

"Go head and kick the shit outa him," Big George said. "Get on there, Stevie boy, we're behind ya."

And suddenly it came to pass. Zucker headed for the bunk, limping along like a soldier home from the war, the crowd flooding in behind him. At the foot of Kurtz's bed Zucker stopped. His arms were crossed on his chest like an Indian's. Kurtz was astonished. He was trying to smile without being too successful.

"Zucker has something to tell you, Kurtz," Herbie Levine said.

"You been hittin'm all summer, now he's gonna kick your ass," said Big George.

Kurtz kept looking at the crowd in disbelief. "O yes," he said, lisping and screeching, "nobody else hits him."

"Yeah?" Big George said, "yeah? Whatsamatta, Kurtz, ya chicken?"

For a moment everything was frozen, then Zucker made a funny sound and lunged trying to swat Kurtz's book out of his hands, and Kurtz growled and jumped for him. Big George stepped in. That big lug! Suddenly I'd had all I could take.

"Who appointed you referee?" I said, stepping in front of Big George. "You hit him plenty too."

First Big George looked bewildered. Then suddenly he got this wild look in his eyes, and the next thing I knew he was barreling into me and I was on the floor. It wasn't just that he was surprisingly fast. Zucker's trunk was sticking out from under his bed, and I got pushed backward over it. All these years I'd wondered how I'd do against Big George, and I had to trip over Zucker's trunk.

I got up slowly. My wrist hurt. I went over to the back door and looked out. Zucker was getting killed. He fought like a girl, flailing away stiff-armed, his eyes closed half the time and his face back as far as he could get it. His face was all twisted up, and maybe that alone might have scared Kurtz for a minute. No more. Kurtz came in and ducked under and before long Zucker was a bloody mess. Big George kept pushing him in to fight, but I ran out to stop it, and this time no one interfered.

Somebody got a counselor, and they took Zucker to the infirmary. There were all kinds of rumors the rest of the day. Everybody thought we'd get sent home. Kurtz thought he'd go to jail. That night everyone hurried to the infirmary as soon as visiting hours began. The nurse wouldn't let the mob in, so we went around to the window. "Steve?" Herbie Levine called. Zucker's bandaged form appeared behind the screen. "How you feel, kid?" Herbie Levine said.

"OK," said Zucker.

"OK?"—"What'd he say?"—"He's OK."—"OK? Hey!"—"Really OK? Really Zuck?"

"You didn't break anything, did you?" said Herbie Levine.

"Nah, I don't think so," Zucker said.

"You don't think so?" Herbie Levine said, a little doubtfully.

"Hell, I didn't break anything," Zucker said. "Just a little bloody nose, that's all. Break? Hell, you can't break steel, can you?"

Everybody laughed.

"Hey, Zuck," said Sammy Nagler, "what do you want us to bring you?"

"Bring me?" Zucker said.

"Hey, we're your friends, right. We don't want you to get bored in there."

Zucker's bandaged form hovered dimly behind the screen. "Bring me Bunny Bond," he said. Bunny Bond was this great-looking girl from the girl's side, and everybody laughed.

"Hey, Steve," Herbie Levine said, "Kurtz wants to tell you something."

A path was made, and Kurtz edged up to the window. "Steve?" he said, lisping softly.

"Hi, Jerry," Zucker said.

"How you doing, boy? We put on quite a show, huh?"

"Yeah," said Zucker, "we should have charged admission."

"Seriously, Steve, I didn't mean to hurt you. It was a fight fair and square."

"I know that, Jerry."

"Heck, I guess I'm pretty lucky I'm not in the hospital."

Zucker laughed. "Maybe you would be if my ankle didn't throw me off," he said.

"Jesus, that's right, his ankle!" Kurtz shrieked. "Wait'll his ankle gets better. He'll probably get out and kill me."

All I knew was that my wrist hurt like crazy. The next morning, when everyone went back to Zucker's window, I went inside and had the nurse look at it. Sure enough, I'd broken it.

When the head counselor investigated the Zucker business, everybody said it was nobody's fault and a fair fight and a square fight and all of that. I said my broken wrist had nothing to do with the fight. An accident, I said, a fall. Nobody got in trouble, and nobody got sent home. They didn't even fire the counselor, since it all happened on his day off.

When Zucker got out of the infirmary, everybody in the bunk except me treated him to a dinner and movie in town. Before the week was out, he was getting punched in the arm again. He got his share of black-and blue marks that last part of the summer too. Still, it was different now. Sometimes he'd hit back, and even when he didn't, it wasn't the same. Because I think everybody was a little afraid of Zucker. It was as if he were back from the dead: next to winning that fight, the best thing he could have done was lose it as badly—or as bloodily, anyway—as he did. "Watch it," Zucker would say now, flashing his crazy smile, "it takes a lot to get Zucker mad. But when Zucker gets mad, look out." Everybody would laugh, but nobody could be quite sure what he'd do. Herbie Levine paid him the supreme compliment one day: "I'm not the crazy one any more," he said. "Zucker is."

Fighting Kurtz had made him a celebrity, and, by God, he was going to keep it that way. He was up to all kinds of ridiculous dares now. Once they dared him to sneak over to the girls' side of camp and get a kiss from Bunny Bond. He made it over to the girls' side and even to Bunny Bond's bunk, but the girls all started screaming, and he got caught. The prize, though, was when some of the older guys offered him five dollars to throw a can of paint on this girl counselor they didn't like. Zucker went through with it, but missed —on purpose, he said. They were ready to send him home for that, but it was the last week, and the whole camp always seemed to go crazy the last week, and what he'd done seemed almost normal.

I didn't say a word to Zucker in the weeks after the fight. He ignored me too at first, but then he seemed to make peace offerings. He returned *Les Misérables,* and made a big point of thanking me for it. He wished he'd been able to read it, he said, he wished he'd read half as much as I had. I just mumbled something. I remembered what he said once about not being so dumb. I remembered that all right.

The last day of the season, I was walking, and a voice came out of nowhere. "How's the wrist coming along? Think we'll play softball again?" I turned to confront Zucker.

"What do you want to play softball for?" I said. "You're afraid of the ball."

"How'd you break your wrist anyway?" Zucker said.

"How did I break it? How did I break it?"

"Big George says he didn't do it, you know. He says you got it the next day."

"Take a walk, Zucker," I said. He didn't, so I did. Zucker followed me.

"Look, Noah, what's got you?"

"What?" I said. "Are you kidding?"

"I'm not kidding, Noah. What's the matter? I notice you're not talking to me and all. But why? I don't know why, Noah. I don't."

"Are you kidding?" I said, laughing. But in a way he had me. Because all along I'd never really been sure just what he'd done wrong, to me at least. Was it him I really ought to be angry at or was I just taking something out on him?

"Noah, look, will you help me make the team next summer?"

"What? Are you kidding? Go throw paint on a girl, Zucker."

"Noah, I didn't throw paint on any girl. Forget about that, Noah, will you? She's just a louse anyway."

"How do you know?"

"Everybody knows—look, you think I tried to hit her? You think I wouldn't have hit her if I tried?" He looked at me with those washed-out blue eyes of his. Maybe he had missed on purpose. How could you tell with Zucker? "Noah, I know how you broke your wrist. But why is it my fault? You always told me to stick up for my rights."

"Not that way," I said.

"What way?"

"That way, with half the camp behind you. Anybody could have done that, Zucker. But what about the day your mother came and Kurtz insulted her. I didn't see you stick up for *her*."

"What? Kurtz insulted who?. . . When?. . ." And suddenly he got mad. "Look, Noah, nobody asked you to butt in."

There I had him. "You're just lucky I did butt in, Zucker. I stopped that fight, remember? And, boy, you're just lucky I did."

That seemed to get him. For a moment I even thought he'd cry, but he didn't. He even smiled a little.

"You think that's funny, Zucker?"

"No, Noah, no, no, I was just thinking of something," he said, smiling secretively. Zucker had let his hair grow, and he had this big mop of blond hair now, and he brushed it back and fixed a look on me. "You knew I was faking that day, didn't you."

"What day?"

"You know what day. When Kurtz knocked me against the wall and those guys were asking me if I was all right. You knew I was faking."

"You were?"

"Sure I was. I mean, I didn't plan it or anything, Noah. But my ankle was all right. It didn't hurt." He kept staring at me, waiting for me to get it, Zucker waiting for me now to see the light.

"A faker, sure, I figured that," I said, and maybe in a way I had. But that didn't seem to matter.

"Noah, Noah, look." Leaning in secretively, he said, "Nobody has to know about any of this." He winked. It was as if he'd grown up in a few weeks, leaving me, dull and mulish, behind.

"That fight sure wasn't a fake," I said.

"You're the only one who knew, Noah. I knew you knew." He kept smiling this little smile over our great secret. Suddenly I was aware of my heart beating like crazy.

"That fight sure wasn't fake," I muttered.

But Zucker only gave me this big pained look, and I could see he was asking me to relent. And suddenly I wanted to. It was flattering in a way—he really was a kind of celebrity. Whatever he'd done, he did want to be my friend. Hell, he didn't owe me anything, I knew that: one of the things that pissed me off was that, with all my fussing, I'd never really helped Zucker. And he was right, it wasn't really his fault I'd broken my wrist. God knows, it wasn't the first time I'd broken something. Wasn't I bound to do something like that every summer anyway?. . .

But what if I was? It was my wrist, that was the thing. It wasn't my fault either, and it just happened to be my wrist. It was just that. It seemed somehow there ought to be more, and that's all there was. . .

"Too bad about your wrist," Zucker said finally. He seemed to hesitate a moment, then turned and walked back to the bunk. And that was it.

FIVE POEMS

PETER GLASSGOLD

SCARS

It rustles
leaves to sun   sun, the fylfot's whorl
the back of one scarred hand
four limbs splayed out
all from a dead heart radiant

Your palms once warmer than these are
stronger drier and more broad
fingers tapered where mine are thick
and the back of one hand scarred

—In your father's factory near Stump Lake,
Making mattresses for the Catskill trade,
Before the Great War, maybe nineteen-twelve.
"Hey Georgie, hold this here for a while."
The button man was fired, his machine
Stitched right through your hand. For six months, you said,
You squeezed daily on a rubber ball—

were cool now to the touch
your head rolled back
eyes unfocused into vastness
the mouth half wide that murmured, dying,
"I'm not afraid"—
                    I was.

BASIC ENGLISH

Knowledge by name is wisdom
Call me by my name and
I am called

My name is not my name

When we have held each other in the dark
Our smells combined
Our hearts in complementary beat
Our names touch

BEYOND WORDS

A poem becomes you—
    if meaningless words
    are soundings merely
    reminding me of more
    than just your image

BHASTRIKA / THE BELLOWS

Zion is the balance of every balanced breath,
Citadel of winds sucked back and forth,
Flowing conjunctive teetering on pinnacles of madness:

Upon what ground does David's city stand?

OLD BONES'S CURSE

He intones upon the mountain.

"You are the blight carved on the bole,
smear on the pavement;

"Your breath is smog,
the brush of your hand stains yellow.

"The nightflyer flit in the corner of your eye,
plucking, boring at what crawls there;

"Slithers stick to the ruddy tongue, the jowl,
they will bloat and fatten;

"The nameless gorge on the lowermost bowel,
till it sag in rupture;

"While your body bent in a five-fold knot
twitch in its smother sack—

"But your heart, your brain,
your liver and your foreskin they will save,
sundry artifacts in memoriam."

THE MAN WITH THE MANDOLINE

JUNICHIRŌ TANIZAKI

Translated by Donald Keene

CHARACTERS

THE MAN WITH THE MANDOLINE, *a blind man*
UKIKO, *his wife*
THE SHADOW-MAN

Scene One

(*The interior of a room with thick white walls that give the impression of a vault. One window to stage left and two in the center are entirely covered with green curtains. To stage right is a door. Next to the window on the left is a desk and a chair. Between the two windows in the center is a small bookcase with a clock on it. An easy chair stands in the middle of the room. A small table and a sofa are to the right. The furniture is simple and rather worn.*

As the curtain rises a mandoline is heard playing a quiet nocturne. It is an autumn night. On the table there is a lighted lamp with a green shade. To the right, facing his wife, the Blind Man sits on the edge of the easy chair, playing a mandoline. He wears black trousers and a grey sweater. His wife is leaning back on the sofa as if listening to the music, although in fact she is reading a book with a pink cover. She is wearing a plain winter kimono with a cloak. Next to her on the sofa are two cushions and a white blanket. One end of the blanket hangs from the sofa to the floor.)

BLIND MAN. (*stopping the music*) Tonight I'm playing better than usual. Maybe it's just my imagination. (*His wife goes on reading the book in silence. She turns a page very softly so as not to make any noise.*) You know, I sometimes have the impression on a night like this—I'm sure there must be a fine moon tonight—that someone on the outside is listening to this mandoline. I'm sure someone has taken a boat out on the lake and is looking up at these windows. (*His wife remains silent.*) Ukiko, don't you have that feeling too? I'm sure my mandoline can be heard out on the lake.

WIFE. (*taking her eyes from the book for a moment*) I don't think that's likely.

BLIND MAN. Is that what you really think?

WIFE. But after all. . .

BLIND MAN. No, I'm sure it can be heard, and you, in your heart, think it's probable too, don't you?

WIFE. Oh, do stop talking about such things! The windows are tight shut. There's nothing to worry about. Play me that piece again.

BLIND MAN. Have you been listening with absolute attention? Without thinking about anything else?

WIFE. I *was* listening, without another thought in my head.

BLIND MAN. I was remembering the time when I first played this piece for you. That and nothing else.

WIFE. Yes, that's all I've been thinking of. (*The Blind Man plays the piece again. The wife secretly resumes her reading. A fairly long pause.*)

BLIND MAN. (*suddenly stopping*) What are you doing?

WIFE. What is it?

BLIND MAN. Are you listening?

WIFE. Of course I'm listening. (*The Blind Man puts down the mandoline, gets up and gropes his way over to his wife. In the meantime she shuts the book and hides it under the blanket. The Blind Man runs his hands over his wife, then feels around the top of the sofa until he at last comes on the book.*)

BLIND MAN. (*fingering the book*) What is this book?

WIFE. A manual of knitting instructions.

BLIND MAN. What good paper—very luxurious for a manual of knitting instructions! (*His wife remains silent.*) Ukiko, you know, in the three years since I became blind I have learned to tell most things with my hands, by their feel. The cover of this book is pink.

WIFE. Is its being pink so peculiar?

BLIND MAN. This is a book of poetry. You were secretly reading it just now while I was playing.

WIFE. No, I wasn't. I read it some time ago.

BLIND MAN. I'll take this book. (*So saying, he goes to the bookcase. He takes a key from his pocket, unlocks a drawer and puts the book away. He locks it again. Then he goes up to the lamp and stands there, seemingly measuring the distance between the lamp and his wife.*) Ukiko, is your shadow reflected on the curtain?

WIFE. It's dark by the window. The lamp shade cuts off the light.

BLIND MAN. Even if it's dark, are you sure there isn't a faint shadow falling on it?

WIFE. (*turns and looks at the window*) No, not a suggestion of a shadow.

BLIND MAN. Are all the curtains drawn, without a crack showing? They're not wrinkled or twisted, are they? (*She looks at him in hatred.*) Why don't you say something?

WIFE. Do you distrust me so much?

BLIND MAN. It's not that I don't trust you. I'm afraid of whoever's on the outside. There's a man secretly peeping through the window into this room.

WIFE. But the house is at the edge of the lake, on top of a steep cliff.

BLIND MAN. I'm sure he comes to the edge of the lake in a boat, then climbs up the cliff.

WIFE. How could anyone possibly climb up here? It's so high up here it's like a fortress tower.

BLIND MAN. It was to forestall him that I put the iron grill outside the window, but it was a bad idea. If somebody dropped a rope from the grill he could climb up it. Every night I have that nightmare.

WIFE. Well. then, why don't you examine the grill, and see whether or not there's a rope tied to it?

BLIND MAN. I know you despise me because I haven't the courage to open the window. That's why you say that.

WIFE. Even if someone managed to climb up outside the window, what could he do? Those bars on the window—it's like a prison cell.

BLIND MAN. I know exactly what he would do. That's why I must make sure your shadow isn't reflected on the curtains. Often in my dreams I hear a pistol shot.

WIFE. Yes, it's all in your dreams.

BLIND MAN. But sometimes I also hear a noise which is not in my dreams. There, from that wall. *(He points to a place between the two center windows.)* Night after night, those scratching sounds.

WIFE. I told you it was mice.

BLIND MAN. I've heard that noise for over a year now. Whenever it gets late, not a night goes by without my hearing that noise. A noise like someone persistently cutting through these thick walls from the outside.

WIFE. How could anyone cut through such thick walls? They're like a vault.

BLIND MAN. If he has been cutting away, bit by bit, every night for a whole year, he might break through. That's not a sound of mice. It's some kind of sharp instrument chipping at the wall.

WIFE. That's just your delusion.

BLIND MAN. Aren't you praying that it is *not* just my delusion?

WIFE. We've been through all this before. . . *(She puts one hand on the other, leaning on the arm of the sofa, and bends her head. The Blind Man sits in the easy chair.)*

BLIND MAN. You think that it's all an empty delusion on my part, just the warped mind of a blind man?

WIFE. Yes, I'm sure of it. There's no doubt in my mind.

BLIND MAN. I don't suppose you realize how tenacious he is.

WIFE. You're frightened by your own shadow.

BLIND MAN. It was thanks to him I lost my eyes. I've only recently come to realize it. That was his first act of vengeance, and now he's working on the second.

WIFE. It's not true. It's not true. You're making it all up. *(Her head is still lowered, and she appears to be weeping in secret. Pause.)*

BLIND MAN. What time is it now? Look at the clock.

WIFE. Yes. *(She answers in a clear voice so that he will not be aware she has been weeping. She gets up wearily and looks at the clock on the bookcase.)* It's twenty-five minutes to twelve.

BLIND MAN. Time for bed then. Five minutes later than usual. *(She sighs and leans limply against the back of the sofa. The Blind Man goes to the bookcase and opens the door with a key. From the shelf he removes a bottle containing a white powder. He goes to the desk, takes a piece of paper lying on top, then returns to the table. Meanwhile his wife sits there, her head hanging, not looking at him, exactly as if she were waiting for her execution. The Blind*

Man's movements are deliberate and careful, and require some time. He spreads open the paper on the table, uncorks the bottle, and shakes a little of the powder onto the paper. His wife raises her head at this moment.)

WIFE. Please, that's enough.

BLIND MAN. No, a little bit more. . .take a little more tonight. *(So saying, he increases the quantity.)*

WIFE. I can sleep even without taking so much.

BLIND MAN. It's barely two grams. Medicines lose their effect unless you keep adding to the dose.

WIFE. You make me take so much sleeping medicine I feel groggy all day long. I'm sure it's harmful.

BLIND MAN. There's nothing to worry about with this medicine. Maybe it *is* a little harmful, but it won't kill you. I have no intention of letting you die just yet.

WIFE. When *will* I be allowed to die?

BLIND MAN. Five years, ten years—who knows?—perhaps twenty years from now. As long as I'm around I'm going to keep you alive too. *(He finishes preparing the medicine and returns the bottle to the bookcase, which he locks. He next goes to the door on the right, takes out a key, and unlocks it. He goes out, locking the door behind him. A brief pause. His wife remains motionless in the room. He returns shortly with a tumbler of water, locks the door and goes to her. He places the glass on the table, puts the paper on his palm and measures the dose again.)* Now stand up. *(She stands facing him and opens her mouth. With one hand he holds her chin, with the other pours the medicine into her mouth. He shakes in the medicine again and again, then makes her drink every last drop of the water.)* That'll be enough. Now lie down. You'll be able to sleep peacefully thanks to the medicine.

WIFE. I hope I never wake up.

BLIND MAN. Not until tomorrow morning, you mean. *(Hiding her face with her hands she staggers over to the sofa and lies down on her back, her head to stage left. The Blind Man props up her head with the cushions and covers her to the neck with the blanket. She lies there peacefully, her eyes shut.)* Pleasant dreams! And now I'll play that piece for you again. *(He fondles his wife through the blanket, then returns to the easy chair and picks up the mandoline.)* Listen to this music, listen to it, even in your dreams. You're not to see or hear anything else. *(He begins to play, stopping occasionally*

*to listen to the sound of his wife's breathing. A fairly long pause.
He puts down the mandoline gently and, on tiptoe, approaches the
sofa. He listens intently to her breathing, then begins to shake her
body, gingerly at first, but at the end almost wildly. She does not
stir. Kneeling, he takes her face in his hands and strokes her cheeks.)*
Ukiko, forgive me. I don't want to hurt you. It's just that I'm so
afraid you'll run off to him. *(He strokes her cheek again and re-
arranges the pillows more comfortably under her head. He moves
to the hems of her kimono and embraces her legs. Then, turning
back the blanket a little, he removes her linen socks and rubs his
cheek against her insteps. After a while he stands.)* Sleep tight. . .
You really *are* asleep, aren't you? *(He picks up the socks and stuffs
one inside the other. He puts them in his pocket, then pulls down
the blanket again.)* Wait there for me. Now that you're asleep I'll
get to bed too. I'll be back in a moment and take you to my room.
*(He returns to his chair, loosens the strings of the mandoline, un-
locks the door on the right and goes out, leaving the door open. A
long pause. A sound of scratching is heard from the wall between
the windows. It stops for a while only to start again. Gradually it
becomes more distinct. The woman lies so motionlessly on the sofa
she might be dead. The Blind Man, wearing white pyjamas, returns
just at a moment when the scratching has stopped. He leaves the
door open. He goes to his wife, strips off the blanket, and lifts her
in his arms. At that instant the wall begins to make a noise. He
gently puts her head back on the pillow and quietly moves to the
wall, where he listens. The noise becomes louder and louder. The
moonlight shining through the window causes the shadow of the
iron grill to bar the curtain. At the same moment a man's shadow
appears in the window to the right. The shadow seems to be stuck
like a lizard to the grill. The blind man listens intently. The char-
acter of the sound gradually changes and becomes a cracking noise.
The part of the wall near the right window starts to crumble.)* He's
come! *(He utters a sharp cry, recoiling so violently he all but rolls
over to the sofa. He clings to his wife, seeming to implore her help,
and shakes her fiercely.)* Ukiko! Ukiko! He's come at last! *(Even as
the wall crumbles, the whole frame of the window begins to shake,
and gradually detaches itself from the wall. It finally falls into the
room, the iron grill still attached. A rope tied to the grill hangs
outside the house. Through the square opening left by the window
the Shadow-man lightly and soundlessly crawls in. The Blind Man
leaps back from the sofa and crouches behind the easy chair. The*

Shadow-man pounces on him like a bird of prey and immediately begins to throttle him.) Ukiko! Ukiko! Save me! (The Shadow-man pushes him farther and farther back until he falls backward over the window frame on the floor. He straddles the Blind Man, takes a cord from his pocket, and twists it around his neck. After a brief struggle the Blind Man dies. The moonlight streaming in from the window casts a pale circle of light around his body. The Shadow-man, having made sure he is dead, stands and, passing before the easy chair, goes to the sleeping woman. His foot strikes the mandoline left lying on the floor, and the strings sound. The man angrily picks up the mandoline, snaps the neck, and smashes it to the floor. He turns, as if struck by a sudden thought and, returning to the body, unfastens the rope tied to the window frame. He pulls it to him, then ties it to the iron grill on the left window. He lifts the sleeping woman on his shoulder and goes out along the rope through the break in the wall. The stage grows dark.)

Scene Two

(The edge of the lake. To the left, on top of the cliff, a white building with a broken window from which a rope hangs down the cliff. The window is completely dark. It is a beautiful moonlit night. The Shadow-man sits in the center of a little boat on the lake. Ukiko sleeps, her head resting in his lap.)

SHADOW-MAN. Ukiko, there's nothing more to worry about. It's all over now.

UKIKO. *(suddenly opening her eyes):* You've got rid of my enemy.

SHADOW-MAN. I have removed him, the hateful enemy of us both.

UKIKO. You have delivered me from prison.

SHADOW-MAN. I have been cutting at the wall for over a year to get into that prison and rescue you.

UKIKO. I have been waiting for you, such a long time. . . I had given up hope, but still I waited. But now my prayers have been answered, and I don't care how soon I die. *(The two embrace. From the window of the house on the cliff the sound of a mandoline is heard. It is the melody the Blind Man always played. The two of them are petrified with horror.)* Ohh—he's still alive, still. . .

SHADOW-MAN. *(looking up at the window)* So that's your revenge, is it? But we're not afraid of you. I'm going to take this woman, my precious wife, to a place where we'll never hear you again.

UKIKO. Hurry! Take me with you! As long as we live, we'll hear that music. Let's go together, quickly! *(The Shadow-man pulls a stopper from the bottom of the boat. He sits in the middle and takes her hands.)*

SHADOW-MAN. Ukiko!

UKIKO. My dearest!

SHADOW-MAN. Hold tight to me! We'll never leave each other again.

UKIKO. Oh, we can die together! You and I, together. . .

(The boat gradually sinks. The mandoline continues playing until the boat has completely disappeared. Then it stops abruptly.)

CURTAIN

NOTES ON CONTRIBUTORS

Born in Belgium at the outbreak of World War II, ALAIN ARIAS-MISSON was raised and educated in the United States. Since 1964, however, with America's overt involvement in the Indochina war, he and his wife, the painter Nela Arias, have been living in Brussels and Madrid. His essays and experimental poetry and fiction have been published internationally, and he has participated in several collective exhibitions of visual poetry in galleries and museums throughout the world. In this country, his work has been included in a number of anthologies, among them *Once Again* (New Directions), *Concretism* and *Experiments in Prose* (The Swallow Press), and *Concrete Poetry* (Indiana University Press).

JÜRGEN BECKER, who lives in Cologne, has contributed to a literary revolution with three short prose works. His "Texte," brief and subjective lyrical pieces, are gathered in *Felder (Fields), Ränder (Margins)* and, most recently, *Umgebungen (Surroundings)*. Becker's approach to reality is enhanced by a limpid style, incisive observation, and an ear able to penetrate the cacophony of the world about him. His authorship of three radio plays and a work broadcast simultaneously on radio and television bears further witness to his ability to evoke realities with a distinctive linguistic flair. A. LESLIE WILLSON, Professor of German Languages at the University of Texas at Austin, is the founder and editor of *Dimension,* a magazine devoted to contemporary German literature. He has translated numerous works by authors writing in German, including Uwe Johnson, Martin Walser, and Günter Grass.

E. M. BEEKMAN was born in 1939 and is Associate Professor of Germanic Languages and Comparative Literature at the University of Massachusetts at Amherst. He is the author of two books—*Homeopathy of the Absurd* (Martinus Nijhoff N. V., The Hague, 1970) and a novel, *Lame Duck* (Houghton Mifflin, 1971)—and edited and translated from the original Flemish *Patriotism Inc.: Tales by Paul van Ostaijen* (University of Massachusetts Press, 1971). His translation of Van Ostaijen's *Ika Loch's Brothel* appeared in *New Directions 21.*

The work of DOUGLAS BLAZEK, a California-based poet, has appeared in dozens of periodicals throughout the country. He is the editor of *Ole Anthology* (Poetry X/Change Press) and *A Bukowski Sampler* (Quixote Press), and has published several collections of his own. Some recent titles are *Baptismal Corruption in the Sunflower Patch* (Runcible Spoon Press), *Climbing Blind* (Second Aeon Press), *Skull Juices* (Twowindow Press), and *This Is What You Wanted, Isn't It?* (Augtwofive Press).

Biographical information on CARLOS BOUSOÑO will be found in the translator's note preceding his "Ten Poems." LOUIS M. BOURNE, a former editor of *The Carolina Quarterly*, lives in Madrid, teaching English and translating modern Spanish poetry.

PETER GLASSGOLD is an editor at New Directions. His work has appeared in *The Nation* and *The New Leader*.

BENJAMIN HAIMOWITZ, born in New York City, was graduated from Columbia College in 1959. He has written critical reviews for *The New Leader,* and portions of his novel *Fool* were published in the Fall, 1967, issue of *Ararat*.

DANIEL HALPERN is editor of the magazine *Antæus*. His work has appeared in *Choice, The Malahat Review, Saturday Review, The Paris Review, Transatlantic Review, Sumac, London Magazine, New Work, Perspective, The Mediterranean Review, The New Yorker,* and *Mademoiselle.* He was a prizewinner of the 1971 YMHA Discovery Award and the *Southern Poetry Review* poetry competition. Halpern has been spending the current academic year teaching at the New School for Social Research in New York.

EDWIN HONIG is a member of the Department of English at Brown University. His translation of Fernando Pessoa's *Selected Poems,* the first collection of the poet's Portuguese work to appear in English, was recently brought out by The Swallow Press, with an extensive introduction by Octavio Paz. Honig's rendering of Pessoa's "Maritime Ode" was included in *New Directions 23.* Among his other works are *García Lorca,* a critical guide (New Directions), *Dark Conceit: The Making of Allegory* (Oxford University Press), and *Spring Journal: Poems* (Wesleyan University Press).

Biographical information on ATTILA JÓZSEF will be found in the note preceding his "Nine Poems." JOHN BATKI, the translator, is a fellow of the International Writing Program at the University of Iowa. He was born in 1942 in Hungary and has been living in the United States since 1957.

YUMIKO KURAHASHI has developed an entirely new area of fiction unique in the literature of Japan. Breaking away from conventional styles and themes, she has introduced a narrative which exploits the force of modern intelligence without losing the sensitivities of Oriental intuition. Her work has been appearing in major literary journals since the early 1960s and has been given the highest praise by Japanese critics. Miss Kurahashi has published six volumes of short stories, as well as four novels and a collection of essays. Much of her work has been rendered into French, German, Italian, and Spanish. "The Ugly Devils," from *Scorpions* (1968), is the first authorized English translation to be brought out in this country. The translators are SAMUEL GROLMES, an American poet teaching at Tezukayama University in Osaka, and his wife, YUMIKO TSUMURA, also a poet, who is connected with Baika University in Osaka.

JAY PETER OLWYLER has lived on and off in Mexico for the past several years, teaching photography and doing freelance writing. He served in the Pacific area with the First Cavalry Division in World War II and later returned to spend some time in the Philippines, Japan, and Hong Kong. His story "Clin Slot Wipe and More Tomorrow" appeared in *New Directions 17*.

Biographical information on ELIO PAGLIARANI will be found in the introductory note to his "Four Poems." FAUSTA SEGRÈ, who teaches Italian literature at the University of California at Santa Barbara, has translated some plays of Carlo Goldoni and is presently working on an English version of Ruzzante's *La moscheta*. LUIGI BALLERINI is a member of the Department of Italian at the University of California at Los Angeles. He has translated several books from English into Italian, the most recent being William Carlos Williams's *Kora in Hell,* and is now putting together a collection of essays on contemporary Italian writers.

JAMES PURDY's new short novel, *I Am Elijah Thrush*, will be published this year by Doubleday. His story "On the Rebound," which appeared in *New Directions 23*, was brought out, together with some poems, in a limited edition by the Black Sparrow Press in 1970. New Directions has two Purdy collections on its list, *Children Is All* (stories and two short plays) and *Color of Darkness* (stories); recordings of the author reading from his own works have been released by Spoken Arts.

ALEKSIS RANNIT is an Estonian poet now living in the United States. He continues, however, to write in his native tongue, which he describes as "characterized by three strict phonetics quantities (long, short, and overlong) and very rich in vowels." Jean Cocteau called Rannit "prince de la poésie estonienne, artiste d'une solitude, d'une noblesse," while other critics have compared him qualitatively with Wallace Stevens and Paul Valéry. He is the author of six collections of verse, five of them rendered into other languages. Since 1961, Rannit has been the Curator of Russian and East European Studies at Yale University. HENRY LYMAN, an American poet and prose writer resident in Aix-en-Provence, participated in the 1971 Edinburgh Festival.

JOHN RATTI, born in Charleston, West Virginia, in 1933, is an alumnus of Middlebury College. His work has appeared in a number of periodicals, including *Poetry, Harper's Magazine, The New Yorker, The Literary Review, Chelsea,* and *Shenandoah.* Several of his poems have been anthologized; one has been used as the scenario for a ballet. In 1969, the Viking Press released his first collection of poetry, *A Remembered Darkness.* He is now preparing a second volume, of which his "Four Poems" are part, tentatively scheduled for publication in 1972.

The American writer EDOUARD RODITI generally makes his home in Paris, but in recent years he has been teaching at Brown University, San Francisco State College, and the University of California at Santa Cruz. His study of Oscar Wilde is on the New Directions list, and his *Poems 1928–1948* may be had from Old Oregon Bookstore, 610 S.W. 12th Avenue, Portland, Oregon 97260. Kayak Press (San Francisco) has published his prose poems, *New Hieroglyphic Tales,* and his *Dialogues on Art* was brought out by Horizon Press in 1961. He is now completing a biography of Magellan, under a grant from the Gulbenkian Foundation, in the meantime publishing short stories in such magazines as *Antæus, Playboy,* and *The Literary Review.*

JOHN TAGGART was born in Guthrie Center, Iowa, in 1942. He is the editor of *Maps,* an occasional poetry magazine, and teaches at Shippensburg State College in Pennsylvania.

JUNICHIRO TANIZAKI (1886–1965) was revered for many years as the greatest living Japanese novelist. His reputation, founded in Japan with the publication in 1910 of his short story "The Tattooer," was spread abroad in the 1950s and 1960s especially, thanks to the English translations of such novels as *Some Prefer Nettles, The Makioka Sisters, The Key, Diary of a Mad Old Man,* and the collection *Seven Japanese Tales.* Tanizaki also enjoyed popularity as a playwright, and some of his plays, including *The Man with the Mandoline* (first published in January, 1925) have recently been successfully revived both on stage and in the films. DONALD KEENE is Professor of Japanese at Columbia University. He has translated work from both classical and modern Japanese and written on the Japanese theater. At present, he is writing a history of Japanese literature.

NANCY WILLARD teaches in the English Department at Vassar. She is the author of *19 Masks for a Naked Poet* (Kayak Press), *The Lively Anatomy of God* (Eakins Press), and *Testimony of the Invisible Man* (University of Missouri Press).

WILLIAM WITHERUP has spent the last few years teaching creative writing at Soledad Correctional Training Facility in Soledad, California; with Joe Bruhac, he coedited a selection of prison writings, *Words from the House of the Dead,* published by the *Greenfield Review.* Witherup's own work has appeared in a number of literary magazines and anthologies. He is the author of a small book of poems, *The Sangre de Cristo Mountain Poems,* and cotranslator of *Twenty-five Poems of Enrique Lihn,* both brought out by Lillabulero Press.